TRESPASSERS

TRESPASSERS

A Novel

Andrea Miles

SHE WRITES PRESS

Published 2014
Printed in the United States of America
ISBN: 978-1-63152-903-0
Library of Congress Control Number: 2014933560

For information, address:
She Writes Press
1563 Solano Ave #546
Berkeley, CA 94707

To my husband

And to my parents

Finally!

Our Father which art in heaven,
Hallowed be thy name.
Thy kingdom come.
Thy will be done in earth, as it is in heaven.
Give us this day our daily bread.
And forgive us our trespasses,
As we forgive those who trespass against us …

—Matthew 6:9-13

PROLOGUE
May 1983

The moment her mother's car pulled out of the driveway, her step-father Carl thundered into twelve-year-old Melanie's bedroom where she lay on her bed reading. She jumped in surprise.

"You think you're so smart, don't you?"

She frowned. "No."

"You were the one, damn it. It was your fault!"

Melanie bit her lip, uncertain how to react to her stepfather's vague accusations, if at all.

Her Siamese cat Yoda jumped down from the windowsill and sat down to wash his face. Melanie smiled slightly at the sight of his eyes closed, his right paw curved and rubbing around his ear as he balanced on three legs. He was just so adorable when he did that. But then he was adorable all the time.

Carl reached out and snatched the cat up with one freckled hand, resting him along his forearm, his fingers by Yoda's head. Before Melanie had time to react, he grabbed her wrist with his other hand and yanked her to her feet, her book falling to the floor. He would teach his wife's brat a lesson she wouldn't soon forget.

"Carl! Stop it!" Melanie yelled, her free hand attacking his grip. She tried to grab the doorframe, but she was no match against his strength and stumbled clumsily behind him as he hurried into the hall and down the stairs.

He released her when they entered the galley kitchen, which

1

seemed even smaller with the two of them breathing in each other's faces. She rubbed her wrist, red from the strong grip of his pale fingers, and watched him uneasily. He removed a cigar box from the cabinet above the refrigerator. Lifting the lid, he stared at the perfectly polished gun. All his life, ever since his own father had killed his uncle almost twenty years ago, he'd admired the power of firearms. Even a small caliber like this one could settle the score in a nice convenient way. He held it up to her and smiled. "What do you think? Pretty fucking nice, huh?"

Melanie stared at the gun and suddenly knew what all this was about. Her mother had broken her promise. Her mother had told him Melanie's secret. And now he was going to kill her.

Carl moved towards her, laughing as Melanie flinched and backed away. He didn't touch her, though, only moved past her and out onto the screened-in porch. "Better get your ass out here, girlie, so you can say adios to your damn cat."

Suddenly pale, Melanie moved to the porch, her dark eyes large. "What are you going to do?" She raised her voice, moving closer to him. "Leave him alone."

He shook his head. "Nope. Not after you told your mother that fucking lie." He tucked the gun into the waistband of his jeans.

She raised her chin slightly. "I didn't lie." Her voice trembled slightly, betraying her.

"I know the signs of a bitch in heat. You wanted it and you know it. And then when I give in to you, you go off and tell her some lie and she gets pissed at me. So now I'm going to kill this fleabag as a lesson. I can't stand a liar."

He turned to unhook the screen door and Melanie grabbed his arm, the one holding Yoda, and began to pull. "Please, Carl, I'll do anything," she promised, her pale face wrinkled as she squinted up at him. "Just give him to me. Please? Please don't hurt him."

He spun around and raised his hand to backhand her, annoyed. Melanie flinched, ducking her head and raising her arms to protect herself. Yoda opened his mouth wide and bit down on Carl's hand, his back claws digging into the fleshy arm and stomach.

"Shit!" He punched the cat in the head and then as the cat's back legs began to kick against him, he wrapped his hand around the cat's neck and squeezed, shaking the animal. He punched the cat again, who finally went limp, its breathing labored. Irritated, he swiped at the beads of sweat breaking out across his forehead and turned, flipping the latch with one finger. Pushing the screen door open, he lumbered down the cement steps. Melanie stumbled behind him, tears blinding her, her head pounding.

"Stop it!" she cried. "Please. I promise I won't lie anymore. Just give him to me!" She pounded her small fists on his back. Suddenly he swung around and Melanie reached out for Yoda, her fingers touching his soft fur. "Yoda!" she cried, tears wetting her cheeks.

Carl wrapped his empty fingers around Melanie's small neck. Her eyes bulged, but she stared at him boldly, looking up at him with fear and anger and hate. He watched in fascination as tears dripped along the soft curve of her cheeks. A few fell onto his wrist where it jutted out beneath her chin. Releasing her, he lifted his wrist to his mouth and licked the salty tears from his skin. She hiccupped, breaking him from his spell. He squinted at her. "You little slut," he whispered. But how he liked feeling her silky skin pressed against him late at night when his frigid wife locked him out of their bedroom and drank herself to sleep. Just thinking of her tight body made him hurt. *Tonight*, he promised himself. *I'll teach her a lesson now so that tonight she'll welcome me with open arms.*

She shook her head slightly as another hiccup escaped and more tears fell.

"Hit me again," he said, his voice deep, deeper than usual, and calm, "and I'll bury you. Alive. Right here in the back yard." He raised his pale eyebrows as though punctuating his threat.

She gasped, instantly dropping her eyes to stare at Yoda. Her lips began to tremble. "Please, Carl," she whispered, "Please don't hurt him." If only she could hold Yoda one last time. If only her mother was here to save them. Because surely if Yoda died, she would die. He was her best friend; she told him everything. She loved him more than she loved herself.

Carl shoved her out of his way and chuckled softly as she stumbled, off balance. "No, you can't hold the fucker. Now or ever."

Melanie gasped in surprise. How had he known exactly what she was thinking? Behind her a car pulled up in the driveway beside the house and suddenly Melanie screamed, "Mama! Mama!"

"Shut up!" he ordered, pointing the gun at her and backing away, moving closer to the fence lining the back edge of the property. "It's too late for anyone to save your useless cat. Even your bitch of a mother!" He dropped the cat in the corner of the fenced-in yard and removed the gun from the waistband of his jeans. "Say your prayers, kitty-cat."

Annie hurried into the backyard, alarmed by her daughter's voice. Melanie hadn't called her that in a very long time. She stopped as soon as she spotted the gun clutched in Carl's beefy hand. She paused, her hand pressing against her chest as she tried to slow her breathing. "What's going on?" she asked, stepping closer to them. She stopped a few feet behind her daughter. "What did you do, Melanie?"

He tilted his head to one side. "This is about telling the truth, Annie. I won't have anyone lying about me, especially your brat there. Now you go on inside and get yourself a drink." He smiled slightly. "Hell, get us both one."

Melanie pointed to where Yoda lay in the grass. "He's going to kill him, Mama." Her voice was high, shrieking, out of control as fresh tears fell from her dark eyes.

"What?" She looked in the direction Melanie pointed and, spotting the cat, strode past her daughter.

Carl cocked the gun. "Don't go near him, Annie, unless you want to take the chance of my aim being off."

"You don't have any bullets in that thing."

"Oh?" He raised one eyebrow. "Are you sure?" He pointed the gun at Melanie. No one moved. Annie said a quick prayer, the words jumbling in her mind, tripping over her fear, never reaching her mouth. Reveling in the power he held over them, Carl smiled and moved to point the gun at his wife. Melanie took a step closer, a tiny cry escaping past trembling lips, but he didn't notice, again remembering the moment when his father had shot his uncle in front of him. He'd certainly respected his old man after that.

Annie stretched her arm behind her and held out her hand. "It's okay, Melanie. Carl's only playing a game, aren't you, Carl? You're just playing a joke on us, right?" She fought to keep her voice smooth, even, respectful. She said the words slowly, allowing them to form in the back of her throat, roll over her tongue, and slip carefully from her dry lips.

Carl frowned and moved to point the gun at Yoda, who was struggling to get to his feet. What a disappointment his wife had turned out to be. "You always make the mistake of underestimating me."

Melanie whimpered, pressing her hands over her ears as she sank to her knees.

"When," he asked, "will you learn?" Had she learned nothing about him these past years they'd been married? He shook his head slightly and then fired the gun. The force of the bullet lifted the cat up and dropped him a few feet away, closer to the fence.

The shot echoed in their ears. Annie cringed at the blood that had splattered in all directions. She moved over to her daughter who sat on her knees with her hands pressed against her ears and her forehead buried in the tall grass.

"Yoda," Melanie cried. "I'm sorry, Yoda. I'm sorry. I love you. I love you so much," she repeated over and over, her voice breaking. She wiped her runny nose with the back of her hand. How could she live without him?

Annie knelt beside her daughter, wrapping her arms around the trembling child, and cried with her. Why hadn't she stayed in bed this morning? It wasn't fair that she had to deal with this crap. She glanced up to see Carl carrying the dead gray cat, limp and dripping blood, over to the metal trashcan. He lifted the lid and dropped the cat inside. The clang of metal hitting metal as he replaced the lid seemed very loud in the silence of the gunshot.

Melanie jerked her head up. "No!" she screamed and, shoving her mother's cool, soothing hands from her, jumped up and ran over to the trashcan.

Carl shook his head and stuffed the gun into the waistband of his jeans. He walked towards the back steps, humming a song he made up as he went along.

Melanie lifted the lid and flung it behind her. She reached in and pulled the cat out. Pressing his still warm body to her, she petted him, kissing the top of his head. "Oh, Yoda," she whispered, her voice soft with the pain she didn't know how to express. Did he know? Did he know how much he meant to her? Did he know how sorry she was that she couldn't have saved him? But she would get Carl back. And he would be sorry. She rocked back and forth, cradling Yoda in her arms and pressing her lips against the place between his ears where she'd planted millions of kisses over the past six years. Her stepfather would be very sorry. She would make sure of it.

Annie jumped up and caught Carl's swinging hand. "How could you do that?"

He tilted his head and stared at her, his eyes flicking past her to momentarily focus on Melanie, who was crooning incoherently. His lips hardened. "Someone has to teach her the difference between right and wrong."

"I told you I'd handle it."

"Yeah, well, shit, Annie, she's twelve years old. I thought it was time to take action, rather than just say the damn words. I don't need your little brat telling lies about me."

"As you keep pointing out, she is my child and not yours so . . ." She stopped, noticing too late his clenched jaw.

"So what?" he asked, his tone light despite the anger she saw in his face.

Taking a deep breath, she finished quietly, "So let me handle her."

Carl slammed his fist into her stomach and she doubled over, falling to the ground in a heap. "Don't you ever insinuate I'm not an equal in this fucking family. Do you hear me? Never!" He stormed up the steps and into the house, the screen door slamming behind him.

Annie lifted her head, searching for her daughter. Melanie was sitting by the trashcan, blood smeared on her hands and her clothes, Yoda cradled in her lap as she petted him from his head to the tip of his tail. Annie grunted as she attempted to get to her feet. They needed to bury Yoda, now, as soon as possible. She bit her lip and dropped back onto the grass. She closed her eyes and listened as Melanie's voice floated on the breeze.

"Don't worry, Yoda. When I get to heaven, we'll be together again."

Annie licked her lips. God, she needed a drink. Why couldn't Melanie stay out of Carl's way? Benjie was a perfect child. There was never any trouble with him. But Melanie . . . damn her for getting Carl riled up! There'd be no peace now. Forcing herself to her feet with a groan, she stumbled to the porch steps. She wrapped her arms around her sore stomach. First, she had to search for a shoebox and find a shovel to dig the grave. Second, she had to perform a funeral. And third, she had to fix herself a drink. A very strong drink. Or maybe that should be first? *Yeah, a drink first,* she thought, stepping into the coolness of the porch. And then she'd deal with her troublesome daughter.

CHAPTER 1
October 1997

Melanie awoke with a start, her feet tangled in sheets damp from her sweat. She ran her fingers through her hair. Turning her hands over, palms facing up, she studied the scars slashed across both wrists. "Why had she bothered to save me?" she wondered aloud. Things would've been better had her mother just let her die. Tomorrow she'd be twenty-six and yet she still mourned Yoda, her childhood pet. She glanced at the clock on the bedside table. Two-thirty. If she hurried, she could stop by her mother's house before work and ask her why she hadn't just let her die fourteen years ago. This time, she promised herself, she wouldn't let her mother's cruel, drunken remarks get under her skin. She wouldn't.

"Jesus Christ, you're not out of bed yet?" Rick asked, entering the bedroom. "You gonna sleep the fucking day away or what?" He pulled the top dresser drawer open and rummaged through the clothes.

Melanie glared at her boyfriend before reaching for a discarded shirt on the floor by the bed. "You know I have trouble sleeping."

He slammed the drawer closed and opened the one below.

Shoving her arms through the sleeves, she yanked the shirt on quickly. "What are you looking for?"

He ignored her, slamming that drawer closed and opening the third one.

"You're messing everything up. I had everything folded, you know."

He slammed the drawer shut and stooped down to open the

9

bottom drawer. "So you'll just have to fold it all again. If you put things where they belong, I wouldn't have to go through this."

"Well, what exactly are you looking for?" She got up and walked over to stand behind him.

"My lucky shirt, that's what the hell I'm looking for. Now where is it?"

She walked over to a pile of clothes heaped on the floor and pulled a black shirt from it. "You mean this shirt?"

He looked over and, recognizing his favorite shirt, jumped up and snatched it from her. "Yes! Why the hell isn't it clean?"

"Because I haven't had time to do laundry, obviously."

He reached out and smacked her across the face. A red handprint formed almost instantly. "Don't you get smart with me. I need this shirt. How do you expect me to win tonight? You know I've got a big match against Hardings."

Melanie pressed her hand against her stinging cheek. Fighting back tears, she moved away from him. "You're good enough to beat him without that shirt."

He sighed and reached out to her. Pulling her close, he pushed her hand aside and studied the cheek he'd slapped. "Yeah, baby, but, that was before. And tonight we're playing for some big money. If I win, I can get that Harley I've been wanting. And you know how much I want that bike, don't you?"

She stared at him silently, cautious.

He began to stroke the back of her neck. "You know that, right? We talked about you and me riding somewhere cool, anywhere we wanted, once I got that bike." He leaned closer. "Remember?"

She started to relax, allowing herself to be soothed by his gentle caress and silky voice. "I remember. You've been dreaming about your own bike for months."

"Longer than that." He pulled back. "So you'll wash it today?" He held the shirt out to her.

"I can't. I've got to go to work."

He frowned. "Skip it."

She pulled away, moving out of his immediate reach. "I can't. You know I can't."

"Why the hell not? Its not like you're doing brain surgery. You're just a waitress."

She cringed, but didn't defend herself. "I can get it started in the wash, if you can put it in the dryer. But we can't afford for me to lose my job, Rick. Especially when you're playing for such high stakes. What'll we do if you lose? We can't afford to lose that kind of money—"

"Damn it, Melanie. I let you move in on the condition that you do my fucking laundry and keep this place clean. Not to nag me to death." He balled the shirt up and threw it at her. He didn't bother to see that she'd caught it; instead, he turned immediately to walk out of the room, but tripped over the open dresser drawer. "Shit!" he yelled, kicking the drawer angrily.

She hurried into the bathroom, the lucky black shirt still clutched in her hand, and locked the door before he decided to take out the rest of his frustrations on her. Pressing her ear against the door, she listened as his ranting continued, his words becoming muffled as he moved through the apartment. She turned to look in the mirror and inspect the damage he'd done when he'd slapped her. She touched her cheek lightly with her fingertips and winced. There'd be a slight bruise, nothing major. She could probably hide it with a bit of makeup. A loud crash reverberated through the apartment. Quickly, she turned on the shower. A long hot shower would be best, she thought. Maybe then his temper tantrum would be spent. She held the shirt up in front of her. It was a simple cotton shirt that buttoned up, nothing spectacular about it. He'd been wearing it when she'd met him and, as a matter of fact, if she remembered correctly, he'd lost his game that night. No, the luck he associated with this shirt had nothing to do with his pool game and everything to do with how he looked in it. Certainly that was why she'd initially been attracted to him. With his black hair, black shirt, and Florida tan, she hadn't been able to take her eyes off him all night. She dropped the shirt on the bathroom floor and began to undress. She was almost happy that she'd gotten behind on the laundry. *Almost*, she thought, touching her cheek as she stepped into the shower. *Almost*.

Forty-five minutes later, Melanie walked quickly along Second

Street. Just after she crossed the railroad tracks, she paused on the sidewalk and stared up at her mother's house. Long ago, when they'd first moved to Florida from New Jersey, it had been a pretty house, but it was hard to imagine describing it like that now. The yellow peeling paint and the sagging porch just proved such neglect had been going on for a long time. Had there ever been flowers blooming in the flowerbeds that bordered the house? She couldn't remember.

What was she doing here anyway? She was being foolish to think she could just walk in and ask her mother about her painful childhood. No doubt her mother was already quite drunk and even if she wasn't, they didn't have the type of nurturing relationship necessary to dredge up, let alone discuss, such painful memories. And even if Melanie could find it within herself to bring them up anyway, her mother would just blame her for everything that had happened. She was the bad child, the one that had ruined her mother's few chances at finding happiness. Melanie turned away from the house. What was the point in seeing her? She glanced back, her eyes sweeping past the overgrown hedges, the peeling yellow paint, and the old newspapers littering the front porch. She sighed heavily. She was already here so she might as well go in. With a last glance along the street she'd just walked, she strode quickly up the sidewalk.

Her mother sat on the floral couch, feet propped on the coffee table, *The Price is Right* on television. "So look who's come for a visit."

Melanie closed the front door behind her and waited for her eyes to adjust to the darkened room. "Nice slippers."

Annie raised one foot high to study her fluffy bright pink slipper. "A birthday gift from my son." She dropped her foot back onto the scratched wood table. "I guess you forgot."

Melanie dropped her purse next to a chair and turned her attention to opening the blinds. "Let's not start, okay?"

Annie held her hand up, shielding her eyes from the bright Florida sunlight that slipped through the open blinds. "Shut that!" she yelled. "Shut it right now!"

Melanie rolled her eyes, but complied with her mother's wishes. "It's so dark in here. I don't know how you can stand it." She sat down across from her mother. "Where is Benjie?"

"I sent him to the store."

Melanie watched as her mother lifted the glass to her lips, exposing her throat as she finished the drink in two long swallows. Once upon a time she'd been a pretty woman, but the years of drinking had done their damage. Like the blue flowers depicted on the couch, she seemed faded. "For more booze?"

Annie set the empty glass on the table in front of her, ignoring her daughter's question. "Still working at that stupid diner, I see."

Melanie pursed her lips, her long fingers absently smoothing the skirt of the old-fashioned blue waitress uniform. She'd never understood why her mother disliked Aunt Betty's Diner, even years ago before Melanie had started working there. Knowing that there was nothing she could say that she hadn't already said many times before, she kept silent and watched the condensation drip along the clear glass until it met the table, hoping her mother would drop it.

"Why you work there I'll never understand."

"It pays the bills, Mother."

Annie shook her head. "You're going to wake up one day and look in the mirror and see an old woman wearing a stained waitress uniform."

Melanie tapped her fingers on the arm of the chair.

"You'll be surprised, too. How could you have gotten so old already, you'll wonder."

"Can we please talk about something else?"

"And of course you'll be alone," Annie said as if Melanie had never spoken. "Who'd want to marry an old, worn-out waitress? And you won't have any friends because you'll have thrown yourself at their husbands. Loneliness makes you desperate, you know, and they'll stop returning your calls . . ."

"Is that what happened to you?"

Annie dropped her feet to the floor and leaned forward. "You know nothing about what happened to me. Nothing."

Surprised by her mother's trembling reaction, Melanie got to her feet before her mother told her to get out. "Can I fix you another drink?" She snatched the glass from the table without waiting for a reply.

Her mother's voice followed her into the kitchen, continuing as though her outburst had never happened. "Next thing you know you'll be asking to move back in with me. And why should I let you? I mean, you don't even remember when my birthday is. I have Benjie here to do things for me and I think we're comfortable with it just being the two of us." She coughed a loud hacking cough, the sound easily reaching Melanie where she hid out in the kitchen. "Yes, Benjie. He's such a good kid, my sweet baby boy."

Melanie leaned her head against the refrigerator. Why had she stopped by? She no longer remembered. She grabbed ice cubes from the freezer and tossed them into the glass. One missed and skidded along the faded linoleum. She picked it up and hesitated, her fingers hovering over her mother's glass before finally tossing the dirty ice cube into the sink. "Good old Benjie," she muttered to herself as she filled her mother's glass with vodka and a splash of orange juice. She stirred the drink with her index finger. "Always there for Mother Dearest." She licked her finger as she put the jug of juice back in the refrigerator before returning to the living room. "Here," she said, reaching the glass out to her mother. "Speaking of birthdays, I have one coming up. I'll be twenty-six."

She accepted the glass. "You say that as if I don't know how old you are. I was there you know. I birthed you." She took a healthy swallow and frowned slightly. "And Benjie, he sure knows how to make a good drink. He doesn't water them down." She took another swallow. "You're not gay, are you?"

"What?" Melanie was startled out of her reverie. She met her mother's bleary eyes. "No, of course not."

Annie stared at her daughter over the rim of her glass. "At twenty-six, I had two kids and a second husband. You certainly don't expect to ever get married, do you? Because as your mother, I feel I should discourage such silly fantasies. No man would consent to marry you if he had one cent of good sense. You are better off alone anyways. You think I've given up? Well, I have. Who needs men? That's what I say."

The front door opened and Benjie entered, his arms filled with bags of groceries. "Hey, sis, long time no see," he said as he swept past them and disappeared into the kitchen.

Melanie frowned at her brother as he walked through, the odor of pot lingering behind.

Annie closed her eyes, suddenly exhausted from her rant. She hated it when her mouth wouldn't stop moving.

Some family she had, Melanie thought. Her mother was a drunk and her brother was a pothead. Where did she fit in?

"Mom, you'll be happy to know vodka was on sale," Benjie called from the kitchen.

"Did you buy me extra then?"

They waited for his answer, Annie suspicious, her eyes narrowing; Melanie indifferent as she studied her mother's wrinkled skin peeking out from the neckline and arms of her faded red robe. The only noise was the rustle of bags and the opening and closing of cabinet doors as he unpacked the groceries. The grandfather clock struck four o'clock.

"Did you buy me extra then?" Annie yelled louder.

Benjie returned to the living room and bent to kiss his mother. "Of course."

"That's my boy," she said, smiling up at him, instantly happy. "Sit down here next to me." She patted the cushion and he plopped down next to her, draping his arm along the back of the couch, his fingers resting lightly on his mother's shoulder.

Melanie tapped her fingers on her knees. Why did she always expect things to have changed? It was always the same. Her brother was the wonderful, doting son while she was the selfish, neglectful daughter.

"Still working at the diner, huh?" Benjie asked, brushing his hair out of his eyes.

Melanie nodded silently, again struck by how similar the two looked. Both mother and son were blonde with blue eyes; both had a long, thin nose . . . She sighed. She'd taken after their father: dark eyes, dark hair, and short, perky nose. Often times, when she was younger, she'd described herself as being the dark one, the evil one in the family, like her father. And she'd described her mother and Benjie as being the good ones, believing with all her heart that blonde was synonymous with good. She'd even gone so far as to attempt to dye her hair blonde and perhaps rid her soul of the evil that lurked there. But her hair had turned a ghastly orangish color and she'd had to give up on ever becoming good. She grabbed her purse and stood up. "I've got to go to work, Mother. As always it was a joy to visit you."

"But I just got here! Sis, sit down. Relax and fill me in on all that's happening with you." He reached over and took his mother's drink from her. He watched his sister over the rim of the glass as he tasted the beverage. "Ugh! Mom, this is awful. Let me fix you a fresh one." He jumped up and hurried into the kitchen.

Annie rested her head on the back of the couch and stared somewhere to the left of Melanie's shoulder. "I know I've been a lousy mother. Maybe if I'd made better choices, things would be different. For both of us." She stretched her arms out, meeting Melanie's eyes. "But this is what it is. And I'm okay with that."

Melanie slung her purse over her shoulder, confused by her mother's words. "What was the real reason Dad left? It had nothing to do with Benjie or me, did it?"

Annie frowned. "Just go away, Melanie. You were always such a needy child." She waved her hand casually towards the front door.

"I'm going. And honestly, Mother, I'm sorry I stopped by."

"Well, what did you come over here for? Money?"

"No, I don't need any money." She opened the front door. "That's Benjie's tune."

"Don't you go badmouthing your brother! He's just a boy."

"No, Mother. When you weren't looking, he became a man." Melanie closed the door behind her. She paused on the sidewalk, blinking back tears. She'd stopped crying over them a long time ago, so why did she want to collapse in tears today? And why did she even bother? But she knew why. Because one day she'd be able to tell her mother she was wrong. Very wrong. And her mother would be forced to apologize. But would she then learn to love her only daughter? Or was that wishful thinking? She glanced back at the house and spotted Benjie peeking through the blinds at her. Even from this distance, she could see the reddened whites of his eyes. What was he thinking? Did he see her as she really was? Or did he see a different Melanie? And what difference did it make really? All she wanted was to make him sorry he'd catered to their mother all these years while turning his back on his sister. It wasn't so bad, really, once she'd accepted herself as being evil. It allowed her to spend many guilt-free hours thinking of the perfect revenge. Of course, so far she hadn't really come up with any kind of plan. In due time she supposed the perfect revenge idea would hit her and then she'd make him regret the day he joined their mother in hating her. Oh, yes, revenge would be sweet. She turned without waving at him and began to walk back down Second Street towards town.

CHAPTER 2

Melanie stepped outside into the cool night air and removed a cigarette from the pack hidden in her apron. Moving away from the door, she was careful to keep under the overhang and out of the rain. Halfway between the door and the end of the building, she stopped and leaned against the brick wall. Flicking her lighter, she stared momentarily at the flame before dipping the end of her cigarette into the fire.

Ida poked her head out and, spotting Melanie, stepped outside. "Figured you'd be out here."

Melanie took a long drag on her cigarette.

"I thought you'd given that up."

She shrugged, releasing the smoke.

"It gives you bad breath, you know."

"Ida, please don't start."

"Fine."

She watched as the older woman reapplied her red lipstick, her dyed red hair in startling contrast to the paleness of her soft wrinkled skin. Was she looking at herself in thirty years? Could her mother be right after all? Melanie rejected that idea immediately. No, she was with Rick now and she would hopefully always be with Rick. If only she could get him to agree to marry her. But he insisted he'd marry no one. Could she be satisfied with not proving her mother wrong? She flicked the ash from her cigarette. No. So she'd have to find some way to convince Rick. But how long would she have to wait? And what if she waited for nothing? Then she would be just another Ida, a dinosaur fighting to keep from being replaced by the younger, prettier, and healthier generation.

"How you think you're ever going to find a decent husband when you have cancer and bad breath, I'll never know."

Melanie almost laughed out loud, but she managed to control the urge. Ida was serious, but to her that just made it funnier. She took a drag of her cigarette, slightly amazed at how close Ida had come to reading her mind. "I don't need to worry about that."

"And why not? Did you get married over the weekend without telling anybody?"

She waved her cigarette in the air. "You don't think I'd be sporting my ring all over the place if that had happened?"

"With you there's no telling. So what aren't you saying?"

"Tomorrow's my birthday. And I think Rick's going to ask me to marry him." Well, she rationalized, it would be a perfect opportunity for him to combine gifts: an engagement ring for her birthday. And maybe he would surprise her, after all. There were a few times she recalled that he'd surprised her, and although they'd rarely been great surprises, that didn't mean it couldn't happen. After all, she was overdue for a bit of happiness, wasn't she? She glanced over to see Ida frowning. "I know you don't like him, but that doesn't matter. I'm the one that has to like him. I know he loves me; he just has a lot of trouble showing it, that's all."

Ida turned to go back inside the diner. "You don't have to explain anything to me. You're old enough to know what you're doing. Just as you're old enough to pay for your own mistakes. I just hope . . ."

"What?" Melanie snapped, suddenly angry with her friend for her pessimism. "You've never held your tongue before so why start now?"

"I just hope the price doesn't become your life." She opened the glass door. "Looks like you have a customer."

"Why don't you take him?"

"I think he'd prefer you."

"Don't be so sure. You're pretty popular."

"It's that policeman, the one who likes you."

"Julius." Melanie nodded and flicked her cigarette into the parking lot. "Anyway, as you've just admitted, I'm old enough, Ida, so why don't you stop lecturing me all the time?"

She smiled, reaching into her apron for a stick of gum. "That's what you do when you get to be my age: lecture the young'uns." She pushed the gum into Melanie's hand and disappeared inside.

Melanie stared at the gum. Begrudgingly, she unwrapped it and put it into her mouth before following Ida inside. She walked over to the policeman sitting alone in a booth reading the menu. His uniform indicated he worked for the local police precinct. "Hi, how are you?" she asked.

"Wet." He laid the menu aside and looked up at her. "But also lucky, if I get you."

"That's not necessarily a good thing," she said, conscious of Ida staring at them from across the restaurant. It was almost impressive how determined Ida was to fix Melanie up with this guy. "You're becoming quite the regular."

Julius smiled. "A man's got to eat."

Melanie smiled. She was beginning to get used to talking to him every day. Not that they ever talked about anything important, but he was nice and polite and far from demanding, unlike other regulars she frequently waited on. And even though he'd asked her out a few times, she still liked seeing him. "Have you decided what you'll have today?"

"I'd like a date with you, but you keep shooting me down."

"You know I'm already involved with someone."

Julius nodded slowly, staring at her. "Looks like I'll be having a side of disappointment with my dinner."

Melanie tapped her pen against her notepad.

"So just to be clear. You love him?"

She raised her chin slightly. What was with everyone today? "Yes, I love him."

He nodded. "I suppose the better question is, does he love you just as much?"

"Not that it's any of your business, but yes. Now are you ready to order? Or do you need another minute?"

"I'll just have the BLT and a cup of chicken noodle soup, please."

She quickly wrote down his order. "On what type of bread?"

"Wheat toast."

She nodded. "And to drink?"

"Coffee."

Melanie walked behind the counter and hung his order up for the cook. She grabbed a coffee cup and filled it with fresh coffee. Returning to his table, she set the cup down next to his tapping fingers and was about to move away when Julius grabbed her hand, stopping her.

"Love isn't supposed to hurt, Melanie."

She untucked the hair behind her ear, startled to realize the slight swelling on her cheekbone must be noticeable. "Then you've never been in love." She turned to leave, but this time Ida looped her arm through hers and forced her to continue to stand by Julius's table.

"How you doing?" Ida asked.

"Good, thanks," he said, his eyes still lingering on Melanie. He glanced over at the older woman. "How about you?"

"Oh, I can't complain." She watched as he poured sugar and creamer into his coffee. "Did Mel tell you what tomorrow is?"

She glared at Ida and tried to untangle herself from the older woman's grip. "Oh, for God's sake!"

"Don't use the Lord's name in vain," Ida scolded. "So did she?"

"No, she didn't."

"I figured she wouldn't. Tomorrow," she said, dropping her voice slightly and leaning closer, "is her birthday."

He picked up his spoon and began to stir the coffee, the metal clinking against the porcelain and watched Melanie's cheeks redden in embarrassment. "Really?"

Ida grinned, immensely pleased with herself. "And can you believe she has to work on her birthday?"

"It's no big deal," Melanie muttered.

"It could be worse; she could have to work a double. Instead, she's working the lunch shift. She has the evening off."

Julius smiled. "That is a big deal. Thanks, Ida, for filling me in."

She winked at him and walked away.

"It's no big deal," Melanie repeated firmly and hurried from the table.

Melanie waved at Julius as he walked out of the diner. Stopping at his table, she put the five-dollar tip he always left in the pocket of her apron before smelling the paper rose he'd created from a napkin. She smiled slightly, and then carefully put the rose in her apron so it wouldn't get damaged while she cleared the table.

Ida stopped beside her. "I see you got another one."

She nodded, taking the paper rose out of her pocket and twirling it in her fingers. "And you're still pleased with yourself." She smelled it again.

The older woman shook her head, grabbing the plate and stacking the soup bowl on top. "I don't know what you're talking about. And why must you always smell it? It's paper. It doesn't smell like anything." She grabbed the silverware and put them in the water glass.

Melanie shrugged. "I know. It's just that I've never gotten a real rose from anyone so these paper roses are real to me." She returned the paper rose to her apron and used a damp towel to wipe off the table.

"He really likes you," Ida said, putting the dishes in the bus tub. "And he seems so nice."

She walked behind the counter and dropped the towel in a bucket of soapy water. "Oh, Ida. I wish you'd stop trying to be my matchmaker. I have Rick and he's all I need."

"How can you be so stubborn?" Ida walked away, muttering to herself about youth being wasted on the young.

Melanie closed the front door of the dark apartment behind her and quickly turned on the light. She knew it was silly, but she hated coming home to an unlit apartment. Years ago, her stepfather Carl used to lock her in a closet when he thought she was bad. Despite all that time in the dark, she was still afraid. Rick sometimes teased her about having nightlights scattered throughout the apartment. If they were off, she couldn't sleep, jerking awake at every sound, real or imagined. She felt safer having even a tiny nightlight to slice through the darkness.

She moved into the kitchen and opened the refrigerator, but seeing how empty it was, she closed it without taking anything out. It was more out of habit than because she was hungry anyway. She'd already eaten at the diner.

Returning to the living room, she turned on the various night-lights as she passed them, thankful that Rick wasn't there to laugh at her for her fear like he usually did. He'd never tried to understand why she was afraid of the dark and she'd long ago lost the desire to tell him. She plopped down on the couch, dropping her apron on the coffee table, the loose change knocking on the table. Closing her eyes, she kneaded the back of her neck, rolling her head slowly from side to side. What was it about rain that made everyone decide to eat out? She and Ida had foolishly anticipated a slow night; instead, they'd been so busy she'd barely had a moment to pee, let alone smoke a cigarette. She grabbed her apron and removed the paper rose Julius had given her and the wad of money she'd made in tips. Finally, her fingers produced the lighter and she lit a cigarette, inhaling deeply.

"Where are you, Rick?" she wondered aloud.

Probably at Ruben's Models of Love, a club located not too far from where her mother lived. And really, it wasn't bad for the type of place it was. There were strippers, but just a handful since it wasn't that big of a club. She had to admit they were pretty. Not the best bodies, if you needed to be critical, but then that's what Ruben's was known for. If you wanted to stare at thin, hard bodies, Mary Jane's Joint, a club on the opposite side of town right off the highway, was the place to go. Of course those girls weren't spending their spare time in the gym. Instead, they were downright bony, no doubt due to a steady diet of drugs, their skinny arms marked with track lines. Mr. Nichols, the owner of Ruben's, insisted his girls remain slightly voluptuous because that was far sexier than being model-thin. Not that they were fat. They just had an inch here or an inch there that kept them "soft." There'd been a write-up in the local paper about the club, mostly negative of course, but the reporter did give Mr. Nichols credit for naming the club after the renowned painter Peter Paul Rubens, a man who apparently preferred painting women with a little substance to their figures. Melanie did not know if that was true or not, but it was certainly interesting.

The strippers weren't the only attraction at Ruben's, though, at least for Rick. He prided himself on being the resident pool shark, unofficially of course. It was a little out of the ordinary to have pool tables at a strip club, or so she'd been told, but Mr. Nichols's son, Giorgio, had loved to play pool and so there were pool tables. Giorgio had died a few years back of an overdose (a terrible scandal because he'd been with one of the girls from Mary Jane's Joint), but the pool tables remained.

Sometimes Rick lost, but more often than not he won and he won big. He had a knack for picking the right drunk to challenge to a game. He'd lose and then insist on being allowed to go for double or nothing. To regain his dignity, he'd say. And the drunken fool would fall for it. Again and again and again. And then Rick, having sufficiently upped the ante, would proceed to clear the table beginning with his first shot without so much as giving them a chance to shoot one ball on the table after the break. Most times they didn't have enough sense to realize they'd been suckered. Every once in a while there'd be someone who'd catch on and try to get physical, but Mr. Nichols had bouncers everywhere who broke things up before much happened. It was pertinent that they ensure the police weren't needed because Police Chief Hal Jackson swore that if his men ever had to step into Nichols's club, he'd make sure the club was forced to close down. Rumor had it that Mr. Nichols had given the Police Chief's daughter a job at the club. She'd been accepted into Princeton University, but was refusing to go. Eventually, though, she'd gone and ever since then Hal Jackson had promised to close Ruben's if there was even one law broken within its walls. Mr. Nichols would get mad at Rick for causing trouble, afraid Rick was going to give his club a bad reputation and attract more troublemakers than his bouncers could handle. He wasn't about to let Hal Jackson enjoy the satisfaction of closing him down. Especially when there was Mary Jane's Joint across town, a club where illegal drugs were used constantly, with owners who thrived on keeping the negative images associated with strip clubs alive and well. Then, so as to pacify Mr. Nichols, Rick would give him a piece of the winnings. The old owner would scowl, disapproving of Rick and his games, before moving on to check on his girls, the money pushed deep in his pockets.

Melanie stubbed her cigarette out in the ashtray on the coffee table and counted her tips. One hundred and twelve dollars. She'd bet this money Rick was at Ruben's, if she could find someone stupid enough to take the bet. She shoved the money in her apron pocket and picked up the paper rose, twirling it between her fingers. Why couldn't Rick ever do anything nice like give her a rose, even a paper one? She lifted the paper petals to her nose and breathed in and then suddenly she laughed at herself. Why did she always smell it? She just couldn't seem to stop herself, kind of like closing your eyes when you sneeze. You just did it.

With rose in hand, she stood up and went into her bedroom. Turning on the closet light, she rummaged in the bottom, finally pulling out an old shoebox. She sat on the bed and removed the lid to reveal twenty paper roses, all made from the diner's plain white napkins. She added the latest to the box and replaced the lid only to remove the lid again seconds later and gently finger the paper roses. Closing her eyes, she lifted the box to her nose and breathed in.

"If only they were real." But then she'd probably smell them so hard, she'd sniff the scent right out of them. Besides, they'd just die in a few days and she'd have to throw them out. At least with these she could always save them. "But just once, real roses would be nice."

Rick, smelling of smoke, entered the bedroom, startling Melanie. She leapt to her feet, the paper roses spilling from the box onto the floor, a guilty flush creeping up her neck to color her cheeks. He squinted, eyeing the mess at her feet and then glared at her.

"How was your night?" she asked, her voice unnaturally high, her fingers beginning to tap lightly against her thighs. She cleared her throat. "Did you win your game?"

He stomped over to her and grabbed her throat. "You been cheating on me?"

Melanie shook her head.

"Answer me!"

"No! Of course not!"

Rick shoved her and she fell back onto the bed. "Don't lie to me. I can see it with my own eyes." He smacked her across the face, busting her lip open.

She winced in pain, but managed to keep from crying out. "I'm not lying, Rick."

He snatched a rose from the floor and shook it at her. "I come home and find you mooning over some dumb, corny-ass roses made from stupid napkins and you still lie to my face?" He threw it at her. "Get out!"

Melanie stared up at him, her lip swelling as tears filled her eyes.

He turned and stomped out of the room, pausing briefly to shove things off the dresser onto the floor on his way out. Melanie pulled her legs onto the bed and curled up into a ball as her hot tears mixed with the blood from her lip. She hated herself for crying, but she was unable to stop the flow of tears. She cringed at the sound of the front door slamming behind him as he hurried down the stairs. The neighbors below were going to complain to the landlord about them yet again.

Slowly, she sat up and picked up the rose he'd thrown at her, now slightly misshapen from being clutched in his big fist. "He didn't mean it," she whispered to herself, bending down and picking up the roses, returning them to the old shoebox. With a last glance, she put the lid on and got to her feet. After surveying the room, she finally knelt and shoved the box under the bed.

In the bathroom she turned on the light and studied her bloody face. How could she be upset at him? He'd reacted this way because he was so hurt to think she might be cheating on him, right? She turned on the faucet and began to wash her face. Actually, she should be screaming with joy. If he loved her so much to react so strongly to the idea of her being with someone else, then surely he must love her. And he must love her enough to want to make her his own. Maybe convincing him to marry her wouldn't be so hard after all. Maybe he really was planning on asking her to marry him tomorrow! That would certainly be the best birthday present she'd ever gotten. She made her rounds, turning on all the nightlights located in the back of the house, before turning off the bedroom light and crawling into bed. She loved him. She loved him and he loved her. He'd only told her to get out because he was hurt. She was sure of it.

CHAPTER 3

On her twenty-sixth birthday, Melanie woke to sunshine streaming through the windows and Rick asleep on the couch, a warm bottle of beer on the floor beside him and the loose change from her apron spilled across the carpet. She picked up her apron and felt inside the pockets. Empty. Except for one dime, two pennies, and an old French fry. She threw the apron on his bare chest and stalked into the kitchen.

"Hey! What'd you do that for?"

Melanie grabbed the skillet and slammed it on the burner. She opened a drawer and slammed it closed without bothering to get anything out. After three more cabinets and two more drawers slamming closed, Rick finally got up and stumbled into the kitchen, his hair sticking up and still wearing his jeans from the night before.

"What the hell is the matter with you? You think I'm dead out here and can't hear this racket?"

Melanie glared at him.

"Well, don't you have something to say for yourself?"

"Go get in the shower, Rick."

He stared at her. "What?"

"You heard me."

"I've got one hell of a hangover, Mel, so don't start with me this morning."

"You smoked all my cigarettes and spent all my money on booze without even bothering to ask? Don't *you* start with me this morning!"

He leaned closer to her. "Your money? Maybe you should move back home with your crazy mother. You live with me rent free so don't even start with your money, your damn cigarettes." He stared at her, waiting for her reply, but she was silent. "Besides, I thought I told you last night to get out." He stormed out of the kitchen.

She smacked the counter in frustration. What was wrong with her? She wanted a commitment from him and yet she was pushing him away. She was going to have to control her temper. What was the big deal? She could always buy more cigarettes and really, there wasn't anything specific she'd planned to buy with that money. They lived together. What was hers was his and vice versa. She began making his breakfast.

Ten minutes later, Melanie set a plate of bacon and eggs on the table as Rick entered the kitchen, his hair still damp from the shower. Sitting down, he glanced over his shoulder. "Where's the toast?"

Melanie grabbed toast from the toaster, placed it on a plate and set it before him. Quickly, he buttered a slice and then took a bite. She sat down opposite him with a cup of coffee warming her hands. "So what are your plans for today?"

Rick shrugged.

"Nothing unusual?"

He ignored her, continuing to eat.

"I'm sorry, Rick. I shouldn't have reacted that way. We are in this together, right?"

He glanced at her, but didn't answer.

"You know the saying: What's mine is yours—"

"Yes," he interrupted. "What's yours is mine and what's mine is mine." He laughed. "I do know the saying."

She studied her fingernails, bitten to the quick and decided to ignore his joke. "Anyway, I thought we could do something tonight. Something fun . . . maybe celebrate?"

He didn't acknowledge even hearing her.

"Well?"

He got up from the table, drinking his orange juice. He put the glass down with a thud and turned away from her, grabbing his keys off the counter. "Already got plans." He opened the front door. "Clean this place up, will you? It's a wreck."

Melanie sighed, picking up a slice of toast. "Happy birthday to me," she sang and bit into it. "Happy birthday to me," she hummed, chewing. She hummed the rest of the song and then tossed the toast onto his empty plate. "Happy birthday, Melanie."

Melanie leaned against the brick wall of the diner, smoking a cigarette, one hand in her apron pocket. She watched as Julius parked his patrol car.

"I didn't know you smoked," he said, walking towards her.

She shrugged.

He studied her face, noticing her swollen lip. "What happened?"

She took a drag on her cigarette and then dropped it to the ground. Avoiding his gaze, she stepped on it. "I fell down the stairs."

He raised an eyebrow. "Funny how that happens."

"The steps were slippery from the rain and I was in a hurry."

He glanced at her legs. "It doesn't look like you injured yourself anywhere else. No visible bruises."

"No." She crossed her arms. "I fell down the stairs," she repeated.

"You deserve better than what that guy is capable of giving you."

She glared at him. "Well, maybe I do deserve better. But then again maybe I don't. Maybe Rick treats me better than you think."

"I'm sorry."

She stared at him. "You are?" She hadn't expected him to apologize.

"Yes. I have absolutely no right to talk about your relationship with Rick."

"No," she said, stunned. "You don't."

He took off his hat and ruffled his hair. "I've never met the man and until I do, it's not appropriate for me to talk about him, good or bad."

She nodded silently, slightly appeased.

"But being a police officer, I can't overlook certain signs. I know the road you're on, Melanie, and I know where it eventually leads. I—"

She held up her hand, not in the least surprised he hadn't changed the subject, but disappointed nonetheless. "I don't want to hear it, Julius. I have to get back to work."

He followed her inside and sat down in a booth. He waited until she brought his coffee. "I'd like to ask you a question. A serious question."

"What is it?"

He began fixing his coffee with cream and sugar. "What do you want? More than anything in this world."

"To win a million dollars."

He stirred his coffee and scowled. "No, really. I want to know. Honestly, what do you want?"

Melanie looked away. She was being honest. Didn't everyone want a million dollars?

"This isn't a trick question." He placed the spoon next to his coffee cup. Interlocking his fingers, he looked up at her. "And it isn't a way to—I don't know—ingratiate myself with you. I'd really like to know."

"Why? What difference does it make?"

"I don't know that it'll make any kind of difference. I certainly don't expect it to change anything. We're just having a conversation." He took a sip of his coffee, watching her stare out of the window. "I'll tell you what I want. That is, if you'd like to know?"

She hesitated, glancing around the restaurant until finally meeting his eyes. "Okay, sure," she said, lifting her chin slightly, challenging him. "Tell me, Julius, what you want most in all the world."

"You might think it's dumb."

"I might."

"OK then . . ." He was suddenly nervous. "I want to find someone who will love me as much as I love her. I want to build her a rose garden."

"That's it?" she asked, her voice sharper than she'd intended.

"That's a lot. Some people would say it is almost impossible. You don't think so?"

A customer waved his hand, trying to get Melanie's attention. "Mel!"

Melanie nodded at the customer to indicate she'd heard him

before returning her attention to Julius. "I've got to go. I'd recommend the vegetable soup and the turkey sandwich. It's the special today."

"That's fine." He sighed and slouched down in the seat a little. She took a step away from him, but then stopped, biting her lip. He looked up at her.

"It is a lot, Julius. And I do think it is very rare, to be able to experience that kind of emotion with someone. If it exists, well, I hope you find that." She hurried away.

"Ida," Melanie said, walking up to where the older woman stood drinking a soda. "Did Julius say anything to you when he left?"

"No. Why?"

Melanie glanced back at his table. "Well, he didn't leave me a paper rose like he usually does. And he didn't say good-bye." He also didn't wish her a happy birthday, but she couldn't admit that to Ida. Not after she'd given her such a hard time for telling him in the first place.

"Did he leave you a tip?"

"Yeah, the usual five. Mary," she said, turning to the elderly cashier who'd suddenly joined them, "How did Julius seem when he paid the bill?"

She shrugged. "He seemed fine to me. He's always so pleasant. And handsome, too, don't you think? I've always liked a man in uniform."

"Don't," Ida said. "You're wasting your breath on this one."

"Ida!" Melanie said, exasperated. "Why are you taking this so personally? I have a boyfriend already."

She shook her head. "Boyfriend. I don't think you know what a boyfriend is."

"You think he finally got the point? That I'm not interested?"

"A man can't take rejection too many days in a row without some sort of encouragement."

"Yeah, you're probably right." She knew she sounded disappointed, and she also knew it was a little crazy to be disappointed. She had Rick, after all, and actually, if she had any sense, she'd be happy there wouldn't be any more paper roses in the future. She'd have felt obligated to keep them and Rick would've eventually found them and then she'd have worse than a fat lip to answer nosy questions about.

"We were so busy this morning I never had the chance to ask you—although I can't believe you wouldn't have been shouting the news when you first walked through the front door—did you get that ring yet?"

"My birthday's not over, Ida."

"Wouldn't that be wonderful?" Mary gushed. "I just love weddings."

Ida glared at her.

"Oh, shoot. Why is it that the moment I walk away from that cash register, someone always wants to pay?" She smiled slightly and hurried over to the register.

Ida set her glass down and stared at Melanie.

"What?"

She shook her head. "You think you're fooling me, missy, but in reality, all you're doing is fooling yourself."

Melanie stared at Ida, but didn't say anything.

"But if you don't like Julius, okay. I guess. Why don't you come to church with me this week? Lots of cute, single, God-loving men would fall over their feet just to get to open the door for you."

"That sounds a bit exaggerated."

"Most women at our church your age are already married. Come and see for yourself how I'm not exaggerating. Well, would you look at that," Ida said, staring past Melanie's shoulder.

Melanie turned around to see a man walking towards them carrying a large bouquet of peach roses. It had to be Julius because of the policeman's uniform, but the flowers he carried hid his face. He stopped in front of them and both women were speechless.

Julius poked his head around the side. "Happy birthday, Melanie."

She stared, her mouth slightly open.

"Put them here," Ida instructed, patting the counter with one hand as she cleared a space with the other. "They're beautiful."

He smiled. "Thank you. I grew them myself."

Melanie continued to stare at the flowers. Finally, Ida nudged her and she turned to stare at Julius. "I don't know what to say." She turned to look at the flowers again.

"Well, I thought it best to give you these now, rather than let them wilt by waiting until later, hoping I'd see you tonight when it's pretty obvious I won't."

Melanie leaned closer to the roses and breathed in deeply.

Ida giggled. "Finally some roses she can smell!"

Melanie smacked her lightly on the shoulder. "Ida!" Overwhelmed, she glanced at Julius. "They're really beautiful, Julius. I love them. I really do."

He smiled. "Yeah?"

She nodded. "I'm so surprised. I just never expected . . ." She took a deep breath. "It's the best present I've ever gotten. Thank you."

A scratchy voice rumbled over the walkie-talkie at his hip. "Excuse me," he said, already turning away and lifting it to his mouth.

Ida and Melanie nodded, unable to stop staring at the flowers.

"Don't they smell wonderful?" Melanie murmured.

"Aren't you glad I told him it was your birthday?"

She smiled. "No."

Ida laughed. "Liar."

"Well, looks like duty calls. Happy birthday again, Melanie."

"Thank you very much," she said, tearing her eyes away from the flowers to meet his gaze.

Ida grabbed his arm. "Listen, why don't you come by later? I'm going to try and convince Melanie to go out with you for a little while tonight."

Melanie gasped, her face instantly flushing with embarrassment.

Julius glanced at her, but turned his attention back to the older woman. "Thank you, but I want Melanie to go out with me because she wants to, not because she's been talked into it, or worse, guilted into it."

"Just come by around . . . I don't know . . . eight?"

Melanie pinched her arm. "Quit meddling in my life."

Ida scowled, rubbing the spot where Melanie had pinched her. "We both know she deserves better than that low-down coward she's with."

"She should have plans with that low-down coward tonight, it being her birthday and all."

"I do," she lied, her voice quiet, unable to meet his eyes.

"Go on, Julius. Criminals are waiting. I'll see you at eight on account of I'm working a double."

He nodded and left.

Melanie crossed her arms. "How could you do that to me? I've never been so embarrassed in my life!"

"Someone had to do something before he gave up on you. How can you be so blind? He is perfect for you!"

"It doesn't matter if he is perfect for me or not. Rick and I are very happy. Don't start trouble."

Ida put her arm around her shoulders. "I'm trying to get you out of trouble. Eventually you'll see that and be glad I was looking out for you. Not everyone can be so lucky."

"Lucky?"

"I pray for you every day, Melanie. Every day I ask that the Lord protect you, that the Holy Spirit opens your eyes to what a scoundrel that boyfriend of yours is. Every day we work together I wonder if you'll show up or if he's killed you."

"Ida!" Melanie shook her head. "That's crazy. Why would you think that?"

"Why? Do you think I'm blind? Don't you get that you are a victim?"

Melanie crossed her arms. "A victim? You are nuts."

Ida studied Melanie and finally shrugged. "Maybe so." She changed the subject. "Those flowers sure are pretty. And he grew them himself. I just can't get over that. Maybe I should try to get him to marry me." She laughed at the thought. "Then you could smell roses whenever you felt like it."

Mary joined them again. "Henry would be awful jealous if he heard you say such a thing, Ida."

"But I bet Henry would bring her ten bouquets if he thought she'd go out with him. In fact, you should focus more on Henry and less on me and my love life, Ida."

Ida blushed. "Oh, hush up the both of you. I swear, you can be such silly gossips!"

"Now you know he doesn't come here every day just for the coffee, Ida. I'm his cashier just as often as you're his waitress and yet I bet that he wouldn't be able to pick me out of a lineup. Julius, however, is at least aware of the rest of us, even if his attention is focused on Melanie."

Melanie smiled, pretty certain Mary was right, but refused to enter further into the conversation. Instead, she allowed her attention to return to the roses. They were beautiful. And they smelled wonderful, even better than she'd imagined when she sniffed all those paper roses she'd saved since meeting the green-thumbed cop. Sure, she loved Rick, but right now, at this very moment, she wished it were Julius she loved. Julius, the man who wants more than anything to grow roses for the woman he loves. She sighed. Whoever she was, she'd be a very lucky woman.

"Melanie?"

"I'm sorry, Ida. I didn't hear what you said."

"So I noticed. What were you thinking?"

"I was thinking I can't take these home with me."

"Because of that dastardly Rick, I suppose. But if he really loves you, he must also trust you."

"Well, of course he trusts me. I never said that. It's just that I'm here more than I'm home so I think I should leave them here so that I can enjoy them as much as possible."

"Good idea," Mary agreed. "And you can come and visit them whenever you want."

Melanie smiled slightly. "I sure can."

"I know that nothing can compete with those beautiful flowers, but Mary and I got you a little something."

She turned to her friends in surprise. "You did?"

Mary retrieved a small wrapped present from where they'd hidden it among the extra napkins and straws in the bottom cabinet. "It's not much now."

"Pens!" she said, tearing the paper to reveal the gift. "And they have my name on them!"

"You're always losing them and blaming Mary or me or one of the other girls for stealing them. So now you'll know exactly who swiped your pen," Ida said.

"Thanks, Ida. Thanks, Mary. That was thoughtful of you."

"And the cooks wanted to get you something, too." Ida handed her an envelope.

She laughed. "I hope this is what I think it is!" Opening the envelope, she pulled out a couple of lottery tickets. Waving them triumphantly over her head, she walked over to the kitchen window and banged on the bell to get their attention. "Pedro! Felipe! These had better be winners!"

They grinned happily. "Okay, *mamacita*. Happy birthday."

"Looks like the fun's about over, girls," Mary said, as she hurried to seat the customers who'd just walked in.

"Time to get back to work. Here comes the lunch rush." Ida grimaced.

With a last glance at the roses, Melanie sighed and headed to her new table.

CHAPTER 4

M elanie stopped just inside the door of Ruben's, waiting for her eyes to adjust to the darkness. The dim lighting reminded her a little of her mother's house. There was a blonde on stage, wearing only a garter and a pair of tiny thong underwear as she danced to the beat of an unfamiliar song playing from the jukebox in the corner. She watched as the blonde flirted with a drunken Japanese man, his brown fingers reaching to tuck crisp bills into the skimpy strap of her black thong. The girl moved along the small stage, pausing to smile and fondle herself as various men tucked money into her garter and panties, their fingers eager to feel her pale skin as they risked getting reprimanded by the chaperoning bouncers. Melanie surveyed the sparse crowd, but she recognized no one. She walked towards the bar stretching along the back wall.

"Melanie, I haven't seen you around lately."

She turned to the old man who'd approached her, a fat cigar clenched between his lips. She smiled, recognizing him as the owner. "Mr. Nichols. How are you?"

He reached out and hugged her, squeezing her tightly. She was a little surprised that such a frail-looking man would have such strength. But then he only looked old. His true age was a mystery. He probably wasn't sure exactly how old he was himself. "Couldn't be better." He pulled away from her and let his eyes roam over her body. "You could stand to put on a few pounds, Melanie. And what's with the fat lip?"

"Oh, it's nothing." She averted her eyes, looking past his shoulder. "It's rather embarrassing to admit, but I fell down the stairs."

He puffed on his cigar, squinting up at her. Finally, he removed it from his lips and waved it towards the back room where the pool tables were. "If that son of a bitch hit you—"

"Oh, no, Mr. Nichols. Rick wasn't even home when it happened. It had been raining and well, I . . . uh . . .," she tried to explain, her tongue thick with the lie. Waving her hand as though erasing the words she spoke, she continued, "I hadn't been paying attention, day-dreaming about something or other and so I slipped on one of the wet steps and down I went." She snapped her fingers.

"You're lucky you weren't hurt worse than a busted lip."

She nodded, tapping her fingers against her thighs. "That's what Rick said. He was very upset with me for my clumsiness."

"Clumsiness," he repeated softly.

She nodded vigorously and then smiled to compensate for her rather over-the-top adamancy.

He grabbed her hand and squeezed it. "If he ever gets out of line, you let me know, Melanie, and I'll teach that prick some manners."

She nodded, unable to say a word. She'd only met him a few times and each time she was always taken aback to realize that he was nothing like you'd expect a strip club owner to be like. Bizarre as it was, he really seemed to care about women. All the strippers liked him as far as she could tell. In fact, many of them confessed that the only reason they stayed there rather than moving on to a bigger, busier club in a neighboring town was because of Mr. Nichols. He considered each of them to be the daughter he'd never gotten to have before his wife had died of cancer early on in their marriage.

"Go on," he grumbled. "You know where he is."

She smiled slightly. "It was nice seeing you, Mr. Nichols."

"Yeah," he mumbled, puffing on his cigar.

She walked away, feeling his eyes on her back.

Around the pool tables were about a dozen or so people, mostly guys, but a couple of girls who were obviously trying to fit in with their sweet-smelling cigars, racy talk, and hoarse laughter. They pretended they didn't even notice the cocktail waitresses dressed in skimpy feathered negligees, but when the waitresses walked away, their eyes searched for flaws and they always managed to find something to feel superior about.

Melanie hung back on the edge of the room, watching Rick as he prepared to take his next shot. He was losing this game and the bald black man he was playing against was looking pretty happy with himself. Rick missed. The man took his turn, an easy shot of the eight ball into the side pocket, and then the game was over. Rick made a big show of being disappointed, begging the man for one more game, and doubling the bet.

"Come on, Mo, give me another chance. I've got to get lucky sometime."

"Shit," he said, a big smile on his face, "an ugly white boy like you ain't never going to get lucky."

"One more game. That's all I ask. What's the big deal? You've already taken quite a chunk of my dough as it is."

"Yeah, it's mighty generous of you."

Rick smirked. "Maybe you're worried your luck's run out. Because I have yet to see any skill."

"Luck? How can one scrawny white boy be so dumb?" Mo wondered, turning to the few bystanders. He grinned. "Or maybe you're just blind? You must be awfully dumb to say my beating your ass isn't skill."

"Then why are you so worried about playing me again? I've got a whole 'nother pocket of dough just waiting to cross those sweaty palms of yours."

"Shit, you might as well just hand it over then. It's a lot less time consuming, you know what I mean?"

"Fuck you. I am not so dumb as to fall for that. Here I am, begging you to let me try to get my dignity back. You going to walk away without offering me just one last chance?"

"Dignity? That's ripe." He laughed, shaking his head. "All right, you dumb-ass fool. I'll play you one more game, but this time pay attention and maybe you'll learn something."

Rick moved to the end of the table to rack the balls. "Now that's some bold ass talk. Maybe I've just been having a run of bad luck."

"Shit, I've beat you so bad your momma don't even want to claim you."

Melanie walked over to Rick, smiling. He was really sexy.

He frowned the moment he saw her. "Damn it, Mel. What're you doing here?"

She kept a smile plastered on her stiff lips. "I came to see you."

"I'm busy. You know I'm busy here," he grumbled. He tightened the rack with his fingers and then gently lifted it from the table. Mo chalked his cue at the other end of the table. "Give me a sec, Mo."

"That can't be your lady?" he said, nodding towards Melanie. "Baby, you get bored being with a loser, you call on Big Mo because I am a gen-u-ine winner."

"Yeah, in your dreams maybe. I'll be right back."

"Take as long as you need, but you're still going to get schooled." He grinned, his teeth bright white against his dark skin.

Rick grabbed Melanie's elbow and pulled her away from the pool table.

"Ow, Rick, you're hurting me," she complained, trying to pull her arm out of his grasp.

"Now," he said, releasing her, "what the hell are you doing coming in here?"

"It's obvious you've forgotten, Rick, so I might as well remind you." She took a deep breath. "Today's my birthday."

He stared at her. "So?"

Her heart dropped. There went the idea of getting an engagement ring for her birthday. "So I thought maybe we could spend some time together tonight."

"I am busy, Mel, trying to make some money. Can't you spend your birthday with someone else?"

She folded her arms, biting her lip and looking at a spot over his shoulder. "You don't want to spend time with me on my birthday?"

"I do. Of course I do. But not right now."

"Come on, Rick. I'd like to get this ass whipping over with so I can have some time spending your dough on a few of those fine chicks out there."

Melanie swallowed, fighting to keep her tears in check. She would not cry in front of him and all these people over this.

"So are you leaving? Because I'm about to beat that cocky black bastard over there. And then I'll be home. Okay?"

"Yeah, okay." She hurried away from him and practically broke into a run the closer she got to the door. Once outside, she stopped. She leaned against the brick building and closed her eyes, breathing deeply. Hearing footsteps scuffing along the cement, she looked up to see Mr. Nichols strolling towards her.

Wordlessly, he held out a cigarette.

She stared at him and then accepted the cigarette, wondering briefly how he knew she needed one and which stripper he'd bummed it off of. Putting it to her lips, he struck a match and she leaned forward to reach the flame. She inhaled as he dropped the match to the ground, the flame extinguished and a thin thread of smoke curling up from the cool cement. "Thank you."

He stared silently at her, puffing on his cigar, his blue eyes intense through the thick smoke surrounding his face.

"I wish I didn't love him so much," she admitted unhappily. But she did love him. He'd taken her in when she'd had nowhere to go. No one forced him to do that. She knew he was a good person deep down; she just wished he'd show it a little more often.

"If you love, you will suffer, and if you do not love, you do not know the meaning of a Christian life."

Melanie stared at him in surprise.

He smiled slightly, noticing her shock. "My wife read that in Agatha Christie's autobiography and quoted it often to me and Giorgio."

"The mystery writer?"

"Yes. I'm not about to pretend I'm a religious man, although my wife did her best to turn me into one, bless her soul; I mean, I own a strip club and I think the Church would frown on that. But I do believe the first part."

"Sometimes love makes you suffer?"

"Exactly."

"That sucks," she said, flicking the ash from her cigarette so hard she almost broke it in half.

"I couldn't have said it better." He moved to stand next to her, and together they smoked in silence.

Her thoughts turned to what she should do now, tonight, for her birthday. She didn't want to sit at home, smoking cigarette after cigarette, her tears and self-pity the only company in the dark and smoky apartment. There was no telling how long Rick would be. He'd said after that game, but there was always another game to be played, another guy to beat. And it'd be suicidal to go and see her mother and Benjie again when she was already feeling so worthless. It sounded silly, but really, she wouldn't have minded sitting in front of her peach roses, her whole body filled with their scent.

"What time is it?"

Mr. Nichols glanced at his watch. "Oh, a little after eight."

She nodded, drawing on her cigarette. After eight. Julius would be gone by the time she got there, if he'd even gone to the diner in the first place. He hadn't actually said he'd be there at eight; he'd only nodded, and that could've just been as a good-bye. She studied the dull red glow of her cigarette and then dropped it and stepped on it, extinguishing the flame.

"Thanks, Mr. Nichols. I've got to go."

He waved slightly, but she'd already hurried across the street to the parking lot.

Quickly, she unlocked her car and got in, starting the engine before her door was even closed. "I'm not going to see Julius," she said firmly. "I'm going to see my roses." So what if she was in a hurry?

CHAPTER 5

Julius was leaving the diner when Melanie pulled into the parking lot. She stopped in front of him and rolled down the window.

"How are my roses?"

He studied her face, the way the streetlight glinted off her dark hair loose around her shoulders. "They're fine."

Uncertain what to say next, she nodded.

"How's your birthday?"

She shrugged, watching her fingers trace the outline of the steering wheel.

He stepped closer to the car and leaned in, breathing the soft scent of her perfume into his lungs. "What are you thinking right now?"

She glanced at him and smiled nervously. "What am I thinking? I don't know. I wasn't thinking anything really."

"I don't believe you."

She stared at him. He actually wanted to know what she was thinking? Rick never seemed to care what she was thinking, certainly he'd never bothered to ask. "Okay, I was thinking that I don't know what to say to you."

"Who said you have to say anything?" He glanced around the parking lot. "Would you like to go somewhere else?"

"Where?"

"Anyplace has to be better than sitting in this parking lot, doesn't it?"

She nodded, smiling. "Okay. But let's take my car."

He turned to walk around to the passenger side of the car, but Melanie stuck her head out of the window and called to him. "Julius, you're driving."

Returning to the driver's side, he opened the car door.

"You don't mind, do you?"

He shook his head and she climbed over the console to the other side. Julius got in and they drove off.

Ten minutes later, without a word said between them, Julius parked the car and turned the engine off. He glanced over at Melanie.

"We're stopping here?" she asked, looking out the window at the empty baseball field lit only by the light of the full moon.

He smiled and, without a word, got out of the car. Melanie watched him as he walked, his head high, his shoulders back. He walked with confidence, not like Rick who walked, or rather swaggered, with cockiness. She didn't think she'd ever seen him out of uniform, but tonight he wore jeans and a polo shirt. He seemed more . . . real somehow. She opened her door, the sound of his footsteps in the uncut grass instantly reaching her. What was she doing here? She should've stayed at Ruben's and waited for Rick. He'd been stressed out over the game he was playing against that black guy Mo. That was the only reason he'd been so cold to her, so anxious to get her away from there. If, instead of overreacting, she'd hung out at the bar until he was through, he probably would've taken her someplace for a late dinner or something. And Mr. Nichols probably would've given her a few drinks on the house as a birthday present while she waited. But instead, she was at a baseball field in the dark with a customer from the diner who liked her and gave her beautiful peach roses he'd grown himself for her birthday. She should take him back to his car. Rick wouldn't like it one bit if he found out.

"Well, birthday girl? Are you going to sit there all night? Come on!"

She climbed out of the car. It was her birthday and Rick most likely wouldn't be done at the club for at least an hour. She closed the car door. She had time to figure out what Julius was up to. Besides, it wasn't like she was attracted to him or anything. He wasn't her type. There was nothing wrong with hanging out with a friend for a bit, right? And hadn't Rick asked if she could spend her birthday with someone else?

Julius waited for her to reach him. Taking her hand, he squeezed it. "You've got a brave heart, Melanie."

She stared at him. What did that mean? She started to pull her hand away, but suddenly he laughed happily, squeezing her fingers tighter.

"Tonight, I want you to forget about everything you stress about during the day. Let's relax, maybe even have some fun." He raised her hand to his lips and kissed it. "Race you to the swings!" Releasing her hand, he bolted towards the fenced-in playground.

Melanie was momentarily stunned, her mind unable to command her body to move, but then the challenge suddenly became clear and she chased after him. When she reached the playground, he was leaning casually against the fence.

"Cheater," she said, and smiled.

Julius pretended outrage. "What? How dare you accuse me of being a cheater! I'm offended."

Melanie crossed her arms and stared him down. "Cheater," she said softly.

He broke into a grin and shrugged. "You think my ego can handle being beaten by a woman? I," he said, adopting an English accent, "am a mere mortal, my dear." He opened the gate and gestured inside. "In!"

She laughed, walking past him. "Race you," she whispered once she was inside the gate, and took off running. The gate clanged shut as he yanked it closed and ran after her.

It wasn't much of a race. For one thing, the distance was only a few feet. And with legs as long as Julius's, he could've easily beaten her. But he kept behind her and she won, jumping on the swing first.

"Okay, so now who's the cheater?" Julius asked, his eyes glittering in the darkness.

Melanie smiled. "All's fair in love and war."

"Which is this? Love? Or war?"

She hesitated and then decided to ignore the question. "Loser has to push so get pushing, mister."

He shrugged and walked behind her. Grabbing the chain on either side of the swing, he pulled her back and then released her. She swung forward.

"Harder!"

"Demanding, aren't you?" he asked, pushing her harder.

Higher and higher she swung. Finally, he stopped pushing her and sat on the swing next to her. Together, they swung back and forth, the creaking of the swingset and the chirping of the crickets the only sounds in the darkness. It was exhilarating, Melanie decided, with the cool October breeze in her face and butterflies in her stomach whenever she swung really high. Perhaps one night when she couldn't sleep, she'd come to the ballpark and swing for a while.

"Having fun?"

She glanced over at him. "Yeah, I am. Thank you, Julius. I really needed this."

"Well, if nothing else, at least you'll be able to say you had an interesting birthday."

"You know, you are different tonight. Less like Julius the Policeman and more like Julius, a guy who happens to be a police officer. Does that make sense?"

"Is it a good thing?"

She smiled slightly. "I suppose it is."

He shrugged. "I am just a guy who happens to be a police officer. I used to be a gardener. Landscape architect. Now, I'm a cop."

"That's a bit of a leap, isn't it? But it explains your roses."

"*Your* roses." He smiled. He slowed his swing down. "My father was a cop, but he died on the job."

She stopped swinging. "I'm sorry."

"It was stupid. A regular traffic stop, but the kid was high and paranoid. And armed. A triple threat. But my dad was so passionate about eliminating crime and creating safe communities that I decided to pick up where he left off. I joined the force."

"Traded in your spade for a gun."

"More like badge. The gun is just along for the ride."

They fell silent, their swings swaying slightly, their feet skimming the dirt.

"Are you ready to take me back to the diner?" Melanie asked uncertainly.

"I suppose he'll be wondering where you are."

She glanced up at him in surprise. "What?"

"Your boyfriend. You probably have to go because he'll be wondering where you are?"

"Yes. Yes," she repeated, realizing she didn't want to leave. Julius was a nice guy, the type that would take care of his wife, sacrificing everything to make her happy. Exactly the kind of guy she needed, except he was too predictable. Predictable was boring. Rick didn't even know what predictable meant. Being with him was like riding a different rollercoaster every day. If she'd grown up in a stable, "white bread" household, would she prefer someone like Julius over Rick? Or would she still have fallen for the bad boy? What if she'd moved in with a great guy like Julius all those years ago when her mother kicked her out of the house? Her life would be completely different. "He will be worried. In fact, I really shouldn't have stayed so long."

Julius grabbed her hand. "Thanks for spending this time with me. I wasn't expecting it." He laughed then. "But I'm a terrible friend because I don't even know how old you are!"

She stared at him. Were they becoming friends? It would be nice to have a friend like Julius who would look out for her, but it was silly to entertain any other ideas. And if she let him get close to her . . . well, she just couldn't. Rick would make her stop talking to him the moment he found out. "You know a lot about me, all the important stuff."

"The important stuff?" He raised his eyebrows. "Like what?"

She smiled. "My name, my birthday, my favorite flower, where I work."

"Tell me what you love about him."

With a frown, she turned and started towards the car.

He jumped to his feet and chased after her. "Wait a minute."

She stopped and faced him.

"I suppose you think I've got a big mouth? That I'm pushy? But I'm afraid you'll never give me the chance after tonight and I know so very little about you—"

She placed her fingers over his mouth. "I'm twenty-six. I've been with Rick for about six years. He can be charming when it suits him, but I suppose that's not what I love most about him. It might be that he's strong enough to be able to put up with me every day and I'm very grateful for that. Or maybe I love him because he's fun and exciting and dangerous. I never know what to expect from him next. He's my rollercoaster. He took me in when I had nowhere to go. The few times he's let his temper get the best of him, I think of the kindness he showed me when I was at rock bottom. Underneath it all he is a good guy. And that's why I cannot dump him to go out with you." She smiled slightly. "Thank you, Julius, for this," she said, waving her hand at the swings. "I'll always remember this birthday because of you."

He reached for her hand, his eyes serious. "Just because he was there when you were vulnerable doesn't mean you owe him your life. You are loyal to a fault, Melanie. You know, I've met a lot of people through my career. God orchestrates that—"

"Julius—"

He held up his hand. "A conversation for a different night. Don't you think there's something between us?"

"It doesn't matter what I think. I'm with Rick and that's that."

He dropped her hand. "But he doesn't love you!"

She raised her chin, suddenly angry. "What do you know about it? About us?"

"I know he hurts you, Melanie! I've seen your bruises!" He ran his hand through his hair and took a deep breath. "That's not love."

She smiled sadly. "Love can be very painful, Julius."

"I don't believe that."

"What? That love is painful? It's no accident that love is a four-letter word, you know."

He smiled at that. "There are other four-letter words that represent positive things."

"Like what?"

"Good is a four-letter word."

"So is evil. It depends on how you look at things. I might believe something you'd call good is really evil."

"I think you're reaching on that one. How about home?"

"That's just another word for prison."

"Now that is far-fetched."

"Not if you're a free spirit looking to roam from place to place."

He shook his head. "Are we talking about you? Because you're not looking to roam from place to place. I think you're scared to be alone, so you've latched onto Rick as if he was a lifeboat. But he's going down and you're about to hit rock bottom together."

"Everybody needs someone. There's nothing wrong with that."

"I know that. God made Eve for a reason. I'm saying that you've latched onto Rick because you are too scared to jump into another boat, a safer, better boat, even if the boat you're in has a leak."

Melanie's fingers fluttered by her side. She'd been right to try to keep her distance from him. If only she'd stuck to it! Julius saw too much and she hated feeling so exposed, so vulnerable.

He reached out and caressed her cheek. "I can see that you've made up your mind about this theory. But I don't believe it. Rick doesn't love you because he beats you, Melanie. That just means he's a coward."

"You don't know what you're talking about."

"Who taught you love was a four-letter word? Your family?"

"It doesn't matter."

"It matters to me."

"I really have to go."

"You're running away."

"No," she said. "I'm not." She turned away from him and began walking toward the parking lot.

Julius watched her and sighed. "I'm falling in love with you," he said, but she didn't show him that she'd heard him. Slowly he followed her to the car.

The ride back to the diner was a silent one, the radio playing softly in the background. And by the time Melanie parked the car next to Julius's at the diner, she'd convinced herself she'd only imagined he'd told her he was falling for her.

He sat with his hand on the door handle, but didn't attempt to open the door.

"We're here," Melanie said needlessly.

He turned to face her. "Marry me."

She frowned and opened her mouth to say something, but Julius held his hand up.

"Just listen to me for a minute. I'm not joking about this, Melanie. It may seem crazy, and maybe it is." He ran his hand through his hair. "In fact, it is a little crazy. A lot crazy. Everyone I know can tell you I don't rush into things, but if I get out of this car without telling you what's in my heart, I'm afraid I'll never get another chance. I am falling in love with you. I don't know where you stand with God, but it isn't a coincidence that you were my waitress. And I'm beginning to think God put us together at the diner so that in the end I could take care of you."

"Julius—"

"Let me spend the rest of my life making you happy. I can take care of you better than he can."

"You're talking nonsense."

"Are you saying that because you don't feel anything for me?" He held his breath as he waited for her answer.

"How can you want to marry me when you know nothing about me?"

"I know your name, where you work, your favorite flower, your birthday. Didn't you say that was all the important stuff?"

"That isn't funny."

"I'm sorry. But maybe you were right when you said that."

"You also know I'm not available. How can I marry you when I'm living with Rick?"

"That can't be your excuse."

"It's not an excuse. That's just how it is."

"He doesn't love you—"

She banged her hand on the steering wheel. "Yes, he does!" She sighed. "You don't hang out with us so you have no right to say such a thing."

He was quiet for a moment, staring out the window. Finally, he turned back to her. "You're right. I'm sorry. Maybe he does love you—"

"Thank you—"

"—but his kind of love isn't healthy. I want to protect you, not hurt you. It kills me to think of him giving you even the faintest of bruises."

"I think you should get out now."

He frowned. "You have nothing else to say?"

Melanie shook her head, staring out into the parking lot. "Why do you think you could love me? What about me can you possibly love, Julius? I'm not special."

"You haven't smoked all night. Why is that?"

"Now who's changing the subject?"

"Can you please just answer the question?"

She shrugged. "Fine. I haven't smoked because I know you don't like it. And the moment your feet hit the pavement, I'm lighting up."

He smiled. "I love the sound of your laugh. I love the color of your eyes because they remind me of fudge brownies, my favorite dessert. You have a generous heart, Melanie. And you deserve so much more out of life than what you're getting. You are painfully difficult to get to know, but it is worth the effort."

"Aren't you exaggerating a bit? Overstating things? I'm not perfect, Julius. I'll never even be close to perfect." She shook her head. "I can't listen to this anymore, okay? Please, let's just blame this conversation on the moon or something and forget it."

Julius stared at her silently. Finally, he nodded slightly. "All right. Will I see you again? Outside of the diner?" he added as she opened her mouth to speak.

She hesitated, rubbing her thumb along the bottom half of the steering wheel. "We don't exactly run in the same circles."

"You know what I mean."

She nodded. "You're right, I do. And I don't think that's a good idea."

"At least you're honest." He reached for her hand. "Can I give you my number?"

She frowned. "Julius—"

"This is sudden, I get that. Perhaps you're overwhelmed. You could take some time and think about things, what you want in your future. There's no harm in that, right?"

"I don't need time."

"What can it hurt to think it over?"

She pulled her hand free. "Fine. If you insist." She fumbled through the glove box until she found an old envelope and handed it to him. "I think there's a pen on the floor by your feet."

He found the pen and quickly wrote on the back of the envelope. "I'm giving you my sister's number as well. If I'm not home, she'll know how to reach me. And hey, we're having Sunday dinner at my mother's if you wanted to join us. She's a good cook."

She took the envelope from him. "Good-bye, Julius."

He opened the door and got out, but leaned back in. "I'd be a good husband to you, Melanie. Think about it." He pushed in the car lighter. "This one time I'll encourage your habit. But only because you look a little stressed and I feel like that's my fault." He grinned and then shut the door before she could comment.

As she pulled out of the parking lot, she glanced in her rearview mirror to see him watching her drive away. How could he think about marrying someone like her? He was Sunday dinners with his mother and she was late nights at a strip club. And how could he know what she deserved out of life? He couldn't know. She wasn't great. She was an awful person. Certainly her mother thought so. She crumpled the envelope and tossed it in the back seat. The only thing she had to look forward to in life was living with Rick. But she would convince him to marry her. She had to. She needed to prove her mother wrong. Although wouldn't her mother be speechless if Melanie married someone upstanding and honorable like Julius? The lighter popped out and she fumbled in her purse for a cigarette, careful to keep her eyes on the road. Of course, she couldn't marry Julius. The constant pressure of trying to keep him in the dark about all of her many faults would kill her before her next birthday. Besides, she loved Rick . . . didn't she?

CHAPTER 6

Melanie collapsed on the couch, running her fingers through her damp hair. The diner had been busier than usual for a Saturday and, although the scalding shower had helped ease the tension in her shoulders, she was still hoping for a quiet, relaxing evening. Picking up the remote control, she flipped through several channels. Perhaps she'd luck out and find a good movie just starting.

The door opened and Melanie looked up to see Rick enter the apartment smiling, a grocery bag in his arms. He was followed by two of his friends, Marty and Steve.

He hadn't actually told her he'd be going out tonight, but still she was surprised. "What are you doing home on a Saturday night?"

Rick set the bag on the coffee table and grabbed the remote control from her. Quickly he flipped through the channels. "The fight's on tonight. What's for dinner?"

She turned away, not wanting him to see the displeasure she was sure was written all over her face. So much for a quiet night. And so much for a movie.

"Mel, are you making dinner?"

She stood up. "Why don't we order a pizza?"

Rick glowered at her and she turned hastily to smile at his friends. "Hi, Steve," she said, nodding to the tall, skinny guy. She turned to the heavier man. "Marty, I haven't seen you around in a while."

"I've been in County."

"Oh." She wondered what he'd done and how long he'd been in jail. When Rick stayed out until the early hours of the morning, she often worried he'd been hauled into jail, but so far his luck was holding out. Or else she wasn't the one he called to bail him out.

Rick plopped down on the couch, resting his feet on the coffee table. He waved towards the grocery bag he'd brought home. "Put the beer in the fridge before it starts to get warm."

She picked it up, noticing the tightness of his mouth.

"And put a six-pack in the freezer," he called after her as she headed to the kitchen. He turned to grin at his friends. "A nice icy cold beer is just what we need."

Steve nodded, sitting down on the couch next to Rick and stretching his legs out. "Sounds good to me."

Marty settled himself in the chair next to the couch. "Man, how I missed doing this when I was in lockup. Different vibe and all, you know."

"Mel," Rick called, "bring us three beers!"

She frowned, but grabbed the bottles from the freezer and passed them out, listening as they argued about the fight.

"So, who'd you bet on?" Rick asked.

"Hold up," Marty said, holding up his hand. "Let's order some food before the fight starts."

Rick shrugged. "Yeah, sure. Sounds good to me."

"I could go for some slices," Steve said.

"Mel, order us a pizza," Rick demanded, flicking the bottle cap across the room. He took a long swig of beer. "What do you guys want on it?"

"No mushrooms," Steve said.

"No vegetables at all," Marty said.

"Get us a couple large onion, sausage, pepperoni, ham, and . . . ?"

"Garlic." Marty smiled. "It's been a long time since I've had garlic."

Rick let out a loud burp. "And garlic then." He motioned to the television. "Christy Martin is one tough chick. That's going to be a good fight to watch."

Melanie disappeared into the kitchen and dutifully called in the pizza order, wondering what she would have for dinner since the pizza was obviously just for them.

"Have you seen that new chick Nichols hired?" Rick asked.

Marty grinned. "There's a new stripper at the club?"

Melanie paused in the doorway of the kitchen, listening to the conversation.

"Yeah," Steve answered. "And she's pretty hot."

"She's definitely hot," Rick answered. "She's got tits like cantaloupes, blonde hair that reaches a perfectly rounded booty . . ." He drew an outline of her body with his hands.

"And the longest legs I've ever seen," Steve added, closing his eyes as he remembered.

Marty licked his lips. "Is she single?"

Rick laughed. "Now you know old man Nichols won't let you near her. Least not 'til he's done tapping that ass."

"I only need ten minutes with her. After that, she'll want me so bad she won't listen to that old timer."

Melanie shook her head slightly. Men were such pigs sometimes.

"Ten minutes? You sure you're not exaggerating?" Rick goaded.

"I still think Rick's got the best around," Steve said, peeling the label from his beer bottle.

Melanie frowned. Did Rick have someone on the side?

"Yeah," Marty agreed. "Mel's hot all right. Which is why I can't understand what the hell she's doing with a bum like you. What's your secret?"

"Hey, the fight's starting. Look at that scrawny Mexican. He should be getting his ass beat, but he's fighting hard!"

Steve punched Rick lightly in the arm. "Don't change the subject, yo."

He grinned. "What can I say? I guess I'm good in bed."

Marty laughed. "In your dreams maybe."

"Screw you. For all we know, you could've been someone's bitch in the joint."

"Rick, I should beat your ass right now. Lucky for you I don't want to miss the fight, especially since I helped you rig it so you'd get it for free."

He laughed, raising his bottle in a toast. "Free pay-per-view. Ain't life grand!"

Melanie leaned against the refrigerator, her heart soaring. They thought she was hot?

Rick stood up. "More beer?"

Marty drained the last half of his beer. "Oh yeah."

"Sure," Steve said, reaching his empty bottle to Rick.

Melanie busied herself in the kitchen, quickly grabbing a glass from the cupboard and removing the pitcher of tea from the fridge.

Rick paused in the doorway and watched her fill the glass. "Eavesdropping, Mel?"

She blushed, averting her eyes as she returned the pitcher to the refrigerator. "No."

"No?" Rick set the empty bottles on the counter and moved closer to her. He ran his finger lightly over her bare arm.

"You weren't exactly whispering."

He grinned. "So you admit it, do you?" He grabbed a handful of her hair and yanked her head back. She flinched and he dropped his head to kiss her, his lips rough as his hand slid under her shirt to play with her nipples until they became taunt and aching.

"I want you," he whispered as he moved to bite her neck.

She knew she shouldn't fall so easily under his spell, but it had been weeks since they'd made love. And to be honest, she needed him to show her he loved her. Julius's proposal had really unnerved her. She closed her eyes, willing herself to forget about Julius.

Lifting her shirt, he impatiently pushed aside the lace cups of her bra before his lips found her throbbing nipple. She moaned, arching her back, momentarily forgetting the two men in the other room.

"Rick," she murmured.

He yanked her shirt down and grabbed her hand. She blinked, taken aback by his sudden withdrawal, and he grinned. "Come on, baby. We need to finish this in the bedroom."

She started to follow him, but stopped before they were out of the kitchen. "We can't. Your friends—"

He planted a quick kiss on her lips. "Like they don't do the same shit when I'm at their place." He grabbed two beers from the freezer and pulled her into the living room. "Here's your beer, bitches. Help yourself to the rest, but you'd better save me a couple."

"You're gonna miss the fight!" Marty said.

"We've got some business to take care of, if you know what I mean. But not to worry, the main fight's not starting yet."

Marty grinned as Rick pushed Melanie ahead of him into the bedroom and turned to Steve. "Lucky bastard!"

"More beer for us." Steve twisted off the cap of his beer and flipped it across the room. He raised the bottle in a toast and farted. Both men laughed.

In the bedroom, Melanie didn't have a chance to say anything. Rick yanked her shirt over her head and tossed it across the room. With a flick of his fingers, he unhooked the clasp of her bra and snatched it from her body, tossing it behind him. He pushed her back on the bed and took first one nipple and then the other in his mouth, sucking so hard she cried out, her hands tangling in his hair and tugging sharply.

He pulled away from her. "Get naked."

She stood and removed her jeans and underwear as he watched. When she had undressed, he forced her back onto the bed. "My turn."

She watched from where she lay on their unmade bed as he quickly stripped. He had an incredible body and she was very lucky he wanted her and not that new stripper with the "tits like cantaloupes." She glanced at her own breasts and wondered how he'd describe them, but she didn't have time to think of a description because Rick was spreading her legs and climbing on top of her.

He thrust into her so hard she bit her lip, her short, jagged nails digging into his shoulders. He grinned and pulled out until he was barely touching her. She trembled, looking into his dark eyes.

"You want me?"

She nodded.

"Say it."

"I want you."

"Say it with my name."

"I want you, Rick." She lifted her hips to receive him and sighed with pleasure when he thrust into her again.

He pressed his hips against hers and she squirmed, wanting him to keep going. He grabbed a handful of her hair and crushed her lips with his own. "Who do you love?" he whispered hotly in her ear as he threatened to yank the fistful of hair he clutched out of her head.

"You. I love you."

"And who's the king?"

"You're the king, Rick."

He smiled and thrust a couple more times before his face turned red, the veins in his neck thick and bulging. He groaned and climaxed. Melanie squeezed her eyes shut, feeling him shudder one last time before rolling off her to sprawl across their bed, his body sweaty, his breathing harsh.

She turned on her side, facing away from him, and listened with eyes closed as his breathing became slower. When it was normal, she felt the bed shift slightly as he stood up to dress.

He buttoned his jeans and reached over, slapping her bare skin. "Come on, baby, get up. Watch the fight with us."

"I'll be out in a minute."

Rick put his T-shirt back on and hovered over her. He bent down and took her nipple in his mouth, sucking hard.

She bit the inside of her cheek to keep from crying out.

"Damn, baby, I'm still hot for you." He glanced at the door, hearing Marty and Steve yelling excitedly. "Maybe tonight." He strode out of the bedroom, slamming the door behind him.

Melanie stared at the closed door, her body throbbing with unfulfillment. Her hand smoothed over her stomach, stopping to rest on the top of her thigh. She clenched her fist and sat up, reaching for her cigarettes on the nightstand. If only she could learn to masturbate, she could stop the throbbing that made her grit her teeth. But she just couldn't bring herself to do it. She knew people did it; she read *Cosmo*. And yet, she still couldn't convince herself to try. It was wrong, she thought, lighting the cigarette. She inhaled and lay back on the bed. Wrong and . . . and dirty. Her stepfather Carl had taught her that.

She frowned, remembering the day she'd learned that lesson. She'd been searching through her mother's dresser for a scarf to wear to school for Fifties Day when she found her mother's vibrator. She'd been so shocked at first that she'd quickly slammed the drawer shut. But her curiosity got the better of her and she'd taken a second look. It was smooth and heavier than she'd expected, but maybe that was due to the weight of the batteries in it. She'd flicked the switch on and was startled by the immediate vibration in her hand.

When Carl walked into the bedroom and caught her holding it, she'd been so surprised she'd been unable to move. She'd known he was drunk; she could smell it from where he stood in the doorway. How had she not heard him enter the house? She supposed she must have made a move because he'd crossed the room and slapped her, busting her lip open. Had she cried out? She couldn't remember. As if in a trance, she'd watched as he fumbled with the button of his pants, finally popping it off, but she'd remained frozen to the spot, unable to move or even say anything.

He'd pressed his forearm against her throat, pinning her to the bed while his other hand ripped her panties. "You little slut," he'd growled. "Dirty slut. I got something you'll like more than that. Flesh and blood. Just what you need."

He'd been rough with her, but she hadn't screamed or yelled or even fought back. She'd just kept her eyes locked on that small brown button he'd torn from his pants and listened to the dull buzz of the vibrator from where it lay on the floor by the bed. He was teaching her a lesson and she needed to learn it.

Melanie cringed, stubbing her cigarette out in the ashtray. It hadn't been her first lesson and it certainly hadn't been her last, but it had been one of the worst. She remembered the moment she'd looked up to see her brother pausing in the doorway as he realized Carl was on top of her. He had looked at her with such revulsion, as if she had seduced their mother's husband, and then he'd walked away without a word. Later, once Carl had passed out, she'd returned the vibrator to her mother's drawer and headed for the bathroom. She'd passed her brother in the hallway and he'd refused to look at her.

"Benjie—" she'd whispered, tears threatening to fill her eyes.

"Don't you talk to me. Don't even touch me," he'd growled, hurrying past her and down the stairs.

Shaking her head to clear her mind of the memory, she stood up and began to dress. There was no use in thinking about all that. It had happened a long time ago and Carl was gone. She took a deep breath, smoothing her hair away from her face. Carl had been gone a long time and her life was so much better now with Rick. That's what she needed to focus on.

In the living room, Rick pulled her down to sit next to him. She smiled, happy. He didn't usually show her much affection, especially when his friends were over. Could this be a sign that he was ready to commit to her now? Maybe she could convince him to marry her after all.

He put his arm around her and kissed her on the cheek. "Baby, will you get us three more?" he asked, holding his empty beer bottle out.

She took it from him. "Of course."

He pinched her butt when she stood and she blushed, hurrying into the kitchen.

What would Julius think now about her unhealthy relationship? She paused in opening the refrigerator. Why did he keep coming into her thoughts at the oddest times? She supposed it was because of that stupid marriage proposal. She twisted the caps off the bottles, listening as the guys in the next room argued about the prowess of certain fighters. She hadn't seen him in about a week. Perhaps he'd regretted his irrational proposal of marriage and was avoiding her out of embarrassment. She didn't care, of course, but she was getting annoyed with Ida for moping around and sighing dramatically as she smelled Melanie's roses. Ida had foolishly convinced herself that Melanie would drop Rick for Julius after spending time with the cop on her birthday. When he didn't show up at the beginning of the week, Ida hounded Melanie with questions. What had she done to make Julius avoid the diner? By the fourth day, when he still hadn't appeared and Melanie had continued to refuse to answer Ida's questions, the older woman had taken to moping around the restaurant. Melanie had ignored her and spent her free time marveling at how her roses were still as beautiful as when she'd received them. And they'd probably last another week, if she and Ida continued to care for them diligently. She grabbed the beer and returned to the living room.

"Rick," she said, bending to whisper in his ear. "I'm going for a walk."

He nodded, his eyes glued to the television.

She smiled slightly, tempted to run her fingers through his hair, but turned and left the apartment instead. It was time to bring her roses home. Not to pressure Rick into marrying her, of course, because she knew he'd not like that, but maybe they would encourage him to show the world just how much he really loved her.

The diner was busy when Melanie arrived and since Ida wasn't there, she grabbed her roses and left. A few petals had fallen, but they were still beautiful. She returned home to find the apartment empty, so she carefully placed the vase of roses on the coffee table and stood back to study them. Already the apartment was filled with the scent of them and Melanie smiled, hugging herself. Julius may have strange ideas about his feelings for her, but he sure gave great gifts. She yawned, suddenly tired. She turned out the living room light and turned on the various nightlights before heading to the bedroom, picking up the vase as she passed. She wanted to fall asleep with the smell of them filling her mind and body and she wanted to be able to see them the moment she woke up in the morning. Besides, she didn't want Rick to knock them over as he stumbled through the apartment in a drunken haze. And, she had to admit, he wouldn't be very happy to see them so it'd be best if he noticed them when he was sober and less likely to explode in a fit of jealousy. She placed them on the nightstand next to her bed. Even though they were very visible, he wouldn't see them through his half-closed eyes blurry from a night of too much alcohol.

CHAPTER 7

"Where the hell did you get those?" Rick asked, shaking Melanie awake.

She pulled the covers over her head to keep the bright Florida sunlight from reaching her eyes. "What time is it?" she mumbled.

"Answer the question, Mel." He ripped the sheets from her grasp and flung them towards the foot of the bed.

She sighed and opened her eyes. "What was the question?"

"Where did you get those flowers?"

"Oh." Melanie couldn't keep from smiling. "I got them for my birthday from one of the regulars that come into the diner. Aren't they pretty?"

"They stink. And they're stinking this whole place up. Get rid of them."

She frowned, watching him stride naked to the bathroom. Glancing at the flowers, she reached for a cigarette.

He emerged from the bathroom and glared at the roses still beside the bed on the nightstand. "I thought I told you to get rid of them."

"They don't last very long, Rick. Why not let them die on their own and then get rid of them?"

"Because they smell," he said slowly, clenching his fists at his side.

He wasn't getting the hint about proposing to her, she thought sourly. At this point she could care less about a ring. It was just metal anyway. The vows were what she wanted. The "'til death do us part" promise especially. "If I throw them out, what will you do to make up for them?"

"What did you say?"

She hesitated. "It's only for a couple more days. A week at most."

"I don't care if its hours. Sixty more seconds is too long. This is my place, remember?"

She lifted the cigarette to her lips with trembling fingers and inhaled slowly.

He crossed the room and put on a pair of shorts.

"Do you love me, Rick?"

"Don't start, Mel."

"Let's get married."

"Go to hell."

This wasn't going like she'd hoped, but she couldn't seem to let the subject go this time. "Why are you so against marriage?"

He ignored her, snatching a T-shirt from the dresser and putting it on.

"The guy who gave me the roses also asked me to marry him."

"You cheating slut."

Her hand paused in midair, the cigarette inches from her mouth. Too late, she realized he was furious.

He moved swiftly to her side and grabbed her arm, yanking her to her feet, her cigarette dropping onto the bed.

"My cigarette!" she yelled, fearful it'd start a fire.

He picked it up and took a long drag, watching her through lowered lashes.

She bit her lip, noticing his clenched jaw and dimly aware of his fingers bruising her arm with his grip. She started to apologize. "Rick, I—"

"Shut up!" He shook her. "You got some guy on the side?"

"No!" Her denial came out high-pitched as she fought the urge to laugh hysterically at his ability to talk with the cigarette dangling from his lips.

"You're lying! Why would he want to marry you anyway?"

Silent, she stared into his eyes, no longer fighting the urge to laugh. She was afraid. She had been foolish to think she could pressure him into marrying her.

He dropped the cigarette on the floor and extinguished the butt with his bare foot.

"I-I'm so sorry, Rick," she stammered.

He grabbed her throat, his thumb resting on her pulse and began to choke her. She flailed at him, the uneven edges of her fingernails cutting his face and shoulders. And still he choked her. She stopped attacking him and instead, attacked his hands, her fingers desperately trying to pry his hands away from her before he killed her. She was very tired; her strength had diminished considerably. And suddenly she began to think that this is what she'd been hoping for all along, to finally breathe her last breath. Dizzy, her legs gave out and he allowed her to drop to the floor in a gasping, naked heap.

"You fucking bitch," he said, his voice loud over her raspy breathing. "I'll kill you."

She looked up as he grabbed the vase of Julius's peach roses and raised it above his head. "Do it," she whispered thickly, her fingers fluttering against her neck.

Rick cracked the vase against her head and roses and water went everywhere. He walked out of their bedroom and out of the apartment. He never glanced back.

Eventually Melanie came to her senses. It was dark out, but she had no idea how much time had passed since Rick had hit her over the head with the vase. She tried to lift her head to see the clock, but it hurt too much and she had to close her eyes and wait for the pain to subside to a more tolerable ache. She was very tired. Perhaps if she slept a little longer, she'd feel better.

When she next awoke, it was daylight and someone was in the bathroom. Hearing footsteps, she closed her eyes and pretended to be asleep still. Someone knelt beside her and she felt a cool damp cloth against her cheeks and forehead.

"Melanie."

Her eyes fluttered open. "Julius?" Had she called him?

"Good. You're awake." He rubbed the cloth along her arms and over her chest.

"Stop," she whispered, realizing she was still naked.

"I have to wipe away the blood to see just how hurt you are."

Blood? "I'm bleeding?"

"You were. Just from a few cuts," he assured her. "I don't think it's serious. This time you lucked out."

She closed her eyes.

"I'm going to lift you onto the bed, okay?"

She didn't answer, but he gently lifted her anyway and stretched her out on the bed, pulling a blanket over her. He smoothed the hair out of her eyes.

She licked her dry lips. "My head hurts."

"Does anything else hurt?"

"Just sore all over. Can I have some water?"

"Of course."

She listened as he moved through the apartment and into the kitchen, picturing him filling a glass with water from the faucet. Where was Rick? Had they arrested him?

"Here," he said, returning to her side and helping her sit up enough to drink from the glass.

"How did you know to come?"

"Your neighbor called the station. When she didn't see you coming or going and she didn't hear you moving around the apartment on Sunday, she was afraid he'd finally killed you. Lucky for him he didn't, but don't think I'm going to let him get away with this."

She heard the anger in his voice and shivered.

He stroked her hair. "You'll press charges and we'll bring him in. Then we'll see how he likes being beaten until he passes out."

She pushed his hand away. "No. I won't press charges."

"Melanie—"

"I said no." She put her hand to her head. "I need to get up."

"Lie still."

"Julius, please. I don't want you to be here when he gets back."

"I won't let him ever hurt you again."

"You have to go."

He stared at her in surprise. "Don't tell me you expect me to leave you here in this apartment?"

She remained silent, uncertain. She had nowhere else to go.

He strode into the bathroom and after a minute of rummaging through the cabinets, returned to the bedroom carrying a handheld mirror. He held it in front of her. "Do you see those bruises around your neck? Do you see them? He tried to kill you, Melanie, and yet it sounds as if you're actually thinking of staying here with him. You're smarter than that. Aren't you?"

She touched her bruised skin, shocked at how horrible she looked. Closing her eyes, she turned away from the mirror. How had this happened? They'd been fine just the night before. Rick had been totally affectionate with her when his friends had been over. A bunch of roses could not be responsible for igniting such rage, right?

"Well?"

She stared up at him and finally, after dropping her head enough so that her dark hair covered her eyes and blocked her view of him, admitted in a whisper, "I don't have anywhere else to go."

"Oh, darling," he said, his voice soft as he reached out to caress her cheek. "You do. I want you to go to my sister's." He pushed her hair aside and raised her chin until she met his eyes. "She'd love to have you."

Melanie hesitated, but finally nodded. There was no reason to argue and even if there was, she was just too tired. Besides, anyplace had to be better than staying at her mother's, if her mother would even have let her.

He helped her dress, frowning over her cuts. "To think my roses hurt you . . ."

"Anything can be used as a weapon, Julius," she whispered softly, glad to be dressed now.

After filling an overnight bag with some of her things, he turned to her. "Ready?"

She stared up at him. Was she ready? Could she really leave Rick and the life she'd made here with him? Could she start all over again? She wasn't sure she had the strength. But Julius wasn't consciously asking her all that. More than likely he wanted to make sure she was ready to leave the apartment and she supposed she was. "Yes."

Ignoring her protests, he scooped her up in his arms. She was too weak, he said, and needed to keep her strength for later when he wasn't there to carry her around.

As they made their way to the front door, she looked over his shoulder at the rooms he passed through. When they were outside, she bent her head. *Good-bye, Rick*, she thought. *I love you.*

Instinctively, Julius tightened his arms around her. "You're free," he whispered, his voice gruff. "And now you're safe."

When they arrived at Clare's, Melanie only wanted to be alone. And for a few days, except for having a doctor examine her, Clare respected her need for solitude. But after almost a week of keeping to herself, Clare insisted Melanie join her in the kitchen while she prepared dinner rather than mope in a dark bedroom, dwelling on her problems.

Sitting on a barstool, nibbling on cheese and crackers, Melanie struggled for something to talk about and break the silence in the tiny kitchen, finally settling on something simple. "What are you fixing for dinner?"

Clare smiled. "Roast beef, mashed potatoes, baked corn, salad, and crescent rolls. You know, your normal after church family dinner."

"Sounds good. You must be quite a cook." Melanie had never planned such a meal for anyone and wasn't so sure she'd be able to pull it off even if she'd had the nerve to try. She could handle breakfast, but dinner was out of her culinary reach. She and Rick often had take-out when they ate dinner together. And when they didn't, she usually had something at the diner.

"I do okay now, but when Brian and I were first married, the only thing I knew how to make was toast and macaroni and cheese. By the time Garrett and Dillon were born, I'd only managed to add meatloaf and sloppy joes to my repertoire. Not exactly the nourishing meals children should grow up on. It wasn't until I started wishing for some time to myself that I decided to enroll in a cooking class. My mother agreed to babysit the twins so I learned how to cook while enjoying the luxury of spending time with adults who could speak in full sentences. And by the time Alexandra came along, I'd managed to become a pretty good cook."

"Where are they? Your kids?"

"Out with Brian. We thought it'd be best if they weren't around when you emerged from your room today."

"I'm sorry." Melanie was suddenly embarrassed. Obviously they didn't want their kids exposed to the likes of her.

Clare reached out and squeezed her hand. "You'll meet them tonight. In fact, they should be home very soon. We just didn't want them to tire you out with all their questions. The moment you'd have stepped out of your room, they'd have bombarded you."

Melanie nodded and smiled slightly, relief relaxing her stiff posture. "Thanks for letting me borrow a scarf."

Clare smiled, slicing tomatoes for the salad. "It looks good on you."

She toyed with the edges of the blue scarf, hoping she wouldn't be asked about the bruises she was hiding.

"I have to tell you I was quite surprised when Julius called about bringing you here. Have you known him long?"

"A few months." Melanie began to wish she'd never gotten out of bed. She didn't want to have to answer questions about her and Julius and she knew there'd be quite a few. She wondered what Rick was doing right then.

"Where did you two meet?"

"Hello, hello," Julius called, stepping into the kitchen.

Melanie wanted to kiss him for his perfect timing, but she only looked up and smiled slightly.

He crossed the small kitchen and brushed his finger along Melanie's cheek, unconcerned that his sister was watching them very closely. "You don't know how happy I am to see you up and moving. How are you feeling?"

"Fine, thanks."

He studied her silently until she looked away. "Brian and the rugrats aren't back yet?"

Clare shook her head and glanced at the clock above the microwave. "They'll be here soon. Where's Mom?"

"Right here," a tall woman answered, entering the kitchen carrying an empty casserole dish and a plastic grocery bag. "I'm finally returning your dish and I brought you some fresh vegetables from my garden."

Clare smiled, wiping her hands on a dishtowel. "Terrific."

Melanie watched as the two women hugged, suddenly nervous to meet Julius's mother.

"What can I do to help?" the older woman asked.

"Not a thing. Just grab a chair and relax."

The older woman turned to Julius and spotted Melanie. "Well, hello. I didn't even see you sitting over there quiet as a mouse. Julius, why didn't you introduce us?" She pretended to swat him on his butt.

"You were busy with your favorite child," he teased, pretending to be hurt.

"I do not have favorites, Julius. I love you both. Now who is this beauty you're hiding from me?"

Beauty? Melanie smiled nervously and stuck out her hand as Julius said the introductions.

"Mom, this is Melanie. Melanie, this is my mother, Gretchen."

"It's wonderful to meet you." She glanced at her son. "You must be very special if Julius invited you to one of our Sunday get-togethers. I've been on him for years to bring a guest and up until now, he's never taken me up on it."

"Mom, please."

His sister laughed. "Julius, are you blushing? Mom, I think you've embarrassed him!"

"Embarrassed who?" a tall man asked, entering the kitchen. "Surely not Julius?"

Clare smiled, lifting her face to accept a kiss from the newcomer. "It's about time you got home. Where are the kids?"

"I sold them, honey. Now we can travel like we always wanted."

Melanie stared as the affectionate couple danced around the tiny kitchen.

"What's going on?" A little boy stood with his hands on his hips as he stared at his parents.

"So much for traveling," the man said and bent and picked up the child, throwing him in the air. The child laughed with delight.

Melanie watched Julius as he laughed with his family. She used to wonder if there were families like this, happy to be together, but she'd always doubted it. And now that she'd seen them interact like a loving family from one of those family sitcoms from the fifties, she still remained skeptical, at least on the idea that there were other families like this one. Julius glanced over at her and their eyes met. She smiled slightly. If there'd ever been any doubt about not introducing Julius to her family, it was now very clear they could never meet.

"Me next!" insisted a little girl running into the kitchen.

"Wait a minute." Clare nodded towards Melanie as another little boy identical to the first little boy appeared in the doorway. "First, we need to introduce ourselves to our guest. And then we need to greet your grandmother."

"I'm Dillon," the child in the doorway said. "And that's my brother Garrett. We're both six because we're twins, but I'm a minute older. And that's my sister Alexandra. We call her Alex. She's four."

"And I am Clare's husband, the father of this brood. My name's Brian." He smiled.

"This is Melanie," Julius said before Melanie could open her mouth.

"You ain't sick no more?" Dillon asked.

"*Aren't* sick *any* more," Clare corrected with a smile. "And she's much better."

He nodded and turned back to Julius. "She your girlfriend?"

"Aren't you planning on saying hello to your favorite grandmother? Or am I suddenly chopped liver?" Gretchen leaned down to kiss Dillon on the cheek.

He giggled, but wrapped his arms around Gretchen and hugged her tightly.

Brian put Garrett down so that he could also hug his grandmother. "Yuck. Chopped liver is gross."

"Gross," Alex repeated, taking her turn to hug her grandmother.

Clare pointed to the sink. "Okay, munchkins. Wash your hands and then up to the table because dinner is ready. And before you ask, Mom, no, I do not need any help so go on and sit down. That goes for you and Melanie, too, Julius."

"Who said I wanted to help? I don't think I offered."

Clare swatted a dishtowel at him. "With that attitude, you get to say the blessing tonight."

Dillon and Garrett cheered, happy to not have the responsibility.

"Wash!" Clare said, pointing to the sink again. "Or you'll both add on to your uncle's blessing."

Dinner wasn't as stressful as Melanie had anticipated. The food, of course, was delicious, and Julius was adept at keeping their relationship from becoming the topic of conversation. The hurricane to the southeast was a big help; everyone wondered if this would be the year to end the town's record of being hurricane free.

After dinner, once the table was cleared and the dishes washed, Clare and Brian took the kids upstairs for their baths before bedtime while Julius and his mother relaxed in the living room.

Melanie knew Gretchen had all kinds of questions about her, but she didn't want to have to deal with it. Like a coward, she thought, giving an excuse when they invited her to sit with them. "I think I'll go outside for some fresh air."

"Are you okay?" Julius asked.

Melanie nodded and stepped outside onto the front porch. It was quieter here than where she lived with Rick. She sighed, sitting down on the front steps. Where she used to live with Rick. It still didn't seem real yet. And maybe—she shook her head. No. There was no "maybe." She'd tried to coerce him into marrying her and it had backfired. She had no one to blame but herself. She leaned against the wood of the porch.

The living room window had been opened earlier to ease the heat emanating from the kitchen and now Gretchen's voice easily reached Melanie. "So, Julius, tell me about Melanie. You have feelings for her, don't you? Stronger than friendship?"

"You could say that."

"Vague doesn't become you."

"No, vague doesn't become *you*," he teased.

"Are you trying to be difficult?"

He smiled.

"She's been here a few days now. Is there a plan? Does she have family? A home to return to?"

He hesitated. "I guess you might as well know that I've asked her to marry me."

Melanie frowned.

"Marry you? But I understood you've only known her for a few months!"

"That doesn't matter. Haven't you always said that the heart knows no time limit?"

"The heart isn't always the most sensible. God gave you a brain, too, you know, to keep your heart's foolishness under control."

"I'm in love with her, Mom."

She watched him silently. Finally, she said, "Well, she is a quiet one. She hardly said a word at dinner."

"She just doesn't know you well enough yet. She's shy."

"And troubled."

"I know what you're getting at, Mom, but you're wrong. I love her. I truly believe we'd be perfect together."

"No one can be truly perfect together and you're just setting yourself up for disappointment if you buy into such a fantasy."

"You know what I mean."

She sighed. "I suppose I do. Have you been praying about this?"

"Of course."

"And?"

"You've said yourself there aren't any coincidences, only God's plan at work."

She nodded.

"I wasn't supposed to be working the other night. But I was. She could've been taken to a shelter by another officer and I might never have known she'd needed help."

"Julius, that doesn't mean you should *marry* her."

"It doesn't mean I shouldn't."

Melanie stood up and hurried down the steps. She didn't want to hear anymore. *He might think he loves me now*, she thought, *but what'll happen in a few months time?* She'd get married and prove her mother wrong, but then what? At the moment, Julius was unaware of her evil heart. Could he eventually help her become "good" or was that goal impossible? She walked around the block, contemplating her predicament, but still had yet to resolve anything upon reaching Clare's house. She was debating about circling the block again when she noticed Julius sitting on the porch swing, drinking iced tea and watching her. She dropped her half-smoked cigarette on the sidewalk and casually stepped on it, hoping he'd missed the telltale red glow.

"Hi."

"I wondered where you'd gotten to."

"I took a walk."

"Anything bothering you?"

"No. Yes." She sighed, glancing up at the darkened windows of the house. "Everyone gone to bed?"

"Yes."

"And your mother?"

"Should be pulling into her own driveway right about now, I'd guess."

She nodded.

"So. Tell me what's bothering you."

She hesitated. "You didn't tell your mother about me before tonight, did you?"

"No."

She bit her lip, uncertain if she should ask why not.

"If I'd told her," he answered before she could ask, "she'd have been over here immediately trying to get you to talk about things. I thought you'd prefer to work through everything yourself."

"You were right," she answered softly.

"Come sit with me."

With hands in her pockets, she stepped onto the porch and sank down next to him on the swing.

"My family likes you a lot."

"They're very nice."

They swung gently back and forth, listening to the gentle chirping of crickets hiding in the grass. The ice clinked against the glass in Julius's hands as it melted in the warm October air. The wooden swing creaked as he shifted, placing the glass on the porch floor.

Julius cleared his throat. "I was wondering, well, I don't want to rush you or anything, but I was wondering if maybe you had, uh, well, thought about my proposal any? That is, my marriage proposal? Or maybe you just have some thoughts about me?"

Melanie met his eyes and then turned to glance out into the quiet street. "Yes."

"Yes, you've thought about it? Or yes—"

"Yes, I'll marry you."

His quick intake of breath showed that he was as surprised as she was. "Really? Are you sure?"

"Are you trying to talk me out of it?"

He laughed nervously. "No, of course not. I just want to make sure I haven't pressured you or anything. Because I would never want to do that."

"Your mother won't approve." She said it as fact, but really she was asking.

"My mother doesn't approve of a lot of things, but she will get behind this. I just took her by surprise. She's not used to that. Apparently I can be a bit predictable." He leaned toward her. "So does that mean you are sure?"

She hesitated. Was she sure? Could she live with this man and his family? She'd have to. It was the only choice she had left. It wouldn't be hard, of course. They were all very nice. She met his eyes and this time, she didn't look away. "Yes, I'm sure."

He smiled, his hand reaching to clasp hers tightly, and leaned towards her. She lifted her face to his and accepted his kiss as she accepted seconds later the lack of passion their marriage would have. But she would be married. And she would be marrying someone who was good and kind, not evil and selfish, as she seemed to be. It was better than nothing, right?

CHAPTER 8

"Well, look who's come to visit," Ida declared.

Melanie smiled, sitting down on one of the barstools at the counter. "Did you miss me?"

"Have you quit smoking yet?"

"Ida, for God's sake!"

"I do wish you'd stop saying that." She poured Melanie a cup of coffee and set it down in front of her. "It's pure laziness."

"Sorry. It just comes out."

Ida lifted her eyebrows, but changed the subject. "How are you really?"

"I'm fine."

She nodded slowly. "You've been busy. Julius said you two were getting married."

"Love is blind, right?" she asked, her tone light. "You saw it. It just took me a little longer. And now I'm getting married this weekend. You're invited of course."

"Will it be a huge wedding with a grand, spectacular reception?"

Melanie shook her head. "Hardly. It'll be a very simple ceremony held in Julius's mother's backyard."

"Where've you been staying? With Julius?"

"No. At Clare's, Julius's sister's. His mother has forbid us to live together. She said since it's only a week, we should be able to deal with spending this time apart. She's pretty adamant that the marriage vows be spoken and the union blessed by the family pastor before I move into his place." She sipped her coffee.

"Good for her. She sounds like a wise, Godly woman, just the kind of influence you need in your life."

"Yeah, I suppose so."

Ida studied her. "Mel, you don't sound very enthusiastic. This is your wedding! Aren't you excited? Nervous? Stressed out?"

She had been afraid Ida would notice her blasé attitude, but she couldn't seem to dredge up any enthusiasm when it came to planning the wedding. She knew Julius's family wondered about her, probably even had serious doubts about her marriage to Julius, but they respected him enough to keep such thoughts to themselves. Julius, on the other hand, teased her about her lack of enthusiasm, chalking it up to pre-wedding nerves.

"Of course I'm excited, but I'm more nervous than anything."

"That's not unusual. But you do love him, right?"

"Has Rick come in looking for me?"

Ida stared at her until Melanie dropped her eyes to focus on her hands wrapped around the coffee cup.

"It's good that you didn't come in an hour earlier. It was crazy in here."

"I figured it'd be best to wait until the lunch crowd had come and gone." She hesitated. "Well?" she finally asked. "Has he come in, Ida?"

"No."

"Has he called at least?"

"Mel, what are you doing worrying about that creep?"

"Has he called?"

"No."

"Maybe he called, but someone else took the message?"

"He hasn't called, Melanie. And he isn't going to."

"You don't know that."

Ida pursed her lips.

"He loves me. He's just afraid to admit it."

"When Julius called to let us know you wouldn't be working for a while, he told me what happened. He told me how he found you. Unconscious and covered in your own blood with a ring of bruises around your neck."

Melanie fingered the scarf she wore. The bruises were barely visible, but she was too self-conscious to take it off just yet. "He shouldn't have told you. And anyway, that is a huge exaggeration. I was not *covered* in blood and the bruises—"

"Tell yourself whatever you need, but that jerk does not love you. Julius does. Do not push him away."

"I'm not pushing anyone away. Now will you promise me you'll call me if Rick calls?"

"He's not going to call."

"But if he does, I want you to call me. Okay?"

Ida shook her head in disagreement, but finally agreed. "Yeah, okay, but I will not tell him where he can reach you."

Melanie smiled. "Fine. Now give me a pen and paper so I can give you Clare's number."

Ida tore a page from her pad and handed it to Melanie with a pen. Quickly, Melanie wrote down the information.

"I'm also giving you the address to Gretchen's house. If you need specific directions, I'll have Julius call you."

"I may be old, girl, but I've lived here my whole life. This town isn't so big I can't find my way around."

Melanie smiled. "Okay, fine. The wedding's at three." She slid the paper across the counter to Ida. "I hope you'll be there. You and Mary are the only people I'm inviting."

"Of course I'll be there. And I'm sure Mary will be thrilled. I'll talk to her tomorrow about it. Now, give me back my pen before you walk out of here with it," Ida said, snatching the pen from Melanie's grasp.

"I've got to go. I'll talk to you later."

Melanie walked out of the diner, mentally scolding herself. Why had she told Ida she and Mary were the only people she'd invited? She didn't want Ida to feel sorry for her. She sighed. It would've been nice to share the occasion with her brother because they'd been very close when they were young. They'd even had a conversation once about her wedding. She'd been hiding in the attic, crying, and he'd come looking for her.

"What's the matter with you?" he'd asked.

"Mandy Jenkins said I could never get married."

He'd sat down next to her. "Married? Why not?"

"Because I don't have a dad." She'd begun to cry again.

"Don't cry." He'd wiped her face with the end of his sleeve. "Who said you had to have a dad to get married?"

"Everyone."

"But why?"

"I have to have a dad to give me away, but since I don't have one I'll be an old maid forever!"

"Now that's silly. I'll give you away."

"You?"

"As man of the house, it would be my obligation to see that you're happily married to Prince Charming or Billy Kaufmann—"

She smacked him on the arm. "He smells."

"Right. Well, either way, I would be honored to give you away."

"Really?" She said, a ghost of a smile forming on her lips.

"Sure. Unless you think I could get something like two dimes and a nickel for you."

She giggled. "You're such a goofball, Benjie."

"You're holed up in the attic crying about Mandy Jenkins telling you you'll be an old maid when you haven't even reached junior high yet and *I'm* the goofball?"

Melanie sighed, surprised at the memory. Would he also remember that conversation when he learned of her marriage? Or was it buried too far beneath the layers of hatred that had started around the time they'd become teenagers? It was then that they'd begun to hate each other. Although actually, it was more like he'd begun to hate her and in self-defense she'd convinced herself into hating him back.

There was no sense in wondering about her brother. He had teamed up with their mother against her and that was that. She turned her thoughts to Rick. Had he called and talked to someone else at the diner? Was he wondering where she was? Maybe sorry for how he'd acted? Perhaps when she returned to Clare's, she'd drive over to Rick's. She had to get her things, didn't she? And by the time she walked back to Clare's and drove to her old apartment, there was a good chance she'd catch Rick at home. She smiled. It would be good to see Rick again. And Julius, bless his kind heart, never had to know.

Melanie hurried up the steps of Clare's house. She wanted to brush her hair and maybe put on some lipstick before heading over to Rick's.

"There you are. I was wondering where you'd gone." Clare stood in the doorway of the house, a glass of lemonade in her hand.

"I walked over to the diner to see a friend."

"Why don't you join me?" She gestured to the porch.

Although Melanie would've liked to decline, she couldn't bring herself to do it. After all, she was a guest in Clare's house and she had a few minutes to spare. She nodded and chose to sit on the porch swing.

Clare relaxed in the chair across from Melanie and smiled. "I just love Wednesdays. The boys are in school and Alex is in pre-K. It's hard to believe that just last month I was crying my eyes out."

"Crying?"

"My baby's first day of pre-K. We were both bawling our eyes out." She laughed.

Melanie smiled sadly, wishing she'd had a loving mother like Clare.

"Anyway, I wanted to ask you, and I hope you don't take this the wrong way, but what are you going to wear Saturday? I haven't heard anything about a wedding dress."

"Won't that be a bit formal? We're just having a simple ceremony."

"Yes, I know, but still, you can't very well get married in jeans."

Melanie tapped her fingers on the arm of the wooden swing she sat on.

"I was asking because I have a suggestion." She hesitated, but Melanie remained silent. "I might have a dress you could wear. Would you like to see it?"

She smiled slightly, knowing there was no way she could politely say no without offending, not to mention worrying, her soon-to-be sister-in-law. Besides, if jeans weren't appropriate, what would she wear? "Sure."

Clare smiled. "Great. It's in my bedroom. Now if you don't like it," she said as Melanie followed her into the house, "it's no big deal, okay? Don't worry about hurting my feelings or anything. This was the dress I wore to my senior prom. Brian had just picked me up and before we'd even gone five miles, we had a flat tire."

"Oh," Melanie said, although she wasn't really paying attention.

"Yeah, I think Brian was pretty embarrassed about it, not that it was his fault or anything. I mean, how could he have known ahead of time that the tire was going to go flat?" She shook her head. "Anyway, as I was standing on the curb waiting for Brian to fix it, some people stopped to help him. They thought we were on our way to my wedding and didn't want him to get his tux dirty. So, to make a long story short, that is why I thought it might work for you as a wedding dress." She reached into the closet and pulled out a long white dress protected by a plastic bag. "Why don't you try it on and then decide if you like it?"

Melanie nodded.

Clare removed the plastic bag and laid the dress across her bed. "Let me know when you have it on, okay?" She stepped out of the bedroom, closing the door behind her before Melanie could answer.

Melanie sighed, fingering the lace that covered the entire dress. It was terribly feminine, not something she'd have chosen, but it was her wedding and she didn't have anything to wear. She undressed and stepped into the gown. She zipped it up and turned to study her reflection in the full-length mirror hanging on the back of the bedroom door.

It wasn't bad. It was a simple dress: little lacy cap sleeves, a scoop neckline, and a straight skirt that reached her ankles.

Clare knocked on the bedroom door. "Are you dressed yet?"

"Yes. Come in."

She opened the door and stared at Melanie from the hallway. "I knew it would fit."

Melanie was relieved Clare didn't comment on the faint bruises on her neck. "Are you crying?"

She laughed, blinking quickly as she walked into the bedroom. "I always cry at weddings."

"The wedding's in three days."

"I know. I'm sure I'll cry then, too. What do you think? Do you like it?"

Melanie turned her head to stare at her reflection in the mirror above Clare's dresser. "I feel pretty."

"You *are* pretty!" Clare crossed over to Melanie and grabbed her shoulders, turning her so that she faced the mirror. Standing behind her, she piled Melanie's hair on top of her head. "I can fix your hair, if you'd like. You could wear it up or," she released her hair and arranged it around her shoulders, "I could curl it for you."

"You don't have to go to all this trouble, Clare."

"Don't be silly. This is my brother's wedding, first of all. And secondly, I'd like us to become friends. As your friend, I'd love to do your hair for you on your wedding day. Just because it's a small wedding and just because you aren't going on your honeymoon immediately after the reception doesn't mean you shouldn't look as beautiful as possible. Right?"

Melanie sighed.

"Or have you decided you don't like the dress?"

"No, no. It's great and it's really nice of you to loan it to me." She shrugged. "Okay. How do you think I should wear my hair?"

Clare grinned. "I think it'd look great if we piled your hair up on top of your head like this," she said, demonstrating. "Only it'll be a little neater. And we'll leave a few tendrils loose to soften the effect and curl them."

She studied her reflection, her eyes drawn to the simple engagement ring Julius had given her after the family dinner on Sunday. She was beginning to get excited. In three days, she'd be a married woman and her mother could eat her words. If Julius had decided she was worth his love, certainly her mother would have to start believing she wasn't quite so worthless, right? And she'd never have to worry about having nowhere to go. Even if Julius realized how black her heart was, he still wouldn't put her out on the street. He was just too nice of a guy. She smiled, too absorbed in her thoughts to notice Clare watching her through the mirror. She'd actually made the right decision in accepting Julius's proposal.

"I like it. Thank you."

Clare smiled and hugged Melanie tightly, oblivious or perhaps just ignoring the stiffness with which Melanie returned the embrace.

Melanie was leaving the house when Julius pulled into the driveway. She frowned, knowing that now she couldn't possibly go to Rick's. She could do nothing but wait for him to step out of his car.

He opened the car door and smiled at her.

Instantly, she felt guilty for planning to secretly visit Rick.

He pulled her into his arms. "Hello, beautiful."

"What are you doing here?"

"I missed you."

She tried to pull away from him, but he wouldn't release her. "You saw me this morning."

"But I didn't see you this afternoon."

Clare stepped out onto the porch. "Hi, Julius."

"My darling sister, you're looking pretty today."

"Aren't you in a good mood."

Julius grinned and turned to stare at Melanie. "How can I not be when I'm marrying this wonderful woman on Saturday?"

"True. Are you staying for dinner?"

"I thought you'd never ask."

"And should I expect you for dinner tomorrow?"

"Lovely of you to ask, sis. I believe I'm free."

"I thought as much." She returned to the house.

"Where were you going?"

"Where—for a walk."

"Do you usually go for so many walks?"

"What do you mean?"

Julius chuckled. "What do I mean? You're always going for a walk. If I didn't know better, I'd think you were secretly meeting another man."

She pushed against his chest harder. "Well, I'm not."

He released her, his eyes serious. "I know."

She brushed her hair out of her eyes with one hand while her other hand nervously tapped against her leg.

"So, have you always gone for so many walks? Clare says you're never here, that you're always out walking."

"I didn't think I had to remain cooped up. I'd never realized your sister was to report back to you as to how I spent my days."

He reached for her hand. "Relax. Clare's not spying on you. You can come and go as you like. I suppose it's my fault for insisting you take some time off from work. You're bored, huh?"

She shrugged.

"I just didn't want you to be stressed out, sweetheart. And I thought you should take some time to heal inside and out after what that creep did to you."

"I know, Julius. We've already discussed this. Okay? I get it."

"But you don't agree with me?"

She sighed. "What difference does it make? I'm not working this week, am I?"

He squeezed her shoulders gently. "I am so lucky to have you in my life."

She smiled slightly.

"Have you talked to Ida?"

"Yes. Today actually."

"Did you remember to invite her?"

"Of course."

He hesitated. "What about your family? You haven't mentioned them once."

She crossed her arms. "I don't have a family."

He sighed. "Melanie, I don't know what's caused this rift, but perhaps it is time to forgive and forget."

"You don't know what you're talking about, Julius!"

"I do know that you're unhappy. Allow me as your future husband to help you. Perhaps if we all sat down and discussed whatever caused this, we could find a solution and you'd have your family back."

She turned to hurry down the steps, but stopped at the bottom. Usually, she would've stalked off, but for some reason she felt compelled to stop and face him. He was watching her, but she couldn't decipher the look in his eyes.

"I wish you'd stop running from me."

She crossed her arms. "I'm not running from you."

"No? Well, when are you going to let me help you, Melanie? Can't you see that I love you enough to want to carry your burdens on my shoulders?"

"My burdens are too big even for your solid shoulders, Julius."

He moved to the edge of the porch. "I think you're underestimating me."

Melanie shook her head, overwhelmed with sadness. She didn't deserve him. She would only cause him unhappiness. The best thing for her to do would be to call the wedding off before she ruined his life. She twisted the engagement ring around on her finger and knew she was too selfish to do anything. "I'm going for a walk."

"Try not to be late for dinner. Clare would be disappointed. She loves cooking for family."

Melanie turned and walked away. *She loves cooking for family.* But she wasn't family and really, she never would be. Sure, she'd be around during the holidays and family get-togethers, but that wouldn't make her a part of the family. Especially a generous family like Julius's. She was too unworthy. She sat down on the curb and rested her chin on her hands. She hadn't expected Julius to offer to help her win her mother's love and to be honest, she'd been tempted to take him up on it. Because if her mother met him and saw what a great person her daughter had married . . . well, couldn't that help her mother see past the black heart she'd inherited from her father? Then again, her mother knew Melanie was evil and Julius didn't. If they met, she might successfully convince Julius that Melanie was no good. She couldn't take that kind of risk. No, it was better if Julius and his family considered her as an orphan. She stood up and headed back to the house. It'd been really nice of Clare to offer her friendship as well as her dress. Maybe she could pretend to be as normal as they were and then she could pretend they really were a family. She would go to Rick's tomorrow, but not to see him. She would go and get her things. That was all.

CHAPTER 9

From the bench, Melanie had a perfect view of the apartment. She'd waited an hour already and was beginning to get impatient. She pulled Clare's red raincoat tighter around her neck and sipped hot coffee from a Styrofoam cup. Of course it had to rain today, right now and not later tonight when she could watch the puddles form from within a warm, dry house. That was her kind of luck. She took a gulp of coffee and winced, burning her tongue. "Damn it!" she muttered. If Rick didn't leave soon, she—no. She couldn't give up. She had to do this today. In two days she'd be marrying Julius. She needed to get her things and maybe then she could put Rick behind her and focus on being the perfect wife for Julius.

Wiping cold rain from her forehead, she contemplated the house that had been converted into two apartments, the top one being the one that she and Rick had shared. Was he thinking about her right now? Wishing he could contact her and apologize? Was she wrong in not facing him? But it was for the best, right? It had been good that she hadn't been able to see Rick yesterday because she'd eventually realized that to make a fresh start with Julius, she couldn't allow her feelings for Rick to interfere. This time she was going to do the smart thing. Her future depended on it.

A battered blue pick-up truck screeched to a halt in front of the duplex and the driver leaned heavily on the horn. Melanie sipped her coffee and searched her memory for a name to match the face of the long-haired guy driving. She didn't think she'd ever met him before. He bobbed his head to music blaring from the radio—a song she was not familiar with—and pounded the horn in a staccato of impatient reprimands. Rick suddenly rounded the corner of the house, scowling as he gave the guy the finger before jumping into the truck.

Melanie bent her head, afraid he'd see her and force a painful confrontation, but the truck sped past and rounded the corner without either of the men glancing her way. *Finally*, she thought, getting to her feet. She was about to step off the curb, but stopped and glanced down the street. What if he'd forgotten something and came back to catch her in their apartment? But then again, so what if he did? She had a right to be there, didn't she? He couldn't possibly expect her to leave everything she owned. She was just going to grab her stuff and leave. He couldn't deny her that.

She hurried across the street and prayed the lady that lived below wasn't looking out her window. She didn't want to answer a lot of nosy questions even if they were well-intentioned. And she didn't have time to listen to the woman's million problems she went on and on about. Quickly, she climbed the steps that led upstairs and fumbled with her keys. As the door opened, she smiled. She'd known Rick wouldn't have thought to change the locks. She closed the door behind her and pushed the hood of her raincoat off her head.

The place hadn't changed any, but then she hadn't been gone for very long. It was messier, but that wasn't unusual. She moved into the kitchen and opened the refrigerator, surveying leftover pizza and bottles of beer. She shook her head and closed the door before moving through the apartment and into the bedroom. The bed was unmade and she sat on it, pulling his pillow into her arms and hugging it tightly to her chest. Burying her nose in the softness, she closed her eyes. She missed the smell of him. She missed him. She stood and, with the pillow still clutched in her arms like a child holds a teddy bear, opened the closet door and gaped in disbelief.

Her clothes were gone. His clothes were there, right where they'd always been, but her clothes were gone. On her hangers hung someone else's clothes. She dropped his pillow and flipped through the vibrant-colored clothes. There were spandex dresses, short skirts, and low-cut blouses, certainly nothing she'd have as part of her wardrobe. Could Rick be playing some sort of cruel joke on her? Or had he actually picked out things he'd like for her to wear? She sifted through the clothes again. He couldn't be living with someone else already, could he? But then she was about to be married so why couldn't he have moved on just as quickly? She spun around and hurried into the bathroom, yanking open drawers. Sure enough, there was make-up and perfume and brushes, all things she usually kept in those drawers, except none of it belonged to her. Where were her things? Whose stuff was all this?

She sank down onto the bed. Clare had been very generous with the use of everything in her closet, and Julius had managed to throw a few things into a bag for her when he'd rescued her, but Melanie wanted the rest of her clothes. She didn't own much and now it seemed she owned even less. She clenched her fists in her lap. He could not replace her so easily. It wasn't fair. She would get him back for this. Oh, yes, and she knew just how to do it. With a determined smile, she hurried out of the bedroom.

In the kitchen, she knelt in front of a small cabinet next to the oven. She hesitated. Maybe she was overreacting? No. She opened the cabinet to reveal plastic grocery bags wadded up and stuffed on the two shelves. Clearing the bottom shelf, she grabbed the coffee can pushed into the back corner. She lifted the plastic lid and was delighted to see the wad of money stored inside. This was the money Rick was saving to buy a Harley. But now, this money was going to give her a new wardrobe. It was the least she deserved. Before she could change her mind, she dumped the money into one of the plastic bags, returned the can to its place, shoved the remainder of bags back into the cabinet, and shut the door firmly.

Having forgotten to check the clock when she had entered the apartment, she wasn't sure how much time had passed, but there was one more thing she needed to get. Back in the bedroom, she flipped the tousled bedsheets up and peered into the dusty darkness under the bed. She smiled in relief and pulled the old shoebox out from where she'd hastily shoved it the night Rick had caught her with it. Tossing aside the lid, she stared at the bouquet of paper roses. At least she still had these. Carefully, she lifted the roses from the box, placed the bag of money inside and then rearranged the roses on top. Satisfied, she reached for the lid.

"You must be Melanie." The words were spoken quietly, but the voice was not soft.

Melanie spun around to face the woman leaning casually in the doorway. She was wearing a tight, low-cut fuchsia dress, which accentuated her large (and from where Melanie was sitting, fake) breasts and showcased her long, skinny legs. She had blonde hair that reached her waist and left little doubt about her identity. Instinctively Melanie knew this was the new stripper at Ruben's that Rick and his friends had been drooling over.

"I suppose you've come to beg Rick to take you back, but you're too late. He found me and we're very happy together."

Melanie realized her mouth was hanging open and quickly clamped her lips together. She shook her head and, with the lid secure on the shoebox, stood up. "No. I'm not here to do anything other than get what belongs to me." She hugged the box close to her chest. "And you may be happy, but you're just the latest flavor. Try not to get used to it."

"I think I will get used to it. Since we're getting married and all. But you're sweet to warn me." She gave her a fake smile.

Melanie managed to keep a straight face, to remain standing, to not rush over and punch the girl, but it wasn't easy. The girl was lying; she had to be. Rick had sworn he wasn't going to be marrying anyone. Besides that, they couldn't have been together longer than a week! She chose to forget for the moment that she was also engaged.

"Where are my clothes?" Melanie demanded.

"Oh. Right. Your clothes." She shook her head. "Bad news. As an engagement party, we had a bonfire downstairs. I'm afraid we used your stuff to keep the fire burning."

"You burned my clothes?"

"It seemed fitting. You know, out with the old, in with the new sort of thing. And you are history, Melanie."

"Aren't you the latest stripper at Ruben's?"

The woman smiled, running her fingers through her hair. "As a matter of fact, I am. My name is Candi. With an 'i.'"

"That's your stage name?"

"My only name."

"And you're not embarrassed to be one in a long list of strippers from the club Rick has screwed?"

"It doesn't matter since I'm the one he's marrying."

"Does Mr. Nichols know about this wedding?"

"Who do you think is giving me away at the ceremony?"

Ceremony? They were having a ceremony? She had to get out of there and away from this woman, but suddenly an idea occurred to her and she changed her mind. "Before I go, I'd like to use your bathroom. If you don't mind."

Candi hesitated, but finally nodded her assent. Melanie pivoted and hurried into the bathroom, locking the door behind her before the stripper could change her mind. Tits like cantaloupes, huh? They were so fake, they were probably molded off of cantaloupes. How gross is that? She shook her head to clear her thoughts. She could think about that later, but right now she had to focus on her reason for needing to use the bathroom. She grabbed the shampoo bottles from the shower and emptied them in the sink, refilling them with the Nair she'd noticed earlier in her search, careful not to fill them too full since they weren't full to begin with. She smiled as she returned the Nair to its spot under the sink, envisioning Candi's long tresses clogging up the drain as they slipped through her fingers. How many clubs would hire a bald stripper? And vain Rick would not take baldness well either. She smiled at the image and then flushed the toilet. Turning on the faucet as though she were washing her hands, she smoothed her hair and then, with shoebox tucked under her arm, returned to the empty bedroom.

She glanced around the room, surprised that the stripper hadn't waited for her so that she could escort her out of their precious love nest. On the dresser, she spotted Rick's lucky black shirt. Unable to resist the temptation, she strode over and grabbed the shirt, fiercely yanking all of the buttons off before tossing the shirt back onto the dresser. Without glancing back, she walked into the living room where Candi waited.

"I assume you'll now be on your way?" she asked, the cordless phone clutched in her fist.

"Yes. I've got everything I need. By the way, congratulations on your engagement." She hurried past the woman, choking on the heavy perfume as she made her way to the door.

"Just a second," Candi called out, dropping the phone onto the couch and following Melanie to the door.

She paused with her hand on the doorknob. Did she suspect what Melanie had just done? Or would this woman have the gall to demand to search her shoebox for stolen property? "What do you want?"

"Our key. You don't need it now that there's nothing of yours left here. This way you won't be tempted to sneak back in and bother us in any way."

Melanie clenched her jaw, but struggled to remove the key from her key ring. "And you might as well hand over the car key, too, since I'm the one driving it now. No sense in you having it. You might be tempted to steal it." She smiled slightly before turning her attention to her fake nails as though bored by the whole scene.

Melanie gritted her teeth, but yanked both keys off her key ring. In a spurt of anger, she threw the keys at the woman, thrilled to see one key hit her in the chest. As she fled the apartment, she knew it was a childish thing to do, in fact all of her little revenge tactics had been rather childish, but doing them had made her feel better, at least for a moment. It was just too bad both keys hadn't found their mark, maybe even putting an eye out in the process. But, she thought with great satisfaction, at least she'd gotten away with Rick's Harley money.

Seconds later her gloating was interrupted when she realized she'd forgotten to take all of her nightlights. There were nightlights at Clare's because of their children; she'd lucked out. But would there be nightlights at Julius's? Of course it wasn't such a big deal. She could just buy more. She certainly had enough money for it!

And apparently the stress she'd been under had affected her memory because she'd completely forgotten she even had a key to the car. Otherwise, she wouldn't have walked all over town! Julius had tried to get her to use his car, of course, but it hadn't seemed right somehow. He'd already done so much for her that she felt guilty for continuing to accept his generosity.

More importantly, the woman, Candi with an "i," had to have been lying about marrying Rick. She just had to! There was probably a very simple reason as to why she was living with him at all. Maybe she was down on her luck or something and since he hadn't heard from her, he decided to let Candi stay with him for a week or so. He probably hadn't known about Candi burning her clothes until he came home and found the evidence, too. After all, he was hardly ever home so she could do anything she wanted really. If Rick ever married (and she highly doubted it) then he'd go to City Hall and get it over with, rather than have an actual ceremony with flowers and music and guests. Of course the girl was lying! She was just trying to make Melanie jealous.

Unfortunately, it had worked.

Melanie stopped walking and stared at the worn shoebox in her arms. She had to get herself under control. She was marrying Julius. She could no longer care what Rick did. She had to remember she was doing the right thing, the best thing she could possibly do. Julius was good for her and hopefully she'd make sure he didn't regret trusting her. Hugging the box to her chest, she sighed, her eyes scanning the gray skies, only then aware that it was no longer raining. "I love Julius; I hate Rick. I love Julius; I hate Rick," she chanted as slowly, she began to walk in the direction of Clare's. "I love Julius; I hate Rick." If she said it enough, maybe it would come true.

CHAPTER 10

Melanie hated malls. She hated the crowds; she hated the sales clerks with their insincerity; she hated the closed-in space. But on the day before her wedding, full of nervous energy, she stuffed her pockets with half of Rick's Harley money and borrowed Clare's car. At the mall, she didn't window-shop; she shopped purposefully: bras and underwear, T-shirts, socks, jeans, and tennis shoes. Careful to keep her eyes averted lest she make eye contact with someone she might know, she accumulated bag after bag of new clothes. It wasn't until she passed the display window of a jewelry store that she faltered, remembering her impending wedding and realizing she didn't have a wedding ring for her future husband. How could that not have occurred to her before now?

She reached out and touched the glass of the display window, wishing she could bang her head against it without causing a scene. How could she have forgotten something so important? And since she didn't have any idea what his ring size was, how could she now buy him a ring?

"Melanie?"

She spun around, startled. "Gretchen. Hi."

"Are you all right, dear? You look a little pale."

"Oh, no. I'm fine. Just," she lifted her shopping bags, "shopped out."

"I can see that."

Melanie nodded.

Gretchen turned to the display window. "Looking at wedding rings?"

"Just . . . looking."

"I'm glad I ran into you today. There's something I've wanted to discuss with you. Do you have time to grab a cup of coffee with me now?"

"I'm supposed to meet Julius for a late lunch."

"This won't take long."

"I . . . well . . . okay." She shrugged, helpless to say no.

"Great. Can I help you with your bags?"

"Oh, no. I've got it. Thank you." She fell into step beside her future mother-in-law, but desperately wished she could run the other way. What did she have to talk to her about? Was she going to admit she didn't think she was good enough for her son? Was she going to ask her to call off the wedding? Maybe Julius had changed his mind, but didn't know how to tell her. No matter what, it couldn't be good, she was sure of it.

Once they were seated with their coffee, Gretchen smiled. "I suppose I should just say what's on my mind and hope I don't offend you. As the woman my only son is about to marry, the worst thing I'd ever want to do is alienate you. I hope that we can develop a close relationship, more than just in-laws, maybe even going so far as to become friends. Anyway, I wondered if you'd chosen Julius's wedding ring yet."

Melanie frowned, surprised at the question. If she answered truthfully, would Gretchen then hold it against her and believe Melanie didn't love her son?

Gretchen sighed, shaking her head and reaching for her purse. "Clare told me I'd offend you, but I didn't believe her." She shook her head again as she searched through her purse.

"No, I'm not offended, really, just taken aback."

"Well, I suppose that's understandable. You were expecting me to grill you about your feelings for Julius?"

Melanie swallowed, afraid to agree.

"Or try to convince you to postpone the wedding?" She glanced up from her purse. "I've already said what I think about this situation, your relationship, to Julius. But I have to trust him, trust that I've raised him right, trust God. Do you know who that is?"

Melanie frowned. "Do I know who God is?"

"Yes, that's what I asked," Gretchen said, looking up from her purse to meet Melanie's eyes.

"Of course I know who God is."

Gretchen dug deep into her purse once more. "Ah, here it is." She placed a man's wedding ring on the table between them. "That was Julius's father's wedding ring. I didn't bury it with him because I thought that maybe Julius would like to have it one day. Some people might think that's crazy, but really, what's a dead man, God rest his soul, going to do with a wedding ring?"

Uncertain what to say to that, Melanie remained silent, picking up the ring to examine it.

"The inscription reads 'Energizer,' referring to the Energizer Bunny commercials. I'd had it inscribed for our twenty-fifth anniversary."

"That's . . . nice," she said, placing the ring back on the table.

Gretchen chuckled. "Nice, but what does it mean? Is that more like what you were thinking?"

She nodded.

"When we were first married, we promised to never take each other for granted. So every year, on our anniversary, we would evaluate our marriage, what was good, what was bad, all that we'd been through together. And then we'd decide that we could remain married another year. Don't misunderstand me. We loved each other very much and would have been heartbroken had either of us wanted out of our marriage. We both believed that a promise like our vows made in church before God was not something we could break, but we both knew it wouldn't be easy."

"Why not?"

She smiled. "We were both very stubborn and certain we were always right. And so when our twenty-fifth anniversary came around, well, it was a shock. Like the Energizer Bunny, we just kept going and going and going." She laughed, shaking her head, her eyes unseeing as she focused on the memories.

Melanie stared at the ring. Would she and Julius still be married in twenty-five years? She wasn't sure. It seemed impossible.

"Anyway," Gretchen said, interrupting Melanie's thoughts. "I'm sorry I got carried away with remembering the past. Will you accept the ring? Don't be afraid to say no if you have another ring for him. I'll understand."

"No, I can return the ring I got him," she lied. "Julius will love it. Thank you."

"Are you sure? I feel bad now that I know you have to return the one you've picked out for him."

Melanie glanced around at the busy food court, uncomfortable with her blatant lie. "Don't feel bad. It's fine. Really."

The older woman breathed a sigh of relief. "Good. Thank you for understanding." She smiled. "How are you holding up with all these wedding plans?"

"It's okay. It should be small enough so I won't feel overwhelmed."

"I agree. And I'm very excited about meeting your mother. What is her name?"

"My mother? She's not—I don't—I don't have a mother."

"But I thought Julius said he'd invited your mother and I believe your brother as well." She noticed her pale face. "I'm so sorry, Melanie. I didn't mean to upset you. I must've misunderstood."

"I have to get going."

"Are you sure? I'm sorry I said anything."

"Yes, this was nice. And thank you for the ring, Gretchen. And the story. It's perfect. And he'll love it. I'll see you tomorrow I guess." Melanie gathered up her bags and hurried out of the mall. How could Julius have gone behind her back and invited her mother? He knew she didn't want them there. And when was he planning on telling her? How had he even found them? Would they actually show up? She stopped suddenly, unaware of the person walking behind her who nearly ran into her. He muttered something but stepped around her and hurried away. Of course they would show up. Why wouldn't they? It was too easy for them to humiliate her yet again. Her mother, of course, would be drunk, and Benjie would be high. It would be a disaster. And then Julius and his family would see that she wasn't good enough for him. They would hear about how horrible of a person she was. And then they would call off the wedding. She couldn't let that happen.

With a heavy heart, she headed to where she'd parked Clare's car. She had to talk to Julius. Something must be done to ensure that her mother did not ruin this for her.

It wasn't until lunch was over and they'd walked out of the little sandwich shop that Melanie finally found the courage to confront her fiancé.

"Your mother and I had coffee today at the mall," she said, digging the car keys out of her pocket.

Julius smiled. "That's great. I hope you two will become close."

Melanie nodded, her fingers fidgeting with the keys. "She mentioned something about the wedding that I wanted to ask you about."

He frowned.

"She said you'd invited my mother and brother. Is that true?"

"Yes, it is," he said, reaching for her hand.

She took a step away from him. "It can't be true. How could—I don't understand."

He stepped closer to her, taking the keys out of her hand, and entwining his fingers with hers. "I'm sorry. I know I should've asked you first, but I just want to help. And then I didn't tell you because I was waiting for them to RSVP, but they haven't yet."

She glanced over his shoulder at the traffic moving along the road. "How did you find their address?"

"Your brother has an arrest record. Just minor offenses like getting caught with illegal drugs, disturbing the peace, being drunk and disorderly." Julius gently massaged her hand.

Suddenly she glared at him, angry. "How could you go behind my back like that?"

"I wish you wouldn't put it like that."

She raised her chin, pulling her hand free from his grip. "It's the truth, isn't it? That's what you've done."

"But putting it that way implies harmful intentions. I only wanted to make you happy. I know how I'd feel if there was a problem of this magnitude within my family."

She shook her head. "However you'd like to put it, Julius, the question remains: How could you?"

He reached out to touch her, but she took a step backwards. "Because I really want you to work things out with them." The radio at his hip crackled and he dropped his hand, turning his body slightly away as he answered the call. It was very brief and he turned back to her, reaching for her hand again. "You haven't talked about what has caused this riff, but can't you forgive them for whatever trespasses they have committed? No one is perfect and I'm sure they'd do things differently if given the chance."

"Trespasses?"

He shook his head. "It's something my mother often says. It's from the Bible. We all need forgiveness at some point in our life, right? Can't you forgive them?"

She pulled her hand away. "You don't know what you're talking about, Julius. Have you spoken to them?"

"No. I just sent the invitation. That's it."

She nodded, crossing her arms in front of her chest. "They don't deserve my forgiveness."

"Do I?"

She blinked, surprised at the question.

He tucked a strand of her hair behind her ear. "I'm sorry I was so insensitive. I just thought that maybe this wedding would bring them back into your life. That if they saw how happy we are, they'd want to be a part of it."

"Were you ever planning on telling me or were you just going to wait and see if they showed up?"

"I had planned on telling you today, but I wanted to check the mail first in case they'd finally responded."

She bit her lip, surprised by how betrayed she felt. "I never expected you to betray me like this, Julius."

"I was very stupid to invite them without first discussing it with you, but betrayal? Isn't that a bit extreme?"

"Maybe you think so, but I don't."

"I would not have let you arrive to your wedding without first being forewarned as to the possibility of seeing your family. I might not be so smart when it comes to women, but I'm not that insensitive. You must know that."

"I thought you were different," she muttered.

"Different?"

"From all the other men in my life."

"I am different." He ran his hand through his hair. "I don't know what else to say."

"I do not want them there, Julius."

"I know. I get that now. I should have left things alone like you wished, but I didn't and I'm sorry, Melanie."

"Sorry," she repeated and frowned.

"Yes, I am. Really. Will you still meet me in front of the minister tomorrow?"

"What will you do if they show up?"

"Whatever you want me to do."

"You'll kick them out?"

"Yes, if that's what you want."

"Even if they start to make a scene?"

"Are you sure you'd want them kicked out? Don't you think they might show up because they miss you and want to be a part of your life again?"

She snatched the keys from his hand. "You can't be an expert on everything, you know. And that includes my so-called family."

He tried to caress her cheek, but she pushed his hand away. "You can be so hard and unyielding sometimes. But okay, if they make a scene, they'll still be asked to leave."

"No, not *if* they make a scene. Because by the time they make a scene, it'll be too late. The damage will have been done. If they show up, I want them bodily ejected. Forcefully. I mean it, Julius."

"Okay." The radio crackled again and he sighed. "I've got to go. Let's finish discussing this later." He kissed her quickly and then stepped over to his patrol car.

She watched him drive off and then slowly climbed into the car. He waited until the day before their wedding to tell her about inviting her family? And even then his mother was the one to tell her. How could she keep them from coming at this late date? Would a case of vodka and a really fat joint left on their doorstep do the trick? Or would that just make them all the more unbearable when they did show up?

She made a U-turn in the middle of the street. Obviously she was going to have to investigate the situation. If she had to do nothing and just wait to see if they might show up, she'd end up killing herself! Her mother probably thought the invitation was a joke anyway. After all, she was always telling Melanie she'd never find herself a husband. Perhaps that was the way to play things. It was certainly something to try.

Though her mother's house was unlocked, there was no one home. Melanie wandered around the dusty rooms, strangely comforted by the familiar stench of stale air, spilled booze, and cigarette smoke. She stopped in the living room to study the photographs in the collage her mother had created years ago. There were pictures of five-year-old Benjie blowing out the candles on his birthday cake; Benjie dressed in his Little League baseball uniform; Benjie and their mother laughing . . . Benjie, Benjie, and more of Benjie. There were no pictures of Melanie.

A stack of mail scattered across the coffee table caught her attention and Melanie knelt on the floor and sifted through it. Bills and junk mail and then there, an ivory envelope. She plucked it from the table and, holding her breath, turned it over. It was their wedding invitation! Melanie held it in her hands, unable to believe her good luck. Maybe things were changing for her now. It had to be a sign or something, right? The envelope was unopened, which meant her family still didn't know about her upcoming wedding. Quickly, Melanie folded it and stuffed it into her jeans pocket.

She climbed the stairs and entered her mother's room. Snatching up a picture frame from the bedside table, Melanie studied another photo of Benjie and his friends smoking pot on the front porch. Their mother had just mumbled that boys would be boys before she'd slapped her daughter for being a snitch. Setting the frame down, she tried to remember if there'd ever been pictures of her on display, but she couldn't remember any. Just as she couldn't remember anything of hers being prominently displayed on the refrigerator.

She paused in the doorway of what used to be her bedroom. Now it was a guestroom, although there were never any guests to use it. The day she'd left to move in with Rick, her mother had ordered everything of hers burned. It seemed that her bridges were being burned for her. Had her mother always hated her? There'd been times when they'd been out at the mall or the grocery store and someone would ask her mother if she and Benjie were her children. Her mother always replied, "This is my son, Benjie. Oh, and then there's the girl." Usually, because of that, the person had an extra smile for Melanie, or even a gentle hand stroking her hair, but it never eased the pain in her heart. Eventually, she'd taught herself to block out the words before the hatred could reach her. But she always knew it was there.

She stepped into the room and opened the closet door, running her fingers along the thickness of it. Even the marks she'd made as a child through the years to show her getting taller were gone. Was her mother trying to erase any signs that she'd ever had a daughter? She rubbed her arms, suddenly chilled. It was almost as though she didn't exist. She turned and fled the sterile room, not stopping until she pulled the front door closed behind her. Taking a deep breath, she reminded herself that tomorrow was her wedding day. And then she would have a new existence as Julius's wife.

CHAPTER 11

She probably should have gone straight to Clare's after she left her mother's, but she didn't. And to be honest, she hadn't planned to go to Ruben's, but when she found herself driving past, she decided to stop in.

Rick was not there, although it was a bit early for him to show up yet, and she was surprisingly relieved not to have to face him. The morning shopping spree had been financed with his money and she was feeling a little guilty about it. Although she still had to buy new nightlights. That was one purchase she wouldn't feel guilty about making.

At the bar, she inquired about Mr. Nichols. It was rare for him not to greet every patron that walked through those tinted glass doors with the fluorescent pink writing. But then the club seemed unusually busy so maybe he had his hands full.

"He's not far," a redhead said as she waited for the bartender to fix her drink. "He never is."

Melanie nodded, her eyes scanning the room. Old habits were hard to break sometimes.

"It's funny, right? The old man?"

"What do you mean?"

"Well, before Viagra, he'd have just been an old perv fighting dementia or some other old-person ailment, don't you think? But because of that pill, here he is, the stud to a stable of money-desperate strippers."

Melanie frowned. "Mr. Nichols? I don't think he's like that."

The woman laughed. "You're not a part of this world, are you? You here for the contest?"

"The contest?" Melanie repeated.

"Yeah, to strip. You here for that?"

She eyed the skimpy outfit the attractive woman was wearing. "I don't think I'm dressed right."

"The clothes don't make the stripper. It's all about the body and what kind of show you can put on."

"Some would say that's like a chocolate cake without the icing, a stripper dressed less than sexy."

Melanie turned to find Mr. Nichols standing behind them. She wondered if he'd somehow heard his name and that's why he'd come over to them. "I was just asking about you. Club sure is busy."

He nodded, his eyes scanning the room.

"Hi," the redhead said. "You're the owner, right?"

Mr. Nichols turned to study her.

She smiled brightly. "Listen, I've been working at Mary Jane's Joint for a while now, about six months, but that's not really my scene, you know? So I wanted to introduce myself and let you know I'd be interested in working here. I think you'll like my performance."

He reached for her hand. "And what is your name?"

She blushed. "Oh, yeah. I can't very well introduce myself without giving you my name, can I? Do you want my real name? Or my stage name?"

"Around here that's one and the same."

She bit her lip. "Stage names aren't allowed here?"

He smiled gently, patting her hand. "How about your stage name so I'll know when you're on tonight?"

"Okay." She smiled. "I go by 'Red.'"

"Because of your hair I presume?"

She nodded.

"Perhaps you should think of something a little more suited to your elegance."

"Elegance?"

"Something like 'Ruby.' What do you think, Melanie?"

"Ruby's good."

"Ruby," she whispered. "I like it." She smiled and leaned in close to Mr. Nichols who didn't back away. "See, that's why I want to work here: classy."

"Well, thank you. I like to think so." He smiled slightly before turning to Melanie. "Walk with me a moment."

She nodded and followed him away from the bar. Had Red been right about Mr. Nichols? Was she naïve to think he wasn't more involved with the strippers he employed?

"Are you here looking for Rick?"

"No."

"No?"

"I was just in the neighborhood and thought I'd stop in."

He nodded, watching her. "Thinking of trying out?"

She hesitated. Maybe this was an opportunity she shouldn't pass up. "Well, I'd hate to be a chocolate cake without the icing."

"I'm sure one of my girls has an outfit you can borrow."

She bit her lip, uncertain. What would Julius think if he found out she'd stripped? He would be furious, but then it was what he deserved. He didn't seem to care about going behind her back and inviting her family to their wedding, did he?

"It's a great way to express yourself."

"Yeah?" She wasn't yet convinced, but it was tempting.

"And I have a feeling you'd be a natural."

"A natural? I don't know about that."

He leaned closer to her. "I have been told I have an eye for talent. My club is successful because of it. You could be quite the star."

She wanted to make a joke, say something about working at the diner all this time when she could've been working here, but no words came. She shouldn't be so tempted. Just to make a stand with Julius? Okay, so maybe the two weren't exactly equal, her stripping and his inviting her family, but she was still her own person. He didn't own her. "Okay. I'll try it."

Mr. Nichols nodded. "Go on back to the dressing rooms. Francine is back there; she helps all the girls get ready. She'll help you find a costume and give you some pointers."

She turned and headed to the back, missing Mr. Nichols's smile as he watched her go.

Backstage amidst a variety of women in varying stages of dress, Melanie found Francine and after a quick discussion, Francine had handed Melanie an outfit and pushed her into the corner to get dressed.

Feeling slightly self-conscious, she quickly changed into the costume. She felt jittery and pretended it was a bit of stage fright that had her tremulous. But the truth, she knew, was that stripping like this was the stupidest thing she'd done in a while. If she was feeling self-conscious in a room of half-naked women, how could she expect to be even less dressed on a stage in front of leering men?

Francine waved her over. "Let me get a look at you."

"I don't know," Melanie said, surveying herself in the mirror as Francine scrutinized her from all angles. "Are you sure I should wear this?" She liked the green color of the costume, but it was so skimpy she felt almost naked. And what was the point of stripping, if you walked out onstage already practically naked?

Francine clucked as she rubbed glitter along Melanie's cheekbones. "This is what all the girls wear. If you can't wear it, then you're not a stripper and shouldn't be about to go onstage."

What would Rick think if he saw her dressed like this? Would he describe her like he described that other stripper, Little Miss Candi with an "i"? She frowned. It didn't matter what Rick would say, but what about Julius? She studied her reflection.

"Okay," a deep voice yelled, "everybody freeze! This is a raid!"

Suddenly everywhere was chaos, but Melanie stood frozen in front of the mirror. How could this be? Was it some sort of joke? Policemen swarmed all around as scantily clad girls yelled and struggled to get away. Melanie was swept up with the rest of them as they were herded outside and into the police transport van. She moved to the farthest corner of the van and sat down, closing her eyes and bowing her head. What a nightmare! And now there was no way Julius wouldn't find out. She sighed, ignoring a couple girls next to her bickering about not having enough room.

By the time they were behind bars, Melanie had decided it didn't matter that Julius would find out about her stripping. She wasn't ashamed. But an hour later when she'd finally called him and he'd become very silent when she'd admitted she'd been arrested, she began to worry. What if he changed his mind about marrying her? He worked here; this could be very embarrassing for him. Could she have ruined her chances of ever getting a decent person to marry her?

Finally, though, he arrived and she was released. After draping his coat across her shoulders, he turned and she followed him outside, keeping two steps behind him. He opened the car door for her and she climbed in. Hurrying around to the other side, he got into the car and started the engine. He sighed and turned the car off again.

"Melanie, I'm so astounded, I don't know what to say."

She bit her lip.

"Do you strip there often?"

"No! I've never stripped. And I didn't even strip tonight, if that makes you feel any better."

"Is this something you want to start doing?"

She shook her head, but realized he wasn't looking at her. "No, definitely not." If he wouldn't even look at her, then how could he still want her? She'd ruined everything. How predictable. Her mother might be right after all.

He grabbed her hand and squeezed it. "I'm sorry. I feel like this is all my fault. I shouldn't have interfered with your family without asking you first. I only had your best interests at heart, but it's not up to me to invite them without discussing it with you first. If you can find it in your heart to forgive me, I'll be a better husband to you. I knew how you felt, but I thought I was right and I wasn't. I believe in you. Can you forgive me?"

She stared at him. He was asking for her forgiveness? She'd been arrested and yet he wasn't angry with her. "Of course I can forgive you. You're not mad about my arrest?"

"It wasn't your fault you were arrested. The club was raided because the maximum occupancy allowed for 195 people and there were 214 inside. The Chief knew about the contest and knew there was a good possibility of a raid. I don't like the idea of other men seeing you half-dressed, but I guess you were trying to make a point."

"Really? I never expected you to say something like that."

"It's called grace, Melanie. I realized today after our conversation that maybe you've never felt that, or seen it. Maybe you can't forgive your family because you don't know how."

"Julius . . . ," she sighed. "You've got to let me handle them my way. I know you want to help. I get that."

"Good. And okay, I will try to back off a bit."

"Thank you."

He hesitated. "So does this mean you *do* want a career as a stripper?"

"No. I was being dumb. I was just mad."

"Great," he said, relieved. "I can't stand the thought of other men ogling you. Does this also mean you'll still marry me tomorrow?"

She glanced at their fingers intertwined. She was still very mad at him for betraying her by inviting her mother and Benjie, but she still wanted to get married. She had no other options. There was no reason to pretend otherwise. And if he could still want her after her arrest, well, how could she say anything but yes? "Yes."

He relaxed, relieved. "Thank you. It would have destroyed me if you'd said no. I'd blame myself for the rest of my life for being too stupid to keep the woman of my dreams."

The woman of his dreams? How could he possibly mean that? She brought nothing to the marriage, nothing of any importance anyway. She yawned, suddenly exhausted. "Clare's car," she suddenly remembered. "It's parked at the club."

"I'll take care of it. I'll take care of everything, sweetheart. Just lean back and rest."

She nodded and closed her eyes. *Sweetheart.* She rather liked the sound of that.

CHAPTER 12

"Are you sure everything's all right?" Clare asked from where she sat on the bed.

"Yes." Melanie leaned closer to the mirror, checking her make-up.

"You can talk to me, you know, even though I am Julius's sister. You don't have to worry that I'll take his side against you."

"Thank you, Clare, but I'm fine."

"He is a man after all and men can really try a girl's patience sometimes."

"That's true."

She stood up, moving closer to Melanie. "Are you sure you're okay?"

"Yes. I'm fine."

Clare nodded slowly and then smiled. "Well, okay. I'm going to go and check on the progress of things."

Melanie smiled and watched as Clare pulled the bedroom door closed behind her, allowing her a few minutes of privacy. She turned to study her reflection in the mirror again. Clare had been right about piling Melanie's hair on top of her head; it was beautiful. Add to that the long, lacy dress and the make-up Clare had talked her into using, and she didn't look like herself anymore. But then who was she? The evil child her mother wished she'd aborted? The unambitious waitress? Rick's ex-lover? Today was a new beginning, wasn't it? So why not become a new person?

She sank down on the bed. She had to become a new person. Otherwise, Julius would discover the evils that lurked in her heart and abandon her. Good and evil do not mix well; all the storybooks she'd read told her that.

Melanie turned at the knock. "Who is it?"

"It's Gretchen. May I come in?"

Melanie stood up, suddenly overwhelmed with anxiety. "Yes, of course."

Gretchen opened the door and studied her future daughter-in-law. "You're beautiful."

Melanie blushed. "Am I? Thank you. Is it time?"

She closed the door behind her. "Not yet. I just thought you could use some support. When I was a bride, I was terrified I was doing the wrong thing, but my mother sat with me and calmed me down. And I enjoyed a wonderful marriage for forty-two years." She tilted her head slightly. "Are you nervous?"

Melanie turned away. "No. Just . . . impatient."

The older woman walked over to the mirror and fluffed her hair. "It won't be long now. But while we have a moment, I wanted to say something to you."

She sat back down on the bed, her hands clenched in her lap. "Okay."

"My son, bless his heart, is a caregiver. Has he told you about Isabelle?"

"Isabelle?" She frowned. "No, he hasn't mentioned her."

"He doesn't talk about her; none of us do to be honest. She was his sister, our oldest, and she died when he was pretty young."

"I'm sorry to hear that. It must've been hard."

Gretchen sat down next to Melanie on the bed. "I wouldn't wish the death of a child on my worst enemy." She shook her head, remembering. "When Isabelle was sick, we were beside ourselves with worry as you can imagine. And so we may not have been the best parents during that time because all our energy was directed towards our sick child. Anyway, it fell to Julius to care for Clare, to do the simple things we couldn't do like reading her a bedtime story or walking her to school . . . you get the picture. And then when Isabelle died, we walked around in a fog for a few months so he ended up taking care of us as well. The point I'm trying to make is that Julius, being the caretaker that he is, cannot turn away from someone who is hurt or lost or just unhappy."

"I suppose that's what makes him good at his job," Melanie suggested.

Gretchen reached over and took Melanie's hand. "I've been praying for you." She laughed softly. "Actually, I suppose I've been praying for you all of Julius's life. Praying for the right woman to come along for Julius to marry when the time was right." She patted Melanie's hand. "I know that you've had some problems in your past and I just wanted to make sure that you are aware that Julius gives his all. I don't want him to get his heart broken. I hope that you're not marrying him because it's so easy. If you don't love him—"

"Melanie," Clare said, knocking on the door as she opened it and inadvertently interrupting her mother. "Oh, there you are, Mom. Well, it's time."

"I was just telling Melanie that it was a shame Julius couldn't get some time off so they could have a proper honeymoon."

"Mom, let it go. How many times have you said that this week?"

"Well, I'm sorry, Clare, but honeymoons are wonderful to think back on when the world is crowding your life and you're both stressed out. Your father and I spent our honeymoon in Hawaii and sometimes long after the actual honeymoon we'd unplug the phone and pretend we were back on the Islands."

"That is not something I want to talk about or hear about. It's just gross."

"Clare, don't be silly. You're too old for such nonsense. And anyway, I really believe if we hadn't had that memory we would've ended up divorced like so many of our friends."

Clare checked her lipstick in the mirror. "At least he has tonight off, right, Melanie?"

"Yes."

"So stop worrying, Mom, and get out there so they can seat you. A honeymoon doesn't have to last a week, you know. One night can be just as memorable. If it doesn't bother them, it shouldn't bother you."

"Okay, okay." Gretchen squeezed Melanie's stiff shoulders.

"Congratulations. You are moments away from becoming a married woman." She leaned in close to hug her, and whispered, "I know you'll do the right thing, dear, and I'll support you in whatever that may be."

Clare threw her hands up as Gretchen walked out of the bedroom. "I swear. Mothers! Personally, I think it's no big deal if you don't have a honeymoon. We racked up quite a bit of debt with ours and when you're just starting out, you don't need such problems. Now, come over here so that I can give your hair one more squirt of hairspray."

Melanie obeyed, but her thoughts weren't on the wedding. Instead, she was thinking about her wedding night. She'd been so worried about everything else, she hadn't even thought about her wedding night, or even about moving in with Julius for that matter. It wasn't like she didn't want to, of course, but—

"Melanie?"

"Yes, Clare?"

"Are you okay? You seem a little pale."

"I'm fine."

"What were you thinking about?"

Brian knocked on the door. "Melanie. It's time."

She took a deep breath. "I'm ready."

The wedding ceremony passed in a blur. All Melanie could remember were the dozens of beautiful white roses arranged throughout the house and the preacher's words "'Til death us do part." And that reminded her of Gretchen's speech before the wedding, something she did not want to think about. She found herself in the receiving line shaking hands and receiving kisses on her cheek as Julius introduced her to their guests. It was overwhelming, but she had very little time to think about everything. Which was why she found herself shaking hands with Ida without even realizing she was someone Melanie knew.

"You're not going to faint, are you?" Ida asked, peering into Melanie's face.

She smiled and hugged the older woman, surprising them both.

Obviously this whole wedding thing was getting to her and making her overly emotional. "No, no. Thank you for coming."

"Like I would have missed it. I threatened to quit if George didn't give me the day off. Mary sends her apologies. She was really disappointed to have missed it."

"Yeah. I was sorry to hear about her father passing. How is she doing?"

"Okay. He'd been sickly for quite some time. You seem happy," she suddenly whispered.

Melanie clasped her hand. "I think I am, Ida."

"You can start thanking me any time since I am the one who forced you to take notice of him."

"That's real good for my ego, Ida. And here I thought she couldn't resist my charming smile."

"I'm sure that was a big temptation, Julius."

He smiled and turned to greet the older man who'd been behind Ida in line and had finally grown bored with waiting and had cut in front of her.

"So you're not coming back to work?"

Melanie glanced at her husband who continued to talk with the guest. She dropped her voice. "Tell George to put me back on the schedule, starting next week. All this free time is driving me nuts."

Ida glanced at Julius. "If you're sure . . ."

"Sweetheart," Julius murmured. "You can catch up with Ida later. People are getting impatient."

Ida smiled. "You're looking very handsome. And are all these roses from your garden?"

"No, not hardly. My garden's pretty small. The flower shop on Seventh Street is to be complemented. They provided all the floral arrangements for today."

Ida moved on and Melanie once again shook hands with strangers, forgetting their names the moment they introduced themselves. She tried to remember, but there were so many and the line seemed to last an infinity. Finally, though, the receiving line ended.

Gretchen had hired a photographer and so, as the guests mingled outside in the backyard, Melanie smiled and posed, conscious of

Julius's strong arm encircling her waist. And she felt safe. Even happy. She gazed at the wedding ring Julius had slipped on her finger during the ceremony. She was actually married. Her mother's dour predictions had been wrong. This was what she wanted. She would always be grateful to Julius for giving this to her.

She watched Julius pose with his mother and sister. They were laughing about something and just seeing them like that made her heart swell. Everything was going to work out. It was such a relief to know that her mother and Benjie weren't going to show up and destroy everything.

Brian stopped next to her. "It's nice to see them so happy, isn't it?" She nodded.

"I love being a part of this family. I think you will, too."

"I'd be crazy not to," she said softly.

After the picture, Melanie grabbed Julius's hand. "Is that it for the pictures?"

"For now."

"Could we have a minute to ourselves?"

He studied her and slowly nodded. "Mom, we'll be out in a second."

"Don't take too long. Your guests want to celebrate with you."

Once they were alone, Melanie wrapped her arms around his waist, leaning her head against his chest.

Surprised, it took him a second before he could react and wrap his arms around her. "Are you okay?"

"Yes." She pulled back and looked into his eyes. "Here we are, on our wedding day, and neither of us has mentioned anything about love."

"Does that bother you?"

"Does it bother *you*?"

"I asked you first."

"Yes, it bothers me. I love you, Julius."

His face remained blank.

"Didn't you hear me? I love you."

He remained silent.

She started to pull away. "It's okay, though, if you don't feel the same way. I mean, I thought you would, but—"

He covered her mouth with his finger to quiet her and then caressed her cheek. "I didn't think I'd ever hear those words from you."

"And you married me anyway?"

"I've been praying about it. Prayed that if it wasn't what God wanted for me, for you, that He would take it off my heart. Marrying you seemed like something I was meant to do. But do you really mean it?"

She smiled. "Yes. I do."

He laughed, hugging her tightly. "I love you, too."

She sighed. So far so good. She'd managed to make him as happy as she was. Now, she just had to keep it up for the rest of their lives. *'Til death us do part*, she thought.

He kissed her quickly. "You're not upset about the lack of a traditional honeymoon?"

"Your mother's been complaining about it to you, too, huh?"

"Maybe I was wrong to rush our wedding. I just wanted to be a husband to you as soon as possible. We can still have a honeymoon. It'll just be delayed for a few months."

"I don't mind, Julius. I'm happy."

He kissed her again. "I was hoping you'd say that. Now let's go mingle with all these guests Mom had promised not to invite. Imagine the mass of people she'd have invited if we'd said we wanted a large wedding."

She reached up and smoothed his hair. "Thank you, Julius, for the beautiful roses."

"I'm glad you like them."

Standing on tiptoe, she brushed her lips across his. "And thank you for marrying me. I'll try to be a good wife."

He didn't say anything, only reached for her hand. Yet she knew she'd done the right thing. Besides, she'd probably end up loving him eventually. He seemed to be a person easy to love. Easier than she was, that's for sure. If he could love her, then it had to be possible for her to learn to love him. Squaring her shoulders, she silently promised him she would make him proud of her, in love or not.

CHAPTER 13

Julius pulled into the driveway and turned the car off, but neither he nor Melanie made a move to get out. Silently, they stared at his house lit by the streetlights and the full moon.

He cleared his throat. "Well, we're here."

Melanie squeezed her hands together and nodded. Suddenly, she was afraid. Not of him, of course. She was afraid of her new life. She'd never been to his house before. She wouldn't know where anything was. She didn't know how to work his coffee maker, or his washer and dryer, or what tricks to use to get the most hot water in the shower. When was trash day in his neighborhood and what was his favorite kind of ice cream? Did he like his socks rolled or folded and which section of the paper did he like to read first? She raised her hands to her throat. *Don't panic*, she thought. *Panic and you'll ruin everything.*

Julius reached out to her and she quickly locked her fingers with his. "What are you thinking?"

"The wedding and reception were wonderful."

"That's what you were sitting here thinking about?"

"Why? What were you thinking?"

"That it must feel strange to be here with me in a home you've never been in and on your wedding night."

Melanie turned to stare at him, surprised. Could she have married anyone more different than Rick? They were such opposites. In fact, if she were with Rick right now he'd be thinking about two things:

getting drunk and getting laid. And yet here she was with Julius, her husband, who was concerned about her feelings. She didn't know him at all.

He began to massage her hand. "You've been through a lot, Melanie, recently as well as in the past and I want to make it up to you."

"Why should you be the one to make amends?"

"Because I love you."

"Still, Julius—"

"Still nothing. I'm serious about this."

"You must be tired, having had to work the late shift last night."

He sighed. "I am pretty tired."

"And what time do you have to work in the morning?"

"Eight."

She began to tap her fingers lightly on the seat. Did he expect her to make him breakfast?

"Melanie . . ."

She waited for him to continue, but he remained silent. "What? What's the matter?"

"Nothing. Nothing's the matter. How are you feeling? About your family not showing up today?"

She looked out at the house, not wanting to meet his eyes. She wasn't sure why she hadn't just told him she'd gotten the invitation back from them, that they'd never opened it. Maybe she would've if she hadn't gone and gotten herself arrested. But after that, stealing the invitation back didn't seem all that important in the whole scheme of things. "I'm glad that we were able to have a nice day without any of their drama."

"I know you don't like to talk about them, but I was wondering when I can meet your family."

Melanie jerked her hand away. "I don't have any family."

"Sweetheart, please let me meet them. I know it'll be hard, but perhaps I can help you work things out with them."

"No. And you promised you were going to let it go." She opened the door and jumped out. But she stopped, leaning back in. "You haven't been completely upfront about your family either, Julius. I heard about Isabelle." She slammed the car door and hurried to the house.

Julius caught up with her as she reached the steps. "Okay. Okay, I'm sorry. Perhaps this was the wrong time to talk about this. And Isabelle . . . that was so long ago. It wasn't a secret. I just don't think of her as a topic I need to tell everyone." He hugged her tightly. "Maybe we're both nervous, huh?"

She remained silent, her head pressed against his chest, concentrating on the steady thump of his heartbeat. Listening to him talk was soothing, the way his voice rumbled in his chest as he held her, his large hands smoothing her hair. She sighed deeply. "I'm sorry. About Isabelle."

"How about I give you the grand tour of our home?"

"Sure." Reluctantly, she released him.

He smiled. "You know, I bet it's been weeks since I used the front door. The back door seems more convenient somehow."

"Okay, I'll have to remember that."

He caressed her cheek. "We'll be happy here, Melanie."

She turned to face the house. "I know."

Later, Melanie stood in the doorway of the bedroom, surprised to see Julius stretched out across the bed, asleep. Had she taken too long in the shower? She'd tried to be quick, but there was so much hot water and it felt so great that she couldn't make herself get out. She'd been too conscious of being a guest at Clare's to linger under the steady stream of hot water. And at the apartment she'd shared with Rick, the hot water lasted all of five minutes. She clenched her fist, angry with herself. Rick was out of her life and it was time she stopped comparing her old life with her new life. But at least her new life was much improved, right? So maybe it wasn't so bad to think about the past when it just proved to her that she'd made the right choice.

She studied her husband. He really had been tired; there was no way she would wake him. She didn't mind that he'd fallen asleep. They'd had an unusual relationship right from the beginning so why should tonight be any different? She tiptoed into the room and reached for the lamp switch. He was her husband. Her husband! She still had trouble believing it. Tomorrow, she'd visit her mother again and tell her the good news. She couldn't wait to see her face when she showed her mother her wedding ring. Hopefully she'd be sober enough to understand Melanie's good news. Would she wish she'd been invited to the ceremony? Probably not, she thought, or at least not unless they'd provided her with an open bar at the reception.

Suddenly sad, she turned off the light and closed the bedroom door behind her. She was tired, but she knew she wouldn't be able to sleep. And this time her sleeplessness was not just because she'd forgotten to buy more nightlights either, although that didn't seem as important as it once had. She felt safe here at Julius's more so than she'd ever felt at Rick's. But she wasn't interested in examining the ramifications of that now. Instead, she'd explore Julius's house, *their* house. He'd given her a quick one-minute tour, but she'd been too conscious of him watching her for a reaction to notice more than that the décor throughout the house was done in blues and greens. Everything had been very neat; the counters were clean, the tables polished; and she'd teased him about trying to impress her by hiring a maid to clean up. Now that he wasn't looking over her shoulder, she wanted to learn more specific things, like which drawer holds the silverware and which cabinet holds plates. Or what areas of the floors creak when stepped on? And where does he keep pens and notepads? The sooner she knew every nook and cranny, the sooner she'd feel like she really did belong.

CHAPTER 14

Melanie hesitated on the sidewalk in front of her mother's house. She'd waited so long to be able to announce to her mother that she was indeed married despite all her mother's dire predictions and yet now she wasn't so certain she should share her news after all. Did her reluctance have anything to do with her marriage having not yet been consummated? No, that would be incredibly shortsighted. There was more to marriage than sex. Besides, it would happen, probably tonight from what Julius had said this morning when he'd found her asleep on the couch.

"Did I snore last night?" he'd asked. "Is that why you slept on the couch?"

Actually, she hadn't intended to sleep at all, but at some point in the early morning hours she'd stretched out on the couch and managed to fall asleep without the comforting glow of any nightlights. And when she'd stretched out on the couch, she had contemplated returning to his—their—bedroom, but she hadn't felt comfortable doing so. She knew she was being foolish, but the couch just seemed like a better idea.

He'd grabbed her hand. "Melanie." Clearing his throat, his eyes concentrating on his fingers massaging her hand, he'd said, "I'm sorry I fell asleep on our wedding night. I guess I was really tired. I'll make it up to you tonight, though. I promise. Okay?"

"There's no need to apologize, Julius. We'll have a lifetime of nights together." She'd bent her head and kissed his hand holding hers. Not because she'd been overwhelmed with affection, but because she hadn't wanted him to see her cringe at the sappiness of her words. Whatever was happening to her? Was it possible that he was already rubbing off on her? *We'll have a lifetime of nights together?* Ugh! He'd been so relieved by her answer, though, that she'd calmed down, having managed for once to say the right thing.

Melanie shook her head and approached the front door. She was being silly. Of course she would tell her mother. She couldn't wait to see the look on her mother's face! Would she finally smile with pride at her daughter? Would she hug her tightly and tell her how happy she was? No, no, no. If she started thinking like that, she was bound to be disappointed. She just wanted to prove her mother wrong; that was all. She'd focus on that, rather than hope for a reaction any mother other than her own would have. And she'd have to stop watching reruns of *Father Knows Best, Leave it to Beaver*, and so on. Life imitates art? Not her life, unless you'd consider *Mommy Dearest* to be art.

Sitting in front of the door was a small gift bag with the logo of the Baptist church located a few blocks away. Melanie picked up the bag. Inside were pamphlets describing the church and a mug that said "Jesus Loves You" on one side and "Jesus Loves Me" on the other. There was also an unsharpened pencil in the bag with the words "We are all sinners. Thank God for Jesus!" printed in gold letters. She carried the bag inside, placing it on the coffee table. The house was dark and cool. She was tempted to open the windows to get rid of the stale air, but she knew her mother would be furious. Besides, it'd just get stale again soon enough anyway. She could hear the blare of the television in one of the upstairs bedrooms. Her mother must be watching TV; she was usually the one who turned the volume up ten times too loud. Melanie glanced at her wedding ring and then hurried upstairs.

Her mother was passed out on the bed, an empty bottle of vodka lying on the floor. Melanie turned the television off, but her mother didn't stir.

"She dead?"

Melanie swung around to face her brother. "Benjie! What are you doing sneaking up on me like that?"

"Scared you, huh?"

She stared at him. When he smiled at her like that, it reminded her of when they were little. The daily arguments between their mother and Carl would frequently escalate into violent free-for-alls and so they'd creep into the attic to hide. There they'd be, crouched in the dark in the farthest corner of the attic, and suddenly he'd grin and tease her about something. She couldn't remember the last time he'd actually smiled at her with affection.

Benjie stepped into the bedroom, a lit joint dangling from his fingers. "So? Is she dead?"

She turned away from him to stare at their mother. "No."

He held the joint out. "Wanna drag?"

She shook her head and he shrugged, crossing the room to rummage through their mother's purse, which rested on top of the cluttered dresser. He pulled out a couple of bills. "Damn. Only twenty lousy bucks." He glanced over at his sister. "So Mellie, got any money I can borrow?"

Mellie was the name he'd called her when he was little and unable to pronounce Melanie. Eventually, it had stuck. Until he'd turned his back on her and then he'd never really called her anything. "No, sorry." She could feel him watching her as he took a drag on the joint. She turned to go.

"That's a pretty nice ring you got there."

She glanced down at her wedding ring. "Yes. I, uh, I got married."

"Well, good for you. Are you sure, Mellie, you can't spare some money for your big brother? I'm in a tight spot, you see, and things aren't looking too good for me right now."

She clenched her jaw. He was asking her to help him? What kind of a fool did he think she was? He hadn't bothered to help her when their mother had thrown her out of the house so why should she help him? Did he think if he just called her "Mellie" a few times, she'd give him anything he wanted? Do anything he asked? But perhaps she was being a little too hasty. She glanced over at him and suddenly smiled. This was a perfect opportunity to get him back, to make him feel what she'd felt years ago. "I certainly don't have any money on me right now, but why don't you come by the house tonight?"

"I knew you couldn't turn your back on your only brother, Mellie."

She kept her face neutral at the use of her childhood nickname, but it wasn't easy. "My husband's a cop, Benjie, so maybe you should come over when he's already in bed. I don't think he'll appreciate you like I do. Say two a.m.?"

He nodded.

She picked up a pen from the nightstand and wrote her address on the back of a liquor-store receipt.

"How much are you gonna give me?"

"We'll talk about it tonight." She handed him the paper and glanced at their mother. "I'll see you later."

Outside, in the bright sunshine, she breathed deeply. Finally! She was going to get her brother back for hurting her like he had. Was that wrong of her? Wasn't this another example of just how black her heart really was? And yet, really, if that was who she was, why fight it? Certainly in this one instance she could let her evil heart lead her, right? Only now she had to come up with the perfect plan. She smiled, crossing the street. Somehow, she would think of something. She would not let this opportunity slip through her fingers.

On her way home, she stopped by the diner. "Ida, did you tell George to put me back on the schedule?"

"Whatever happened to 'Hello, Ida. How are you? Thank you for the lovely wedding present'?" She placed a cup of coffee in front of Melanie and frowned.

Melanie smiled. "Hello, Ida. How are you? Thank you for the lovely wedding present. Did you tell George to put me back on the schedule?"

"You're impossible. I don't suppose you've given up smoking yet?"

"No, but believe it or not I have cut down."

"Well, at least that's something."

"Are you going to answer my question or not?"

"Do you even know what I gave you as a wedding present?"

Melanie laughed, blushing slightly. "Well, no. We haven't actually gotten around to opening them yet. I think we're going to do that tonight."

"At least you're honest, girl. And yes, I did manage to pass the message on to George." She pulled a neatly folded napkin out of her apron pocket and placed it on the counter next to Melanie's coffee cup. "I was going to call you with your schedule, but since you're here, you've saved me the trouble."

"You're a great friend, Ida." Quickly, she unfolded the napkin and glanced at her schedule. "But I'm only working four days!"

"He didn't think you'd be coming back to work so he'd hired some-one new. He can't very well give her nothing now that you've decided to return to work, can he?"

"I never told him I wasn't coming back. Can't I take a vacation?"

"Why are you whining? I'd be jumping for joy if I were you. You've just gotten married to a wonderful man who is willing to support you—"

"Ida . . ." Melanie stopped. There wasn't any reason she needed to work her usual six shifts and it wouldn't be fair to take them from the new girl even if she shouldn't have been hired in the first place. "You're right."

"Good Lord, what has marriage done to you? You've finally gotten some sense!"

"And what has happened to you? Using the Lord's name in vain after scolding me for doing it!"

"I never said I was perfect. God knows I'm a sinner, but I must've forgotten I was talking to Ms. Perfection herself."

"It's Mrs. now, thank you."

"Pardon me," she said and smiled.

Melanie sipped her coffee, glancing around the restaurant. "Business seems unusually slow for this time of morning."

Ida shrugged. "It has been a bit slower lately for breakfast, but lunch has certainly picked up."

"Has Julius been in this morning?"

"You are kidding, right? Don't you know he only came in here to see you?"

"Not necessarily. A man's got to eat, doesn't he?"

"You didn't fix your husband breakfast?"

"Ida, don't start."

"The day after the wedding and you didn't even bother to fix your husband breakfast, your first meal together as a married couple?" She shook her head.

"I never realized you were such a romantic. But really, breakfast is breakfast whether we're married or not, whether I cook it or—"

"So maybe you still don't have much sense in that thick head of yours after all."

"Gee, maybe I should leave. You been abusing all your customers this way or am I just special?"

"Only the ones that need it. You've gotten yourself a good man, Mel. Much better than that Rick character you were mixed up with."

"Let's not talk about him, okay?"

"If you intend to keep Julius as your husband, then you need to start making his life so wonderful, he'll wonder how he ever got along before he met you."

"Don't you think that's a little old-fashioned? Perhaps even a little ridiculous in this day and age?"

"If I did, would I be telling it to you? You young things think you know so much, but you don't know anything. A good marriage means spoiling each other. You spoil him and he spoils you. That's what Robert and I did and we were happily married for over forty years."

"Okay, okay. I believe you. I'll cook Julius breakfast every morning, whether he wants it or not."

"Go on, make smart remarks all you want and when those divorce papers arrive, you'll wish you'd listened to me. Excuse me." She grabbed the coffeepot and rushed off to refill her customers' empty mugs.

Melanie watched her go, slightly taken aback by Ida's vehemence. She'd never realized until today that they always talk about her life, never about Ida's. When had she become so self-centered? She sipped her coffee and waited for her friend to return so she could make a point of asking about what's been new in her life. And she still had to come up with a plan to get revenge against her brother.

"More coffee?" Ida asked, holding the pot over her cup.

"Sure." She watched as Ida refilled her cup, suddenly nervous. It was crazy, she knew, but she felt awkward asking about her friend's life. She cleared her throat.

Ida returned the pot to the burner on the counter behind her and faced Melanie. "I'm sorry. I think I may have overreacted. It's your life and I don't have any say as to how you live it."

"No, I was just being my usual know-it-all self. You were right to scold me. But let's not talk about me anymore. To tell the truth, I'm a little sick of the subject. How are things with you? Anything new or interesting happen?"

She hesitated. "Why do you ask?"

"So something new *has* happened?"

She didn't answer.

"Ida! Come on. No secrets. I tell you."

She sighed. "Fine. If you must know, my place was recently burglarized."

"What?"

"Yeah." She started to say more, but stopped and looked away, her mouth trembling with emotion.

"You weren't there, were you?"

She shook her head, blinking back tears. "No, but they pretty much cleaned me out. Except for my clothes and stuff."

"Did you call the police?"

"Yes, of course."

"And they haven't caught the guy yet?"

"No. But luckily enough, I have good insurance. They delivered a check to me yesterday to cover the expense of replacing everything I lost."

"Thank goodness you weren't home. You could've been hurt!"

"It was probably just a couple of kids, not some mass murderer. I'm fine."

"How long ago did this happen?"

Ida shrugged. "What difference does it make? It's over and done with. I got my insurance check and everything's fine."

"You could've told me, you know."

"You wouldn't have heard me."

"What does that mean?"

"Don't pout, Mel. You've been too swept up in your own problems to spare a moment to worry about mine."

"That's not a very nice thing to say."

"On the contrary, I think it is very nice of me to point it out to you. Sometimes the truth isn't nice, but that's got to be dealt with. But I was once your age and I was the same way."

Unwilling to be lured into a discussion of her faults, however human and universal they may be, Melanie returned to the subject of Ida's break-in. "Aren't you scared at night? Afraid they might come back?"

"Why would they come back? They already took everything there was to take."

"Still, I think I might not want to ever sleep there again."

She tapped her nails on the counter. "I wish you'd learn to think before you talk. I own my house. The mortgage is finally paid off after years and years of working hard. The house is full of memories; I feel closer to Robert there. I will never move, Mel. I'm too old to deal with that kind of headache." She shook her head, her mouth pursed.

"How 'bout some more coffee?" Henry called out, raising his coffee cup to get Ida's attention.

"Keep your britches on, Henry. I'll get over there soon enough. If you can't wait, then get up and get it your own self."

Stunned, Henry put his cup back on the table and closed his mouth, adjusting his hat.

"And take your hat off while you're at the table!"

She turned to Melanie, her back stiff with anger as Henry snatched his hat off his head, his cheeks flushed with embarrassment. "You know, all you do is moan and groan. I'm sick of it. I've kept my mouth shut, but today I can't seem to let anything go. You think you're the only one who's had a hard life? I'm fifty-nine years old, too old for this job. My feet always hurt, my back aches, I get leg cramps. Do you think this is how I pictured my life when I was young like you? Robert was supposed to take care of me. He had good plans for us when we retired. He promised. Instead, he had a heart attack right there at the kitchen table, his mouth full of my homemade mashed potatoes. And so here I am, breaking my back to support myself while some hooligans break into my home and clean me out. Now I can't even soak my sore feet and watch my shows. You've heard the saying 'Life sucks and then you die?' Well, someone said it because it's true. Here you are married to a man who only wants to make you happy and yet you spend all your time worrying about that worthless Rick. He's probably one of the scumbags who broke into my home. Has he ever done anything for you, or even anyone else, that didn't somehow help him out?"

Melanie stared at her in surprise. "I'm sorry. I didn't mean to offend you and now it seems I've done it twice." She stood up, reaching into her pocket for some money to pay for the coffee. "I'll try to think of every angle from now on before I ask you a question."

Ida sighed, her shoulders slouching forward as the anger suddenly left her. "The coffee's on me because I'm being an old bitty. I'm sorry. I think I'm just getting sick of working. It'd be nice to retire, but then I'd probably just be bored silly." She grabbed a slice of pie from the pie display case. "See you next week?"

Melanie smiled. "See you next week."

"Excuse me, but I'd better go apologize to Henry. He can be so sensitive." She smoothed her apron and patted her hair before heading over to Henry's table. "Pie's on me, Henry. I apologize for snapping at you like that."

Outside the diner, Melanie paused to glance back at Ida talking to newly arrived customers. Could she be sick? Never had she snapped at her before in all the times they've worked together and today she'd done it twice. She unlocked the car. And how could Ida have not mentioned her home had been broken into? She'd have to ask Julius about it. He must've heard something. She smiled. Suddenly, she felt like a wife. A wife who needed to ask her husband a question. She laughed. Sometimes, she could be really silly, but maybe there was hope for her yet.

CHAPTER 15

When Julius returned home from work, he found his wife sitting in the middle of the living room floor surrounded by their wedding gifts.

"What are you doing?"

"Oh! Julius, you startled me!" She laughed, suddenly embarrassed. "I was trying to guess what sort of presents could be in these boxes." She'd been so bored, she wanted to add, but knew he'd just be unhappy hearing about her misery.

"Why didn't you just open them?"

"Without you? No way. But now that you're home we can open them together."

"Let me change first."

"Okay." She turned to study the box she held in her lap.

He hesitated in the doorway. "Melanie?"

She glanced up at him. "Yes?"

"Couldn't I have a kiss from my new bride?"

She stared up at him in surprise. It hadn't even occurred to her! What kind of wife was she going to make if she couldn't even remember to kiss her husband hello? She shoved aside the box and leaped to her feet. "Yes, of course, Julius. I'm sorry. I guess I was distracted or something—"

He put his finger against her lips. "No apologizing, sweetheart. Just kiss me now."

She nodded, lifting her face towards his and closing her eyes as he kissed her. She had to admit, she liked the feeling of his arms around her. He was strong and she felt so safe. If a burglar broke in and they were there, she knew Julius wouldn't let them harm her. Before, with Rick, well, he was tough, but he wouldn't have been able to protect her. He talked tough, but he wasn't much of a fighter. He'd let a weapon do the work rather than his fists. Her husband, she felt sure, preferred his fists to his weapon, if it came to that, because he'd been trained to keep the peace.

"Much better," Julius murmured, hugging her tightly. "I missed you today."

"You did? I missed you, too."

"I like to hear that. How'd I get to be so lucky?"

"I'm sure I'm the lucky one." She sat back down on the floor and picked up a present.

He smiled. "I like to hear that even more!"

Once he'd left the room, she sighed, returning the present to the floor. So there'd be no passion in her marriage. Passion wasn't everything, right? It was a friendly kiss at least and certainly that was better than nothing at all. She stood up and walked over to the window. Drawing back the curtains, she peered out into the darkness. Her problems used to be a lot bigger than worrying about having a passionless marriage. She once thought that she'd never survive growing up, but she had. Carl hadn't destroyed her as he'd intended. And the nightmares she'd once had on a regular basis were now few and far between. But the memories . . . well, she'd probably never be able to forget those long nights she'd lain awake listening for his footsteps on the stairs and then as the door opened and the hall light sliced through her room, she'd pretend she was asleep. Not that it ever mattered to him whether or not he was interrupting his stepdaughter's sleep. No, he'd just shaken her until she was forced to open her eyes and then he'd climb into bed with her, his weight causing the twin bed to dip and then his callused hands were suddenly on her nightgown—

Melanie screamed at Julius's touch on her shoulder. She swung around to confront him, her face pale.

"Sweetheart, I'm sorry. I didn't mean to scare you." Julius gently rubbed her arms.

She drew in a shaky breath and hugged him tightly. When he tightened his arms around her, she closed her eyes, leaning her head against his chest.

"You were a million miles away. Want to talk about it?"

"No. I'm fine."

"Are you sure? It might help." He held her tighter, one hand rubbing her back. "You're still trembling."

He wanted to share her troubles, but she couldn't bring herself to put them into words. The one time she had found the courage to confess, things had backfired. It was around then that her mother started looking through her rather than at her. She wouldn't let that happen again. She squeezed him tighter. But she knew he wouldn't let it go so she had to tell him something. "I talked to Ida today. Did you know her house got broken into? They took everything."

"But she's fine, right?"

Melanie pulled away. "Yes. She wasn't there when it happened. But she could've been seriously hurt, you know?"

"What's her last name? I'll find out which officer wrote up the report and see if there's anything I can do."

"Carter. Thank you, Julius. I would feel better knowing everything was being done to catch whoever did it."

"You feel safe here, though, don't you?"

She nodded. "I do. You make me feel safe."

"Good. Are you ready to open some wedding presents now?"

She smiled. "Sure."

He sat down on the couch and she handed him a present.

"You first."

"Aren't you going to tell me what you think it is before I open it?"

"I think it's a bread box and an umbrella all in one."

"All in one box? Or all in one gadget?"

"Gadget, of course."

"That'd be pretty handy." He held up the box and studied it. "You may be right." He smiled and began to tear off the paper.

She sat down on the opposite end of the couch and watched him.

That had been a close call. Thank goodness she'd remembered about Ida's robbery or otherwise, she might've ended up having to tell him the truth, or at least part of it. She didn't want him to know about her stepfather. More to the point, she didn't want him to know about any of her past if she could help it. And in five hours, her brother would be here and she had yet to figure out a plan of revenge. "It's a set of knives," she murmured as he held out the unwrapped gift.

"Who'd have thought?"

"Who's it from?" she asked, picking up the pen and paper she'd left on the floor. "We have to keep track for the thank you notes."

"Bob and Suzanne Myers."

"Bob works with you, right?

"Good memory."

"Just this time." She dutifully wrote down the information. Putting aside the pen and paper, she smiled brightly, sensing he was watching her closely, worrying that she might still be upset. "My turn!"

He handed her a box. "What do you think it is?"

"This one is quite obvious. It's a flamingo."

"Plastic? Or alive?"

She shook the box gently. "Alive. Or maybe pretty close to it."

He leaned back against the couch, shaking his head. "You peeked earlier, didn't you?"

"Maybe. Maybe not."

The doorbell rang and Julius got to his feet. "I ordered us a pizza. I hope that's all right."

"Yeah, of course." She watched him leave the room. Here was another example of why she was a terrible wife. She should've already taken care of dinner. She jumped to her feet and headed for the kitchen. She'd at least make herself useful now and get their plates and napkins.

Last night Melanie had already explored every inch of the kitchen so finding everything proved to be no problem. She moved from cupboard to drawer to pantry without any hesitation.

"You already know where everything is."

Melanie paused to glance at Julius leaning against the wall watching her. "You sound surprised. Is that a problem?"

"No, of course not. I'm impressed. I guess I just expected you to still be learning your way around."

She smiled, stopping next to him with her hands full of plates, napkins, and silverware. "I probably know this house as well as you, if not better. Ask me where something is. Anything at all."

"This could be interesting. You sound awfully confident."

"Just try me."

"Okay. Where is my money clip?"

"On top of the refrigerator."

"That's where I left it? I've been looking for it for days."

She laughed. "Impressed?"

"That was an easy one since we're already in the kitchen. How about buttons?"

"Buttons?"

"Yeah, you know, like those extra buttons you get with a shirt."

"Well, you don't keep them with your sewing stuff like any normal, logical person would, and by the way, I'm surprised you even have sewing stuff."

"The credit belongs to my mother, not me."

"Anyway, there is a small tin at the top of your hall closet that contains a red rubber band, one nail, a gold ring, one cuff link, and last but not least, a variety of loose buttons."

"You are very thorough."

"You did say nothing was off-limits."

"What's mine is yours, sweetheart. I'm astounded at your sleuthing ability."

She dipped her head slightly in acknowledgement. "Now, get our drinks before our dinner gets cold."

"Yes, ma'am! I put the pizza in the living room."

She smiled and returned to the living room. So what if their marriage would be passionless? There's something to be said for being able to get along well with each other. Certainly she and Julius were having no trouble in that respect. And maybe if they worked at it, passion would flare up between them. She set everything down on the coffee table next to the pizza box and hurried to their bedroom.

When she returned to the living room, Julius was putting a slice of pizza on her plate. "Do you like cold pizza, Julius?"

He glanced up and stared at his wife dressed in a skimpy, sheer black chemise. "Tonight I do."

She held out her hand.

He moved to join her. "Have I told you today how much I love you?"

"Show me."

Gently, his hands fluttered to frame her face. "It's weird to think we haven't known each other very long, but I love you more than life itself, Melanie." Slowly he bent his head and kissed her, closing his eyes.

She kept her eyes open, willing him to not be so gentle. Carl hadn't been gentle; Rick hadn't been either. She didn't really understand gentle. Julius, she knew, wouldn't leave behind any evidence of his lovemaking. There would be no bruises. Her body wouldn't ache afterwards.

He pulled away from her. "Are you okay?"

She nodded.

He hugged her tightly. "There's no need to be nervous, sweetheart."

"I know."

He kissed the top of her head before taking her hand and leading her down the hall and into their bedroom. Slowly, by the light of the adjoining bathroom, he stripped her of her chemise, whispering endless words meant to encourage her, entice her, and calm her as he kissed her all over.

She knew he was trying to pamper her, to love her fully, but she couldn't help but wish he'd just get on with it. By now, if she were with Rick, it'd be over and she'd be smoking a cigarette. Clenching her teeth, she closed her eyes, mentally admonishing herself for comparing her husband—her warm, caring, wonderful husband—with Rick. She needed to focus, to concentrate on Julius and maybe she'd get a bit of enjoyment out of it after all.

He undressed as she watched from where she lay on the bed. He had a good body with a light dusting of blonde hair in all the right places. Rick had a body like a pre-teen when it came to having any chest hair. She bit her lip. She was doing it again, comparing the two when there shouldn't be any comparison whatsoever.

"Relax," he whispered as he hovered above her.

She nodded and wrapped her arms around his neck, pulling him closer for a kiss. The curled hairs on his chest and stomach tickled her and she shivered. Instantly, his body lightly covered hers, warming her as his hands stroked her hair. She could feel herself relaxing in his arms, her bones becoming languid and her body temperature rising. His hands moved to her breasts and before she knew it, their bodies were joined.

It felt good, she decided. Not amazing, but then, when had sex ever been amazing? She gripped his biceps, thrilling at the muscles that bulged as he held himself slightly above her. She definitely liked that about him. She allowed her fingers to roam across his chest. Julius was better than Rick. Just look at his muscles. She glanced at her husband's face and knew from the way his eyes were rolled back into his head that he was about to climax.

Suddenly she was overcome with a thought. What if she had her brother burglarize their house, but then arrange to also have him caught? She gasped aloud, surprising herself. Where had her subconscious come up with that idea? Ida, of course. And then Julius collapsed on top of her, his sweaty brow against her cheek as he tried to catch his breath.

She frowned, frustrated because she couldn't continue to flesh out her plan, but quietly mimicked his quick breathing so that he couldn't guess she'd been far away from their bedroom during such an intimate moment.

"I love you," he breathed.

She stroked his hair. "I love you, too." And she actually meant it this time.

He shifted slightly so that his weight on top of her wouldn't be so unbearable and brushed her hair out of her eyes. "I wish we could stay locked together like this all night."

She nodded, uncertain what to say or how to react to such intimacy.

He sighed and rolled over to his side. "Unfortunately, things don't always work out like we'd wish." He kissed her lightly. "Is that your stomach growling or mine?"

She smiled. "I'm not sure."

"How about a romantic dinner in bed tonight?"

"Okay."

He kissed her again and stood up, unconcerned with his lack of clothing. "Don't move, my beautiful wife. I shall return."

She watched him leave the bedroom, noticing the strength of his shoulders, the firmness of his butt, the leanness of his long legs. What would her mother think of her daughter's new husband? She'd probably think there was something dreadfully wrong with him since he'd chosen Melanie. She sighed, pulling the covers up to her chin. She had to stop these negative thoughts and try to enjoy the time spent with her husband. She glanced at the bedside clock and frowned. And she had to make sure he was asleep before her brother arrived looking for a handout.

Julius entered carrying a tray laden with pizza and two sodas and Melanie looked at him happily. "Thank you, Julius."

"This isn't exactly a gourmet feast."

"It doesn't matter." She studied his face, at the tiredness that lurked around his eyes, and relaxed. He'd be fast asleep by the time Benjie arrived. "Thank you for loving me."

He settled the tray over her lap and kissed her on the top of her head. Climbing into bed beside her, he said, "That's easy to do, sweetheart. Now dig in."

She nodded and picked up a slice.

CHAPTER 16

Melanie slipped quietly out of bed, careful not to wake her husband, who'd fallen asleep soon after they'd filled up on pizza, too tired to even notice as she cleared away the remnants of their dinner. Her brother would be there soon and she needed to analyze her idea from every angle. There could not be any mishaps because she might not ever get a second chance. Snatching her robe from the chair by the bed, she tiptoed out into the hallway and closed the door. The hinges creaked and she cringed, holding her breath as she waited for signs that Julius had woken up. But he hadn't stirred.

She hurried through the house and unlocked the back door, turning on the outside light. She hoped that Benjie would be smart enough to figure out not to use the front door, but she wasn't so sure he hadn't lost all his good sense in a cloud of pot smoke. She'd better put a note on the doorbell just in case. Otherwise Julius would wake up and be certain to investigate.

Quickly, she wrote a note directing her brother to use the back door and taped it to the front door. As a precaution, she also taped over the doorbell in case he reached for the bell before he saw the note. Then she stood in the dark kitchen and stared out the window, waiting.

If someone were to break into their house and steal all their belongings, the homeowner's insurance would reimburse them. Your basic run-of-the-mill insurance fraud was the answer to her prayers. She could convince Benjie to rob their house and then sell all their stuff in order to get the money he needed. He wouldn't even have to pay her back, not that he intended to do so in the first place. Of course she wasn't interested in insurance fraud. So if an anonymous caller happened to tip off the police to a robbery in progress and then that thief was to get arrested, well, she had no control over that, right? But by then who cares if he knows she set him up? Revenge might be sweeter that way. And she'd have to press charges anyway, wouldn't she, in order to get him prosecuted? But then again, he'd be caught red-handed so she wouldn't have to; instead, the law itself would press charges. Right? She'd have to remember to ask Julius about that part, using Ida's recent break-in as an excuse.

She jumped as Benjie's pale face appeared in the window. With one hand over her racing heart, she pointed towards the back yard. He ran out of sight and, after taking a deep breath, she moved to meet him at the back door.

He was still laughing when she let him in.

"Shh," she whispered. "My husband's asleep and I'd like to keep it that way."

"You should've seen your face!"

"Benjie! Please. Be quiet or you can leave right now without my help."

He shrugged and walked past her and into the kitchen.

When he headed towards the doorway leading to the living room, she grabbed his arm. "We can discuss everything right here."

"What? Now that's not very nice of you. There's no reason we can't relax a little."

She frowned, but followed him into the living room.

"Pretty nice place you got here, sis," he said, glancing around.

"Thanks."

He flopped down on the couch. "So how much?"

"How much what?"

Rolling his eyes, he elaborated. "How much dough did you get me?"

"I didn't."

He squinted at her. "What do you mean? Mellie, I told you it was important."

"I couldn't get you any money, Benjie. But I do have a plan."

He leaned forward. "Yeah? What kind of plan?"

With a forced smile, she sat down next to him and proceeded to explain to him the first half of her plan. The second half, the revenge half, he'd learn about later.

Finally, after she'd patiently outlined the benefits of her plan several times, he seemed to grasp the concept. "Damn. I never knew you could be so sneaky, Mellie."

She shrugged. "Well, there's a lot you don't know about me." She stood up, ready for her brother to leave. "Next Friday night then?"

He continued to slouch on the sofa. "Friday? Not any sooner? I told you I needed some fast cash."

"Yeah, well, Friday is Julius's birthday. We'll be out late; you'll have the place to yourself. It's the only time. Are you in? Or not?"

"But I've got myself a hot date on Friday."

"Bring her along. Knowing the type of girls you screw, she'd probably be quite turned on by a little B&E. Just wait until you get home, though. No sex in my bed."

Benjie laughed. "Mellie! What a little spitfire you turned into. Used to be all I had to say was 'Boo!' and you'd be on the floor in a dead faint."

"Well, as I said earlier, there's a lot you don't know about me now."

"So it seems. Now, aren't you gonna offer me a drink? Let us talk about old times?"

"Why would I want to do that?"

"Afraid I'll slip something into my pocket while you're pouring me a drink? I can wait until Friday night. Although it might be nice to know now where all the good jewels are hidden. Care to give me a tour?"

"Sorry, no jewels. And no tour. You'll just have to do your best on your own."

"Okay, so no tour. But at least let me have a drink."

She sighed. "Fine. You can have a drink, but just one. And I do not want to talk about our shared past. One word, one syllable about our childhood, Benjie, and you're out of here."

"Nothing wimpy, though. Make it a good strong one. Big, too. It's a long ass walk home, you know."

"What happened to your car?"

He shrugged, averting his eyes. "It's in the shop."

"I'll see what we have." She turned, her back stiff, and disappeared into the kitchen.

Slowly, she grabbed the bottle of Myers Rum from the cabinet by the refrigerator and unscrewed the lid. She smiled. She'd done it. She'd dangled the carrot in front of his nose and he didn't have sense enough to turn it down. Of course now she had to get him out of the house before Julius woke up. What kind of explanation could she possibly come up with if Julius got up to go to the bathroom and found Benjie drinking in the living room? Quickly, she fixed his drink and returned the liquor bottle to the cabinet.

She halted in the doorway of the living room, unnerved to find it empty. Where had he disappeared to?

"Just checking out the layout of the place, sis, since you won't give me a personal tour," Benjie said, coming up behind her.

Melanie jumped, her hand automatically going to her throat as the glass trembled in her hand.

"Better let me take that before you go and drop it. " He grinned. "Guess you're not so different like I thought, huh? Only I didn't even have to say 'Boo!' Maybe you should take a sip of this before you faint at my feet."

She waved him off and sat on the sofa. "You just startled me, Benjie. That's all. I hadn't expected you to go snooping around when you're fully aware that my husband is asleep down the hall."

He shrugged, lifting the glass to his lips for a long swallow. "You didn't put anything in this, did you?"

"What do you mean by that?"

"You know."

Melanie clenched her fists. "I said no reminders of the past, Benjie. Shut up, drink up, and then get out."

"Gee, what a great hostess you are."

She leaned back, pretending to be calm. "I'm just tired and would like to go to bed." And afraid of the memories that crowded her mind as he stood in her living room deliberately, cruelly, dredging up their past.

"Myers and coke, huh? Not bad. Not strong enough, but okay I guess when you're dying of thirst."

She refused to comment, closing her eyes and massaging her temples. She felt him sit next to her, but continued to keep her eyes closed. *Please*, she prayed silently, *don't bring it up*. But she knew it was useless. Once her brother had hit puberty, he'd preferred hurting her, rather than protecting her.

"It was a good plan, Mellie," he said, his voice soft in her ear. He took a sip of his drink, the ice clinking against the glass. "If only we'd increased the dosage, he would've died."

She licked her lips. "I don't know what you're talking about."

He laughed. "Still going to deny it to this day, huh?"

She opened her eyes and glared at him. "*We* didn't do anything, Benjie. You were unavailable. You were always unavailable when I needed you."

"If you'd told me you planned to poison the man, I'd have hung around. For consultation purposes only, of course."

"Are you finished with that drink yet?"

"No." He sipped his drink, his eyes scanning the room. "Mom never did find out the truth, did she? She just thought he was drunk and passed out in the snow. Which would have worked, too, if only he'd passed out face down. What a shame."

Melanie jumped to her feet and snatched the glass from his lips, causing him to spill it down his shirt. "You've overstayed your welcome, dearest brother. Get out."

"Mellie, I'm sorry. I didn't realize you were so damn touchy." He stared at his wet shirt. "Can't I at least have a towel or something before you kick me out?"

"It'll dry before you get home."

"And if the cops decide to hassle me, all they have to do is take one whiff and I'll be spending the night in the drunk tank."

"You'll survive." She walked over to the doorway leading into the kitchen. "I mean it."

He shook his head, but got to his feet and followed her through the kitchen to the utility room.

She opened the back door.

"Are we still on for Friday night at least?"

She hesitated, not wanting to appear too eager for her plan to be put into action. She couldn't afford for him to get suspicious. She couldn't blow this chance.

"Mellie, come on. I need the cash and you're my last chance."

She stared at him, silently counting to ten before finally sighing. "Yeah, sure. We're still on for Friday night."

"Great. See you then. Or rather I won't see you then."

She nodded. "We should be out of the house by eight, but just to make sure, don't come until nine. Okay? Nine o'clock, Benjie. And please be on time. Otherwise, you're liable to mess everything up by being here when we return."

He grazed her cheek with a light kiss. "Thanks, sis."

Awkward, she stared out into the back yard. How long had it been since her brother had shown her any kind of sincere affection? She couldn't remember the last time. Was she wrong to plan her revenge this way? Should she follow Julius's advice and just let the past go and focus on the future?

She grabbed his hand as he stepped outside. "If you get caught, Benjie, you're on your own. I won't let this ruin my marriage."

He smiled. "I'm too good to get caught." With a quick wave, he hurried down the steps.

She waited a minute before turning off the outside light and locking the door. There could never be any doubt as to the color of her heart after Friday night. It was blacker than black. Her mother and Carl had been right all along about her. She really was an evil person. And what would Julius say if he ever found out she'd set her own brother up? But there was no backing out now. The plans were made and she'd just have to wait and see how everything turned out. If Julius turned her away . . . But he wouldn't. He loved her, right?

And as for trying to poison her stepfather by drugging his soup, well, that was years ago. No one except Benjie had known the truth and that was only because he'd caught her dissolving their mother's sleeping pills in the soup she was preparing for Carl. He had no actual proof and back then he was in trouble a lot with the cops and the school, starting to use drugs on a daily basis. No one would've believed him. If Benjie ever tried to tell Julius, she would deny her failed attempt, insisting that Carl had been very drunk when he'd gone outside and passed out in the snow. Sure, she hated him, hated him so much she still got a bitter taste in her mouth just thinking of him, but try to kill him? Benjie must have been hallucinating. And besides, it had happened so long ago that it would be ridiculous to point fingers now anyway. Julius would have to believe her. She would make him believe her. Quickly, she turned off the lights and went to bed, hoping she'd fall into a deep, dreamless sleep where memories of Carl could never follow her.

CHAPTER 17

Melanie stowed her purse in her locker before pausing in front of the full-length mirror to check her appearance. She quickly tied the apron around her waist and plucked a loose strand of hair from her shoulder.

Ida poked her head in. "You're beautiful, girl, now hurry up. You've got three at table two."

She cast a quick glance at her reflection before hurrying out into the dining room.

"Hey, there's the bride! How was the honeymoon?"

Melanie smiled at the old man sitting at the counter, his trembling hands wrapped loosely around a coffee cup. "Hi, Fred. It was great, thanks. How's the wife?"

"Mean as ever," he quipped.

She shook her head and grabbed an order pad. "She probably says the same thing about you."

"I can only hope she does."

Melanie chuckled and, uncapping her pen, headed over to table two. For the next hour and a half, she only had time to answer the regulars' inquiries about her wedding with the briefest of answers. Otherwise, she hurried from table to table, dashing back to the kitchen window to hang orders and pick up hot plates of steaming food, circling around the restaurant with the coffee pot and acting as hostess or cashier when needed. Finally, though, the breakfast rush was over and she could enjoy a cup of coffee while it was still hot.

Ida wiped off an area at the counter where a customer had just vacated. "So, how's Julius?"

"He's great."

"Things are going well with the two of you?"

"Yes, of course." Melanie sipped her coffee.

"I was surprised he didn't mind you coming back to work."

She had forgotten, in fact, to tell Julius she was returning to work until this morning, although maybe the truth was she hadn't mentioned it because she was afraid he'd be upset with her. "He wouldn't tell me what to do, Ida."

"True. He's too much of a gentleman for that sort of thing. Not to be nosy, but have you talked about starting a family yet?"

"For God's—sorry," she said, catching herself. "I know, don't take the Lord's name in vain. But Ida, don't you think it's a little soon?" She added more sugar to her coffee.

"Soon? You're having sex, aren't you?"

Melanie blushed. "Don't you have a table to set or a check to add up or something?"

"No, I don't." She sighed. "You know, I still remember the first time Robert and I talked about starting a family. Back then, girls didn't have sex until their wedding night so it'd never come up. The night before our wedding we went for a walk. It was very clear out and there were so many stars . . ." She smiled. "Of course I was head over heels in love so my vision and my memory may have been impaired. Anyway, there we were walking along and suddenly Robert stopped and turned to look at me. I thought that maybe he wasn't feeling well. He'd had a big dinner, at least two full helpings if not more, which pleased my mother to death, and sometimes when he ate too much, he got gas, but no, he was fine. He said, 'Ida, there's something I need to know that concerns our future together.' Well, that made me instantly nervous as you can imagine. It sounded so darn ominous. But then he entwined his fingers with mine and asked, 'Exactly how many babies are you going to let me father?'" She paused.

"So what did you say?"

"I said, 'As many as God grants us.' I was a good Catholic girl at the time and that meant no birth control."

"Oh, Ida! What does that mean? That eventually you weren't a good Catholic girl?"

"That, my dear, is none of your business."

The door chimed, signaling someone had entered the restaurant and both women turned towards the entrance.

Melanie slowly put her coffee down. "Rick?" She glanced over at Ida who scowled, but remained quiet.

"Mel. It's been a while."

She nodded. Many times she'd imagined him coming to the diner to beg her to come back to him, but now that he was here, she had no idea what to say.

"Tell him he's not welcome here," Ida said to Melanie loud enough for Rick to hear as she stared at him.

"It's none of your damn business, old woman, so stay out of this. Mel, let's talk outside for a minute."

She followed behind him, discreetly removing her wedding ring and slipping it into her apron pocket. She knew it was wrong; she knew Julius would be very hurt, but she didn't want Rick to know that she was married. Not yet anyway. But as to why she felt that way, well, she'd have to brood over that later when she replayed everything they said over and over in her mind.

"Gimme a cigarette."

She pulled the pack from her apron and silently offered him one.

Once they both had a lit cigarette dangling from their fingertips, he studied her. "You look good."

"Thanks. So do you."

"Yeah?"

She looked away, bringing the cigarette to her lips and inhaling deeply. Yes, he looked good. Too good, in fact, because now she wished he would yank her into his arms and devour her. She wondered if he'd lost any of his hair after she'd switched his shampoo for Nair. It didn't seem to be any thinner. Leaning against the brick building, she absently tapped her fingers on the rough surface.

"Where you staying nowadays?"

"Rick, I don't have much time. Why are you here?"

Narrowing his eyes, he watched her as he smoked. Finally, he exhaled and smiled. "I need my Harley money back, Mel."

She should have known that was his motivation. He hadn't missed her. He hadn't come here to ask her to come back to him. He just wanted his money back. "Where are my clothes?"

He shrugged. "That wasn't my fault, Mel. You can't think I'd do something as dumb as that, right?"

She sighed, glancing away. "Well, I certainly don't have the money on me."

"What are you doing after work?"

She shook her head. "Nothing specific."

He took one last hit off his cigarette before flicking it out into the parking lot. "I'll be home. You should come by and we can hang out like old times. You can bring the money with you."

"I don't know."

He grabbed her hand. "I've missed you, Mel. Haven't you missed me?"

She searched his face for evidence of deceit, but he'd always been an exceptional liar. Was this time any different? "Rick . . ."

He smiled and brushed his lips across hers. "I'll see you later."

Startled by the lack of roughness in his kiss, she only watched as he hurried through the parking lot.

"Mel," Ida said, poking her head outside. "You gonna stand out here all day and blacken your lungs or are you gonna come in here and make some money?"

"I'll be right there." She sighed and tossed her cigarette into the parking lot. Rick had certainly confused her this time. But what could she do? She had to give him his money back; she'd never intended to keep all of it in the first place, just enough to pay for more clothes. She'd only taken it all because she'd been so angry. So, she would go home, get the money, and stop off at Rick's. She didn't have to stay, but what would it hurt if she stayed for a few minutes? With a last glance in the direction Rick had left, she slipped her wedding ring back on her finger and hurried into the diner and back to work.

Melanie hesitated outside Rick's apartment. It used to be her home and yet now it seemed forever since she'd lived there. Funny how things could change so drastically so quickly.

Glancing down at the jeans and T-shirt she'd changed into, she wondered if maybe she should've shown up in her greasy uniform. Would this give him the wrong impression? But what did it matter, right? She could hear the television, but couldn't make out what show was on. She knocked loudly.

Rick opened the door. "Mel, what's with you knocking? You could've just come right in."

She held out the bag she'd brought with her. "Here's your money. I didn't spend too much, just enough to replace my clothes your little girlfriend burned."

He scowled. "She's not my girlfriend. You're coming in, aren't you?"

She hesitated, knowing she shouldn't, but before she could even voice a response, Rick pulled her into the apartment and closed the door behind her.

"The place hasn't changed much," she said, looking everywhere but at Rick.

"It's lonelier."

She stared at him. "Really? I thought Candi with an 'i' would've done her best to fix that."

He laughed. "Jealous?" Grabbing her hand, he forced her to sit on the sofa next to him. "Candi is just a friend. I was helping her out by letting her crash here. She was hoping for more, I won't lie to you, but I was too hung up on you."

Melanie listened to his words and wondered if she was dreaming. Or on some type of hallucinogenic. He was hung up on her?

"What's this?" he asked suddenly, grabbing her left hand and staring at her wedding ring.

She'd forgotten to take it off. "My ring. I got married, Rick."

"Married? Who'd you marry?"

She began tapping her fingers on her leg. "You don't know him."

"You're lying."

"I'm not."

"You weren't wearing this earlier. You expect me to believe you got married today between the time I saw you and now?"

"No, of course not. I-I'd forgotten to put it on this morning because I was running late."

"Or maybe you're making the whole thing up? How do I know that ring doesn't belong to one of those bitches you work with? Is this a game to you, trying to play hard to get?"

"Why do you care? You weren't going to marry me. You told me that plenty of times. So I found someone who would."

"You got that right. I'm not marrying anybody. But it doesn't change anything, you know."

"It doesn't?"

He reached over and grabbed her breast. "No."

"Rick . . ."

"You can't tell me you don't want me, Mel. And you got what you wanted, right? A ring? So give me what I want."

"And what's that?"

"You."

She'd wished so hard and so often that he'd say that back when they'd been together that now his words were like alcohol: They went straight to her head and made her dizzy. Before she could think about what she was doing, she was in his arms and seconds later he was attempting to yank her shirt over her head.

"No." She held on to the hem of her T-shirt.

"No?" he mumbled, his lips moving to bite her neck.

She shivered. "Not here. Let's go to the bedroom."

"Right." He grabbed her hand and rushed her into the bedroom with such haste, she had to bite her lip to keep from laughing out loud. All this attention just because she was no longer his for the taking whenever he wanted? If only she'd left him a long time ago!

They had sex twice and it was the same as it had always been with Rick: quick and fierce.

And afterwards, as she lay with the sheet pulled up to her chin and shared a cigarette with him, she wondered what in the world she'd been thinking. And she wondered just what in the world she was going to tell Julius.

"I've got to go," she said, stubbing the cigarette out in the already full ashtray.

"Back to the old hubby." Rick laughed.

She ignored him, hurrying to dress and at the same time come up with a believable lie as to her whereabouts after work. And actually, simple was the safest way to go. She paused, one shoe in hand. Perhaps she'd just say that since he hadn't been home when she'd gotten off work, she went for a walk and lost track of time? Yes, he would believe that.

Once dressed, she turned to Rick, smiling, but he was fast asleep. Slightly disappointed, but also relieved because she would have felt awkward saying good-bye to her ex to go home to her husband, she crossed the room and left without looking back.

CHAPTER 18

"You sure are quiet," Ida remarked the next day when the breakfast rush was over. "Something bothering you?"

"No, I'm fine."

"You sure?"

"Yeah, I'm sure."

Ida watched Melanie stir spoonfuls of sugar into her coffee. "How can you drink that? It's all sugar with just a splash of coffee. It's going to rot your teeth."

Melanie remained silent, ignoring Ida's scolding. She'd been debating with herself all morning as to whether she should see Rick again tonight or not. Julius had accepted her lie last night of having gone for a long walk easily enough. Could she use the same excuse tonight? Should she?

"Mel?"

"What?" She glanced up, realizing Ida had been talking to her. "Oh, I'm sorry. What did you say?"

"I asked what that no-good ex of yours wanted yesterday."

Melanie shrugged, willing herself not to get stirred up by Ida's tone. "Nothing really."

She raised one penciled eyebrow. "You expect me to believe he came all the way here for nothing? 'Nothing really' implies something. Now if it's none of my business, well, that's another story and you can certainly tell an old woman to butt out."

Melanie sipped her coffee, stalling for time. Of course she couldn't tell Ida it was none of her business because then it would seem that Rick had really wanted something important after all, but it was definitely tempting. "He just felt bad for how things ended between us and wanted to make peace."

Ida grunted. "I find that hard to believe."

Melanie shrugged. "It's a small town and we have friends in common so are bound to run into one another every once in a while. This way, when that does happen, things won't be awkward for us or our friends."

"What did Julius have to say about that?"

"Julius?" She blew on her coffee. "Nothing. Why?"

"You didn't tell him, did you?"

She set her coffee cup down. "No, actually, I didn't."

"Mel, already you're keeping secrets from your husband? How in the world do you expect to be married forever if this is how you're starting out? Never, never did I keep secrets from my Robert."

"I'm not you, Ida, and I'm not perfect, okay? And you know how overprotective of me Julius is. He just would've gotten upset for no reason and probably would've either paid Rick a visit and threatened him to stay away from me or else he would've insisted I find a new job where Rick won't be able to stop in and 'harass' me—his words, not mine. Do you think that would be better? Because I don't and that's why I didn't tell him."

"Don't you think Julius deserves more credit than that?"

"He's a man and where my ex is concerned, he can't be rational. You should've seen him the other day. At the briefest mention of my life before? My life with Rick? He had this huge vein throbbing in his neck."

"Because he loves you and wants you to be safe."

The door chimed as customers walked in. "It's your turn," Melanie said. "I'm going to the restroom." She turned and hurried away.

In the employee restroom, Melanie leaned against the door and closed her eyes. She'd totally overreacted to Ida's innocent questions. It was just that she was under enough stress without Ida voicing her worries. Of course she wanted to see Rick tonight; despite her marriage, she was still drawn to him. But she couldn't. She had to remember Julius, who loved her unconditionally. She could not fall back into her old ways. She washed her hands and returned to the dining room.

"There's a phone call for you," Ida said, walking by carrying a tray of drinks. "And you've got two on table four. I've got their drinks."

"Thanks." She hurried over to the phone.

"Mel," Rick said on the other end of the phone. "What time are you coming over?"

She turned away from where Ida could glance over and read her all-too-expressive face. She lowered her voice. "I don't know if I can—"

"Don't be dumb. Of course you can. Just tell your husband you're hanging out with a friend. How can he say no to that? Or is it that you're on a leash nowadays?"

"No, it's not like that. I can do what I want—"

"Then what time will you be here?"

Melanie bit her lip. What was the harm in hanging out with him for a little while? He seemed to really miss her and she had to admit, she liked the idea of being with him without all the drama and tension. "I'll stop by after work."

"Great. I'll be waiting, baby."

She heard the smile in his voice and couldn't stop the smile that answered his. As she hung up the phone, she decided that as long as she didn't sleep with him again, there was no harm done.

"Who was that?"

Melanie jumped. "Oh! Ida, you startled me!"

"Who were you talking to?"

"Who? Oh, that was Julius's brother-in-law."

"Why were you whispering?"

"Was I? We were talking about Julius's birthday and I guess I just got caught up in the whole surprise thing going on." Swallowing her irritation, she smiled and hurried over to table four to take the waiting customers' orders.

Later, Melanie tried to explain the conversation to Rick. "I love her dearly, but Ida's not my mother and I'm getting tired of her always butting into my life."

"So tell her to leave you the hell alone."

"I can't do that. It would hurt her feelings."

"You're making it hard on yourself. The next time she starts in on you, just tell her to shove off and walk away. Then you won't have any more problems."

She sipped her beer, disappointed that he didn't understand. Her husband would've understood, but she couldn't talk to him about it because then she'd have to admit Rick had been the main topic. "How's your pool game?"

He laughed. "Better than ever. Those suckers don't know how I get so lucky when it comes down to the wire. It's so funny to watch their faces as I run the table and then fill my pockets with their cash."

"I hope you're not being too obvious."

"Hey, don't start with me. I know what I'm doing."

Melanie glanced at her watch. "I've got to go."

"It's still early yet." He leaned closer to her, placing an arm around her shoulders, and kissed her.

She didn't pull away, but she didn't kiss him back, at least not right away. "Rick," she said when he ended the kiss. She turned away from him, closing her eyes. Was she asking him to stop? Or begging him to continue?

He took the beer bottle from her and placed it on the scratched coffee table. "Let's do it right here on the couch, baby. Come on." He grabbed her hand and placed it on his crotch. "Can't you feel what you're doing to me? I'm hot for you."

She knew she shouldn't, but then his hands slipped under her dress and she knew she wouldn't stop him. There was some sort of connection between them that kept her from being smart and keeping her distance and it had nothing to do with whether she wore her stained uniform or not. She knew she was hurting Julius by being with Rick, but she couldn't seem to stay away. At least she could be discreet and keep Julius from finding out. She would do her best to protect him from this truth, she thought as she sunk back onto the couch under Rick's persistent touch. This time Rick was more his usual rough self, but Melanie couldn't worry about the possible bruises right then. It was later, much later when she was sorry she hadn't kept Rick from being so rough.

"Where've you been?" Julius asked after he'd helped her off with her jacket.

She tossed her words over her shoulder as he followed her into the living room. "I took the long way home from work. It's nice out and I wanted to take advantage of it before the rainy season hits."

"I've been trying to find you. I asked Ida where you were."

Melanie stood in front of her husband and fidgeted. She'd been a bit unnerved when he'd met her at the door, but now as he stood in the living room and stared at her, her jacket still in his arms, she frowned, wishing she were anywhere else. "What did she say?" she finally asked.

"She said . . ." He cleared his throat. "She said you were probably with him."

"Him?"

He clenched his fist. "That jerk you used to live with."

"She told you I was with Rick?" Melanie frowned, furious with Ida for interfering. Rick had been right; she should've told her to mind her own business. She turned on her heel and stomped down the hall to the bedroom and then to the master bathroom, suddenly anxious to check her skin for bruises, even though it was probably too soon for such evidence to have formed.

Julius followed, tossing her jacket on the couch before moving down the hall. "Were you?"

"Was I what?"

He stopped in the bathroom doorway. "Were you with Rick?"

"What's the matter with you? This feels like the Inquisition. I'm not one of your suspects you can interrogate, Julius." Why hadn't she made sure Rick was more careful about marking her body?

"Perhaps you wouldn't feel like that if you weren't guilty of something."

"Oh, and I suppose now you're going to confess to having a doctorate in psychology?"

"Melanie, I don't want to fight with you. But, well . . . we can talk about this later." He ran his hand through his hair. "I have something important to tell you."

She studied his face. Had he decided he didn't love her after all? Did he think their marriage was a mistake and now he wanted a divorce? "By the look on your face, I'd have to guess that what you have to tell me won't be considered good news."

"Your brother stopped by earlier tonight."

She stared at him, horrified. "I was right. That's definitely not good news," she muttered as her mind began to spin with the possibilities his visit meant. She would almost prefer to talk about Rick than to talk about her family. Why would her brother come by? Had he gotten the day wrong? Had he tried to break in and Julius had caught him? Her brother was worthless!

"He came by because your mother . . ." He hesitated.

"My mother?"

"You mother has been in an accident."

She kept her face expressionless. At least her brother hadn't screwed everything up after all. "She's dead then."

He reached for her hands. "No, sweetheart, she's fine. A few scrapes and bruises, of course, and they're going to keep her overnight because she hit her head pretty hard. She was driving drunk."

"Was anyone else involved?" She heard herself ask, but her mind wasn't really focused on the question or Julius's answer. It would be just her luck for her mother to die before Melanie could prove that she really wasn't the loser her mother believed. "What?" she asked, realizing she hadn't heard her husband's answer.

"No. She ran off the road and hit a tree," he repeated.

"So if she's fine, why did Benjie come here?"

"He thought you'd want to know. She is your mother, Melanie."

She yanked her hands out of his grasp. "Don't say that to me, Julius, as if I'm a confused child or something. I'm perfectly aware of who she is." She snapped her mouth shut, afraid she'd blurt out something she didn't want to say. Quickly, silently, she counted to ten. She lowered herself to sit on the edge of the bathtub. "Did Benjie hit you up for any money?"

"Money? Melanie, no, of course not. He just thought you'd want to know."

"That's a surprise."

"If your family needs money or anything for that matter, I would do my best to help them."

She shook her head. "And I thought you were smarter than that."

"He's family; I would always try to help family."

"Not mine. They don't deserve it so don't ever offer it. And if they have the nerve to ask, turn them down. Okay?"

He studied her silently. Finally, he shrugged. "I'm sorry to hear you say that, but okay. If that's what you want, I'll respect your wishes."

"Good." She looked away, rising to her feet. "If you'll excuse me, I need to go to the bathroom."

"I think we should go to the hospital."

She faced him, angry. "What for?"

"I'll get your jacket."

"You said she was fine, Julius. You said she was fine so why do we have to go?" She hated sounding the way she did, like a child about to burst into tears, but she couldn't let them meet. What if her mother managed to turn him against her? She wrapped her arms around her body, hoping to stop the trembling that had overcome her.

He pulled her into his arms with a weary sigh. "Because it's time we faced your mother together. I don't know your history, Melanie, because you won't talk about it, but if I'm to understand you, to love you fully, I need to know. I need to meet your mother."

She pulled away from him, swiping the tears from her cheeks. "That's a bunch of bullshit, but fine, I'll go." She shook her head. "I can't believe I'm agreeing to this, but whatever. Just keep in mind that I'm not staying very long, okay?"

"When you say the word, we'll leave. I promise."

She stared at him and, finally deciding he meant it, nodded. If her mother so much as said one negative word, she'd yank Julius out of there so fast, her mother would think she'd imagined seeing them.

He walked out of the bathroom, pulling the door closed behind him.

Melanie needn't have worried about spending a lot of time with her mother. Hospital visiting hours were over and it took a lot of convincing of the nurse on duty on Julius's part to be allowed even five minutes.

Julius squeezed her hand tightly. "I love you, Melanie."

She nodded, too nervous to speak, and entered the room. Her mother lay in the metal bed, bandages wrapped around her head and one wrist. Melanie stopped by the bed, noting the scratches on her mother's face and the swollen lip.

She turned to Julius. "She's asleep. Let's just go."

"I'm not asleep," the older woman said, her voice hoarse in the quiet room.

Melanie swung around and stared into her mother's eyes.

"You're the last person I expected to see."

She lifted her chin. "Yeah, well, I'm not staying very long."

"Just came to see for yourself that I wasn't dead yet?"

Julius cleared his throat from where he stood just inside the hospital room, announcing his presence.

"Who's that with you? Benjie?"

He came up behind Melanie. "I'm Julius." He rested his hand on the back of her neck, his thumb gently stroking her sensitive skin.

"Oh?" She stared at his hands offering comfort to her daughter.

"He's—" She stopped, clenching her jaw while she fought to keep herself from shouting the news in her mother's face. "He's my husband," she finally explained, her voice quiet.

She struggled to sit up. "I thought Benjie had been hallucinating when he told me that. I didn't believe him." She frowned. "I didn't think you'd get married without me."

Melanie folded her arms across her chest. She wasn't going to put on the act of the poor, neglected mother, was she? "You thought I'd never get married, remember?"

"But I can't say I blame you, Melanie," she continued, ignoring her daughter's question. "Who'd want an old drunk of a mother embarrassing you at your very own wedding?" She shook her head, not bothering to hide the few tears slipping down her cheeks.

"We have to go," she said, turning away, refusing to acknowledge her mother's tears. Crocodile tears, she thought, for Julius's benefit.

Her mother blinked her tears away, drying her cheeks with her hands. "I guess you do. It was nice meeting you, Julius. Take better care of my daughter than I have."

"It was nice meeting you. Take better care of yourself."

Melanie clutched her husband's hand tightly as she led him through the hospital corridor to the elevator. They didn't speak until they were in the car.

"That wasn't so bad, was it?"

She stared out at the passing scenery cloaked in darkness. "She was putting on an act for you. That isn't how she usually is." She turned to face him. "I hope you're not going to be taken in by it. She could've been an actress."

"Maybe the accident has changed her."

Melanie grabbed his arm. "You're a cop, Julius. You should be a better judge of character. People don't change just like that."

"Some people do."

She didn't answer.

"How is she usually then?" He asked, turning off the music. "I don't have anything to compare her behavior to and five minutes is not very long to formulate an opinion of my wife's mother."

"She's mean and angry more often than not. The mother I grew up with is not a mother who would cry at having missed her daughter's wedding." She shook her head. "She should've been an actress," she repeated, her voice full of disgust.

"Actually, I thought the tears were very real. She seemed to struggle to keep them in check. Why bother to do that when it's so easy to let them fall? It is much easier to wail and go on, using drama and hysterics to mask the truth, don't you think?"

"You tell me. You seem to have all the answers."

"I don't have all the answers. I'm just trying to help."

"You know, I don't want to talk about this anymore."

"Would it be so terrible if your mother really has changed?"

"You can't just flip a switch and suddenly she goes from being Mother Dearest to being Mother of the Year. I know you'd like to get me to believe that, but I'm a realist and I know my mother. Things like that just don't happen. Especially to me."

"Good things can't happen to you? If you really believe that then how do you explain us? Our marriage? That's something good in your life. At least I hope so."

She didn't answer.

He reached out and touched her hand. "Maybe she knew you'd scoff at her tears and that's why she wouldn't let herself really cry and let go. Could that be a possibility?" Julius glanced at her, but she'd turned back to the passing scenery. He shook his head, exasperated, and turned on the radio. "You can be so stubborn," he muttered.

CHAPTER 19

Melanie was grateful to have the bedroom to herself as she dressed for the evening out with her husband. There were only two bruises as evidence of her guilt with Rick, one on her upper thigh and the other on her side. They were very slight, but still, she had to be cautious. If he saw them, he'd be certain to ask how she'd managed to bruise herself.

She sat on the bed. It was Julius's birthday, their first celebration together since they'd married. But more importantly, tonight she'd finally get her revenge on her brother. And that was the reason her heart beat a little quicker than it normally did. Would everything go as planned? Would Benjie remember he was to come by tonight? Or would he screw it up?

She stood up, anxious to get dressed and get out of the house. She could really use a cigarette right about now, but there was no time to waste. The sooner she got them out of the house, the better. What in the world would she do if her brother showed up early? Julius would probably invite him out to dinner with them so he could get to know her family, uncover a few of her secrets, too, no doubt. And wouldn't her brother be happy to talk until the cows came home just because he knew his sister would hate it. She slipped her dress over her head and wondered at the hand fate had dealt her. Why couldn't she have had a brother who'd have stuck up for her instead of preferring to push her further into troubled waters with high hopes that those waters were filled with hungry sharks?

169

"Darling," Julius said, pausing at the door of the bedroom. "You look gorgeous."

She blushed, smoothing the dress. With Rick's Harley money, she'd bought three dresses, two short and one long, so she'd chosen the long red dress because of the cool October temperatures.

"Will you be cold?"

She tugged on one of the delicate spaghetti straps. "I have a jacket. I should be fine."

He nodded. "Almost ready to go?"

"Give me two minutes." She watched him leave the bedroom before turning to enter the adjoining bathroom. After applying her lipstick, she wondered when he'd ask her if she really had been with Rick the other night after work as Ida had suggested. He'd dropped the subject because of the news of her mother's accident, but she'd be foolish to think he'd forgotten Ida's words.

She snapped the lipstick case closed and tossed it in the drawer, suddenly angry. Why had Ida even brought Rick's name up in the first place? She would definitely have to have a talk with that woman. Weren't they supposed to be friends? And why did she think Melanie's marriage was any of her business? She'd been a bit disappointed when Rick had said it, but he'd been right; she should've told the woman a long time ago to mind her own business. Then she'd never have been in this situation.

She started to leave the bathroom, but hesitated, turning to look at her reflection. She didn't look bad, she decided, at least not bad for a woman who seemed to be getting more evil as the days passed. Her wedding ring sparkled in the reflection and she raised her hand to study it. Sleeping with Rick once had been a terrible mistake in judgment; twice had been just plain stupid. She was ashamed to admit that she couldn't seem to resist him. If only Julius wasn't so good to her, but he was kind and generous and giving. Any girl would kill to have such a great husband, but he scared her. What if sometime down the road he changed his mind about her? She didn't deserve such kindness. Rick treated her as she should be treated and that was probably a major part of his appeal. Yet she had to resist him because it wasn't fair to Julius. It was almost a new year; time to make resolutions. *My first resolution*, she thought, *should be to stay far away from Rick.*

"Is there somewhere you need to be?"

"What?" Melanie glanced at her husband, startled by the question.

"I can't help but notice that you've been checking your watch every few minutes."

She held her fork in midair, speechless.

Julius chuckled. "I hope you haven't arranged some sort of surprise for me and I've just spoiled it?"

She placed her fork on her plate, dabbing at her lips with the linen napkin as she hastily tried to think of some sort of excuse.

"Sweetheart?"

She raised her eyes to meet his. "Your sister mentioned that she might join us for dessert if she could find a babysitter. But she wanted it to be a surprise so you absolutely cannot mention it to her. She didn't want to disappoint you if they couldn't make it."

"But why couldn't Mom watch the kids for a couple of hours?"

Damn, she'd forgotten about the mother. Oh, when had she become such a terrible liar? "I don't know. Maybe she didn't want to burden your mother."

He sipped his wine. "You may be right about that. I think there's some sort of social going on at church tonight and Mom's probably going."

She resisted the temptation to sigh with relief. "It doesn't look like they're going to make it."

"I like having you all to myself."

Melanie smiled and abruptly, she was certain, excused herself from the table. But she couldn't wait a minute longer. What if Benjie had already stolen everything and left? She headed to the restrooms where she knew she'd find a pay phone.

Glancing over her shoulder, she picked up the receiver and with trembling fingers dialed 911. When the operator answered, she explained in a voice breathless with excitement (and hopefully well disguised) that there was a robbery in progress. She hung up as quickly as possible in case they could trace the call. In the ladies' room, she took several deep breaths in order to calm herself. Julius would sense her excitement and believe she'd planned a surprise for him when she'd done no such thing. She didn't want him to be disappointed. It was the least she could do, to save him from that. She'd certainly learned the taste of disappointment and it wasn't something someone as good and kindhearted as Julius should have to sample.

Back at the table, as Melanie resumed eating her dinner, she felt her husband watching her, but much to her profound relief he refrained from asking any questions.

As they lingered over dessert, Julius slid a small present across the table. "Happy Halloween, sweetheart."

She stared at the present in surprise. "It's not Halloween."

"Then Happy Friday."

"But tonight's your birthday. You can't give gifts on your birthday."

"Who says?"

"It's a rule."

"Excuse me, Mr. Watson, but you have a phone call."

He glanced at the waiter in surprise, but rose to his feet. "You don't have anything to do with this, do you?"

She shook her head, afraid her voice would give her away if she spoke. Was it possible Benjie had been caught and one of Julius's friends was calling him to let him know about the break-in? As he walked away, his back straight as he towered over the waiter, Melanie began to worry. What would he do if he found out she'd set her brother up? He felt so strongly about family that she might very well have pushed him away from her by finally getting even with her brother.

Pushing her plate away, she eyed the present. It didn't matter. What was done was done and whatever consequences came about, well, it was worth it because now her brother would finally know what it felt like to be abandoned in a time of need. And maybe Julius would understand. She could tell him a little about her past and then he might forgive her. It was a thought at least.

Gently, she picked up the present and, with a quick glance around to make sure no one was paying her any attention, she shook it. Silence. What could it be? She returned it to the spot on the table where Julius had left it and picked up her fork, pretending to still be interested in the little bit of icing left on her plate.

"Melanie," he said, appearing at her elbow. "We've got to go."

She jerked her head up and met his eyes, her fork clattering against the china when she dropped it onto the plate. "What's the matter?"

Removing his wallet from his pocket, he tossed money on the table before grabbing her present and returning it to the inside pocket of his sportscoat. Grasping her hand, he led her out of the restaurant.

"What's wrong?" she asked as they waited for the valet to return with their car.

"That was Joe. From the station. We've been robbed."

She fiddled with the buttons on her coat. "Robbed?"

He held her, kissing the top of her head. "I don't want you to worry or be afraid, okay? They've caught the guy and he's being held at the station. In fact, he's claiming there's been some sort of mix-up."

"Mix-up?"

He clenched his jaw and nodded.

"What does that mean? Do you know him or something?"

He glanced at her, surprised by the question. "Yes, I'm afraid so."

She bit her lip, reluctant to ask who it was. Stiffening her spine, she pulled away. "Who would do that?"

He brushed the hair out of her eyes, watching her carefully. "Your brother."

The valet pulled up in front of them and jumped out, hurrying around to the passenger side to hold Melanie's door open for her. Once inside the car, she watched as Julius tipped him before getting into the car. She remembered what Julius had said before he'd admitted it was her brother. *He's claiming there's been some sort of mix-up.* A mix-up? That had to mean her brother was telling anyone who would listen the truth and blaming her. Could she go to jail if the truth was uncovered? She unclenched her hands and smoothed her dress over her knees. She was being paranoid. No matter what he said, she would deny it and they would believe her. They had to; they didn't know of a reason why she would lie. He was the one who had something to gain by lying. They would know that and distrust everything the pothead said. After all, he'd been caught red-handed.

"Are you okay?"

She nodded.

He reached over and held her hand, squeezing her fingers tightly.

She stared at their entwined fingers and hoped that everything would turn out all right. Not for her brother, of course, but for her. For Julius's sake if for no other reason.

They arrived at the police station in record time and Julius ushered her inside.

"Melanie!"

She swung around to see her mother sitting on a bench. She looked older and more vulnerable than she remembered.

"What is going on? They say Benjie tried to rob a house and as it turns out, it's your house."

"I don't know. I just found out myself."

Annie approached her daughter, grabbing her by the elbow and peering into her face. "He says you told him to do it."

She pulled her arm from her mother's grasp, stepping closer to her husband. "He's crazy."

"We'll get everything straightened out. Don't worry." Julius turned to his wife. "Why don't you wait right here with your mother? I'm going to find Joe and see what's going on." He kissed her lightly and then before she could protest, was gone.

She sighed and sat down on the bench, casting an uneasy glance at her mother.

"This all seems pretty strange to me."

Melanie ignored her.

"Why would he say you told him to do it? That just doesn't make sense."

"Julius will find out the details and then we'll know the story so there's no sense in you speculating."

"That's quite a dress. You look, uh, very, well, just very pretty."

She turned to stare at her mother in surprise. "Julius isn't here; you don't have to play the doting yet misunderstood mother with me. I know you, remember?"

"I've been thinking about my life since the accident and I'm trying to change. To do better. There's something I'd like to discuss with you, but now probably isn't the best time."

"Why not? Afraid someone might overhear you and see you for who you really are?"

"That's not fair."

"Isn't it? Say what you want to say now because I don't know that you'll ever have another chance."

"All right, Mellie. I've decided to accept God into my heart—"

Melanie laughed, cutting her off. "Yeah, okay. Your story sounds good. Maybe you'll convince Julius or whoever you're planning to tell that story to, but you should probably add some tears for the full effect. And don't ever call me Mellie again. That's the only fond memory I have of my childhood and I'd like to at least hold on to that. Besides, you no longer have the right to use it."

The older woman pursed her lips, but to her daughter's relief, remained quiet.

Ten minutes later, Julius emerged, his face grim.

"Well?" Annie asked, jumping to her feet.

He glanced at Melanie still seated on the bench and then turned to address his mother-in-law.

"Basically, he alleges that he asked Melanie for money, but she didn't have any to give him. Instead, she came up with the plan that he would steal whatever he could from our house and we would get reimbursed from the insurance company. He would then sell whatever he took to come up with the cash he needed."

Melanie stood up, her arms folded. "He's lying."

An older cop joined them. "Hello, Melanie. As usual you're looking pretty as a picture."

"Thanks, Joe."

"And you must be Melanie's mother. Nice to meet you. I'm Joe Hamilton."

She shook his outstretched hand. "Annie."

"I'm sorry about these circumstances. I know it must be hard."

"Thank you." She smiled slightly, her hand moving to smooth her blonde hair.

"He's married," Melanie muttered.

Annie's face paled and she dropped her eyes, biting her lip. With hands clenched at her side, she said, "I don't know why you'd say that, dear."

Joe cleared his throat. Glancing at Julius, he became all business. "He's willing to repeat his story in front of all of us if you'd care to hear it."

"Annie?" Julius asked.

"Absolutely. I want to hear it from his own mouth. I can't believe . . . I mean, I know he's got problems; he's not perfect. But I just find it hard to believe that my son would do this."

"Well, let's go downstairs then." Joe led the way, with Annie following close behind.

Julius hung back so he could hold his wife's hand. "What's going on, Melanie?" he whispered.

"I certainly have no idea. Could he be high? He must be desperate," she said, inspired. "Did you test him?"

He squeezed her hand. "I'm not sure about that, but I hoped you'd say that you are just as surprised as I am."

Joe gestured for them to enter a room off to their right. "I'll be right back with Benjie."

The three entered the room. It was pretty bare, a table and three chairs the only furniture and nothing decorating the walls. The two women sat, but Julius remained standing.

"How's your head?"

"Much better, Julius. Thank you for asking."

Melanie remained silent, too busy trying to keep her thoughts in control to notice the look her mother gave her. She had to remain calm at all times. If she let her brother provoke her, she'd blow the whole thing. How great would revenge feel if she ended up in jail with her brother on a conspiracy charge?

"Mellie," Benjie said, entering the small room with Joe following closely behind. "Tell them this is one big misunderstanding. It was just a little prank. Tell them."

Melanie raised her eyes to stare at her brother. "Why would I do that?"

"Because it's the truth!"

She shook her head. "I don't know what you're talking about. You robbed our house. How can that be considered a prank? A misunderstanding?"

He narrowed his eyes. "You told me to do it."

She didn't flinch from his gaze. "What are you? High?"

"I'm telling the truth!"

Joe placed a hand on his shoulder. "Calm down, Benjie. Why don't you sit down and tell us again your side of things."

"Aren't I supposed to have a lawyer here or something?" he asked, sullen.

"Of course you can if you'd like, but this isn't really a formal interview. You're just repeating to your family what you've told me. We can do this big, if that's what you want. You can get a lawyer; they can get a lawyer. But you said you wanted to talk to your sister and your sister has agreed. We're a small department. We don't need to spend a lot of time and manpower on this if we can resolve it with a few simple explanations. Not if it is a misunderstanding, as you say it is."

Benjie reluctantly eased into the vacant chair and glared at his sister. "It's not just my side of things; it's the truth."

"Start from the beginning," Joe said, closing the door and leaning against it.

"I was in some trouble because I owe some guys money. A lot of money."

Melanie shook her head. "This sounds like a bad script from an even worse movie."

"What's a lot? Hundreds? Millions?" Joe prompted, ignoring Melanie's remark.

He scowled. "No, a couple grand. So when Mel came over to Mom's, I hit her up for some money."

"But you knew she worked at the diner so why'd you think she'd have any money to give you?" Annie asked.

"I was going to ask her for the money at first because I'd heard all about that scumbag she'd been shacked up with. Everyone knew he was running tables at that strip club out on Water Street—"

"Ruben's," Joe supplied.

"Yeah, that's the one. So I figured he had some money stashed away or at least could get it pretty easily enough and she would be able to get me what I needed."

"You said 'at first.' Does that mean you changed your mind?"

"When I saw that ring on her finger I knew she couldn't still be with Rick because he wouldn't be dumb enough to let one girl pin him down like that. She had to have been with someone new and although she might not have had any money, she must've known someone who did."

Melanie frowned at the mention of Rick. There was no reason why he needed to be brought into this. It was just another reminder for Julius to wonder about the truth of Ida's words.

"Where was I?" Annie asked.

"You were passed out in the bed."

She lowered her eyes, blushing, and then looked up, challenging anyone to make a comment. "I've changed."

Joe cleared his throat." Okay. Did she give you any money then?"

"No. She said she didn't have any on her, but if I came by after her husband was asleep, she'd help me out."

"And when was this? Do you remember the date?" Julius asked.

"No, but I think it was a Sunday."

Melanie crossed her legs. "You asked me for money the day after my wedding to Julius."

"So you agree with everything so far?"

"What has he said, Joe? A whole lot of nothing. So yes, I suppose I agree. Well, for the most part. He asked me for money and I told him I didn't have any. Then he brought up my ring and I told him I'd gotten married, but I never invited him to my house. Frankly, I didn't want anyone in my family to know where I lived."

"So you didn't tell him to come over when Julius was asleep?"

She turned to stare at her brother, suddenly afraid he might have saved the slip of paper she'd written her address on. "No, I didn't." Her brother had never been a pack rat. That slip of paper had to be long gone by now.

"You're lying. You told me to come over at two in the morning because your husband was a cop and wouldn't appreciate having someone like me in his house."

"Someone like you?" Julius asked.

"Yeah, you know, I've got a record. Cops don't usually hang with criminals."

"Maybe your little tale would sound slightly more plausible, Benjie, if you'd picked a better night. I'd just gotten married the day before. Why would I, a newlywed, invite you over at two in the morning when I could be curled up in bed with my new husband?"

"You did and I came over. You were wearing a robe, a fuzzy blue robe."

"That only proves you've been spying on us, probably scoping out the house so you could rob us. What'd you do? Follow me home after I left that day?" Melanie leaned forward. "You did, didn't you? You saw my ring and all you could hear was the sound of a cash register. Ka-ching, ka-ching."

"What happened next?" Joe asked.

"Well, I got to her house and I scared her. She was looking out the window and I jumped up and she screamed."

"She screamed," Julius repeated.

"Yes."

"Don't you think I would've heard my wife scream?"

"It wasn't like a huge, full throttle kind of scream, but more like a little scream."

"A little scream."

"Yes, almost like a gasp or a yelp or something."

Julius nodded slowly. "Okay, then what?"

"Well, then she let me in the back door. I asked about the money and she said she couldn't get me any. I started to panic. I mean, I was really counting on her coming through with some cash. But then she told me her plan."

"This should be good," Melanie muttered.

"She said that I could rob her house because everything was insured. Then I could sell the loot to get the money I needed and they could get more stuff because the insurance company would give them more money. It would work out for everyone. Then I had a

179

drink, which made her real nervous because she was afraid he would wake up."

"What kind of drink?"

"It was a rum and coke. Myers I think."

Joe glanced at Julius.

"Yeah, we have Myers."

Melanie shook her head. "He probably found that out when he was there tonight."

"Then what happened?" Joe asked.

"She kicked me out before I finished my drink, even made me spill some of it on my shirt. I was afraid some cop would cruise by, smell the alcohol on me and pick me up for being drunk in public. But that didn't happen."

"And so tonight you went to our house and helped yourself, all because I supposedly told you to?" Melanie smiled. "What kind of drugs did you say you've been using lately?"

Benjie jumped up, slamming his fist on the table and startling both Annie and Melanie. Joe grabbed Benjie and twisted his arm behind his back.

"You set me up, Mellie!"

"Calm down," Joe said.

"Why would I set you up?" Melanie asked. Feeling safe with Julius beside her, she shook her head. "You did this to yourself, dear brother. I intend to press charges. Hear me, Joe?" She pointed at her brother. "I most definitely want this common thief behind bars."

Benjie stopped struggling, defeated. "Mom? You can't let her do this to me. You can't believe her. You hate her, remember?"

Annie stood up. "I was wrong to blame her for everything that's happened in my life, Benjie. I don't know what to believe about this, but you have to admit it sounds strange. Please, son, you must ask God for forgiveness, as I have done."

He stared at her and suddenly laughed. "You're crazy. We're all crazy in this fucking family."

Joe led him out of the room.

"Melanie . . . ," Annie said, breaking the silence and turning to her daughter.

She held up her hand. It almost sounded as if her mother believed her and not her precious son and that was just too unbelievable. Was it possible her plan of revenge had worked even better than she could ever have imagined? "Don't."

"But I just wanted to—"

"No. I don't want to hear it."

"Can't you listen—"

"No. It's just too late."

The older woman hesitated and then finally nodded and, with a last glance at Julius, walked quietly out of the room.

"Are you okay?" he asked, kneeling beside her chair.

She licked her lips. "Will you hold me for a minute? Please?"

"Of course."

They stood and he wrapped his arms around her and held her tightly, one hand stroking her hair, soothing her.

"It's been quite a birthday for you, hasn't it?"

"I've had worse."

She pulled away to look into his face. "Really?"

He shrugged.

She smiled, resting her hand on his cheek. "Take me home, Julius."

With an arm around her waist, he led her out of the room.

CHAPTER 20

The drive home was spent in silence and Melanie was grateful. She kept thinking about the confrontation with her brother, remembering what she'd said to contradict his story. She couldn't help but feel as though she was forgetting some important aspect of that night. Something that still needed an explanation. More than likely, she thought as they pulled into the driveway, she was just being a bit apprehensive. She wasn't usually so overly cautious, but perhaps living with Rick had taught her something after all. A long, hot bath would help her relax. There was nothing she had forgotten; worrying needlessly would make her old before she was ready. Hadn't Ida told her that once? Benjie had told his story and she'd been capable of logically contradicting every point he made. It was over. She should be congratulating herself. She'd finally managed to do to her brother what he had done to her so many years ago: She'd turned her back on him when he'd needed her the most.

"Are you okay?"

Realizing they'd parked and Julius had turned the car off, she smiled reassuringly. "I'm fine." Later tonight, when Julius had gone to bed, she would go over all that had transpired with her mother.

She reached for the door handle, but he touched her sleeve, stopping her. "It's a full moon tonight. Do you think that explains all that's happened?"

"Superstitious, Julius? I never would've believed it if I hadn't heard you say that."

"At work we all know it'll be a busy night when it's a full moon." He pulled the wrapped present from his coat pocket and held it in front of him. "Maybe now would be a better time to open your present. It might help take the edge off everything that's happened."

"Here? In the car?"

"Why not? I can't imagine what kind of interruption could delay us this time, especially if we're sitting in the car, completely alone. Can you?"

"You're probably right about that." She reached her hand out to take the gift.

He pulled it out of her reach. "But first," he said, glancing over to smile at her, "shouldn't you try to guess what it is?"

"How many guesses do I get before you'll let me open it?"

"Three."

"Don't I get to shake it?"

"You already did."

She blushed. "You weren't supposed to see that."

"Quit stalling. What's your first guess?"

"Not even going to give me a hint?"

"And make it easy for you? Forget it."

"Is it . . . tickets?"

"Are you planning on being that vague on your other two guesses?"

"Maybe. Am I close?"

"You're not playing fair, but no. It's not tickets to somewhere or something. Your second guess?"

"You sure you don't want to give me a hint?"

"No hint."

"Then why can't I hold it if I've already shaken it?"

"That's my prerogative as the gift giver. When you are the gift giver, you can do things as you like."

"Boy, Julius. I never knew you could be so tough."

"Quit stalling. I don't intend to be out here all night."

She stared at the oblong box. "It's not jewelry because jewelry would've made a noise when I shook it."

"Is that your official second guess or are you just trying to weasel an answer out of me by guessing what it isn't when the game is to guess what it is?"

"Can't I think aloud? Now be quiet." She pursed her lips and stared at the box as if it would tell her what item was hidden inside if she thought about it hard enough. "Is it . . . I don't know . . . a poem you wrote?"

"That's your second guess?"

"Yes. Am I right?"

"Do I look like the type of guy to write poetry?"

"As a matter of fact—"

He groaned. "Don't ever mention that in front of the guys at work or I'll never live it down."

"Does that mean I'm wrong?"

"Yes! You couldn't be further from the truth. Think before you waste your last guess, Melanie."

"Why? Maybe I should just guess and then you'll let me open it and we can go inside."

"Do that and I'll never let you open it, brat."

She sighed. "I pity the criminals that are foolish enough to do wrong deeds during your shift."

When he didn't answer, she looked up to see him gazing towards the house, frowning. She turned to see what could be wrong. "What's the matter?"

"What is that?"

"What's what?" She scanned the yard. Was there someone lurking in the bushes? A friend of Benjie's, someone who'd been helping him with the robbery, but managed to evade police? But why wouldn't they have fled the scene of the crime hours ago? Her brother didn't hang out with the smartest people, but still, a fool would've known to get as much distance from the scene of the crime as possible, right? She bit her lip, squinting to see some kind of movement. At least she was with Julius. He'd keep her safe.

"What is that on the front door?"

Immediately, she knew what he was referring to without having to look. Melanie closed her eyes and swallowed nervously. There it was, the missing piece, the damning evidence, the note she had left for Benjie to use the back door. She heard him get out of the car and opened her eyes to see her husband striding across the yard to the front door. She could sit there all night, but she knew it'd be useless. Eventually she'd have to explain the note. What kind of explanation could she possibly come up with this time? Her mind was blank. Slowly, she got out of the car and followed her husband.

He held the piece of paper in his hand and turned to study her under the porch light as she climbed the steps to stand next to him. "What is this? And why is there tape over our doorbell?"

Her eyes slid from the paper in his hand to the doorbell. *Damn. Damn, damn, and double damn.*

He removed the tape and pressed the button, his hand dropping to his side as the echo of the doorbell chimed throughout the house. "It works."

"Yes," she said, and shivered.

He took the keys out of his pocket and unlocked the front door. "Why don't we discuss this inside where you'll be warmer?"

She nodded, preceding him into the house. She hadn't shivered because of the temperature outside, but because of the ice she imagined forming around her cruel black heart. There was no way she could explain that to him, though. Removing her jacket, she asked, "Would you like me to make you some tea or coffee or something?"

"No." He took her jacket from her and hung it up in the hall closet. "Thank you."

"A soda maybe?"

"I'm fine. Would you care for something?"

She would have liked to have something strong, like a scotch, but knew he wouldn't have liked that and then it would've been a big indication of her guilt. "A glass of water. But I can get it."

"No, let me."

She walked into the living room and sat down on the edge of the couch. Her husband was so polite; she'd never realized to what extent before, but now, well, Gretchen had obviously done an impeccable job of instilling manners in her son. She glanced up as he entered the room.

He stopped in front of the coffee table and handed her the glass.

"Thanks." She took a sip.

"It's your handwriting."

It hadn't been a question, but she nodded anyway, watching as the note fluttered from his fingertips to rest on the polished table. Should she confess the truth? No, she would lose him. But Rick—

"Melanie."

She met his eyes. Enough about Rick, she scolded herself silently. It was time she focused on her husband. Past time really. "Julius . . ."

He sat down in the chair across from her, rubbing his eyes. Tell me your brother wasn't telling the truth tonight. Tell me you had nothing to do with your brother breaking into our home and attempting to steal us blind. Tell me there is a perfectly logical explanation for a note being on the door and directing someone to the back door. And tell me—"

"There is."

He stopped and leaned forward in the chair. "I'm listening."

"I was outside the other day and put that note up because I wouldn't have heard anyone at the door."

"What were you doing outside?"

"I was smelling your rosebushes. I never realized you could grow roses in October." She bit her lip. That sounded lame even to her ears.

"Who were you expecting?"

Who? She thought. His sister? Ida? No, he could ask them and even Ida wouldn't lie for her. Well, to Rick she would, but certainly not to wonderful Julius. Besides, most everyone goes to the back door. The front door was rarely used. She drank some of the water. She needed an alibi that couldn't be questioned. "I was expecting the UPS guy." She smiled suddenly, relieved that she'd managed a believable lie and, if she was honest, proud of herself for thinking of such a clever alibi.

"You were expecting a package?"

She relaxed against the couch. "Yes. And I don't intend to tell you what package."

He leaned back in the chair. "No?"

"No. If I told you, then you'd know what you were getting for your birthday. And since the item was backordered, I don't have it for you tonight." She was on a roll!

"Why did you also tape the doorbell?"

She sipped the water, stalling for time.

He frowned, impatient. "Well?"

She crossed her legs, her foot tapping against the leg of the coffee table. "Well, I was afraid . . . that he . . . wouldn't see the note . . . so I taped the doorbell so he'd think it was broken and then when he went to knock, he'd be sure to see the note."

"You're sure?"

"Well, yes, of course."

"So you didn't put the note on the door for your brother?"

"No."

"And you didn't tape over the doorbell because you were afraid your brother would press the bell before he saw the note, thus waking me up?"

"No. Julius—"

"Why do you hate your brother, Melanie?"

"What? Who said I hate—"

"Can you answer my question?"

"You're confusing me. Which question?"

"Can you tell me why you hate your brother?"

"No."

"No," he repeated. "You don't feel comfortable enough with your husband to discuss your past, is that it?"

"No, I mean I never said I hated my brother."

"You don't have to say it. I know you hate your brother because I can see it in your eyes when he's mentioned. I know you don't like your mother either, but what I don't know is why."

She put the glass down on the coffee table and stood up. "Stop treating me like some criminal. I do not like this side of you, hurling accusations at me as if you don't care about me at all. How can you be so cold?"

"Where are you going?"

"I'm not going anywhere. Can't I get up and stretch my legs?" She glared at him before moving to stand in front of the window.

"I'm sorry."

She sighed. "What difference does it make how I feel about my family? It's not as if you didn't know we were estranged. Isn't that enough information?"

"If you give me a good enough reason why you won't discuss your past, your family history with me, then I'll drop it. But until you do, I want to know."

"Just because you want something doesn't mean you'll get it."

"I'm well aware of that. Can you give me a reason or are you finally going to share your past with me?"

"It's in the past and that's where it should stay. Besides, you think you want to know the truth, but you don't really. And for the record, I think you're being very unreasonable and just downright mean."

"Well, I think you're being unreasonable and stubborn."

"Fine." Arms crossed, she stared out the window.

"Want to tell me about Rick then?"

She closed her eyes. Of course he would bring this up now.

"Well?"

She looked at him over her shoulder. "What about Rick?"

"What were you doing at his place the night your mother ended up in the hospital?"

"I wasn't." She turned back to the window and dropped her voice. "With him."

"Excuse me?"

"I wasn't with him," she said to the window, her voice only slightly louder.

"Does he know you're married?"

She pressed her palm against the cool glass.

"Does he tell you that he misses you, Melanie? That he wished things could be different?"

"Where are you going with this, Julius?"

"You know he only wants you because he can't have you."

She swung around to face him, her fists clenched. "That's not true! Can't a man want me because he finds me irresistible?"

He stood up and crossed the room, grabbing her by the elbows. "*I* find you irresistible! Don't I count?"

She shook him off. "Of course."

"Then why were you at his apartment the other night? Why have anything to do with him at all? Have you forgotten the condition you were in when I found you at that apartment?"

"No. But he's different. He's sorry about what happened, but I was the one who brought home those roses you gave me. It was my fault for pressuring him to marry me. So don't blame him, Julius. I got what I deserved."

He stared at her. "Did you? Did you really? And did he tell you that? That you got what you deserved?"

She refused to meet his eyes.

"Has he even really apologized for that night? Or are you lying to me and to yourself?"

He raised his arm to run his hand through his hair and she flinched.

"You expect me to hit you?" he asked in disbelief. "You actually think I would do that?"

She shrugged, glancing out the window to avoid the hurt she saw in his eyes. "It was an instinct. But maybe you should."

"Oh? And why is that?"

She didn't answer.

"I don't get it. I assume it's because of something that happened to you in your past, but I just don't get why you feel so unworthy of any kindness or love. I love you, Melanie. I'm certainly not about to hit you. There are better ways to express one's love. There are better ways to get one's point across."

They were standing so close that if she only reached out, she knew he'd take her in his arms and everything would work out. But she couldn't bring herself to do it. The distance felt too great. Any minute now he would ask if she'd had sex with Rick. If she touched him now, he wouldn't ask tonight, but eventually he would ask and this temporary reprieve she'd have would be over once she'd admitted the truth, if she was brave enough to even do that.

"You set your brother up, didn't you?"

She jerked her head up in surprise. "What?"

He caressed her cheek. "Were you expecting another question?

190

Were you waiting for me to ask you if you've slept with him since we've been married?" He closed his eyes. "I can't bear to see the answer reflected in your eyes so you can relax. I won't ask." He opened his eyes and smiled slightly, dropping his hand away from her. "Cowardly of me, isn't it?"

She watched as he walked away from her and out of the room. What had she done? She pressed her hot cheek against the cold pane of glass. She'd done what she knew she'd eventually do; she'd ruined her marriage. She'd broken Julius's heart. It certainly hadn't taken her very long. Wouldn't her mother be thrilled to be able to tell her daughter she told her so? She stepped away from the window and idly drew a heart in the spot where her breath had fogged up the glass. She frowned, staring at it. Her mother, if she was to be believed, was now a born-again Christian. Which meant now she'd probably just gloat in private. Hearing Julius's footsteps along the hall, she hastily erased the heart she'd foolishly drawn and spun around.

"You have a suitcase," she blurted when he stepped into the room.

"I'll be at Clare's. If you need anything."

"Julius, wait."

"I think we both need some time apart to think about things. This has been a pretty exhausting night."

"But you don't have to go. I'll go if you absolutely feel we can't be under the same roof. It's your house."

"Where would you go?"

She hadn't thought about that. Where would she go? "I would go to a hotel or something. That isn't important."

"Would you go to his place?"

"No," she said, startling herself because she meant it. "I wouldn't."

He studied her. "I actually believe you. But I'd prefer you to stay here. I won't worry about you so much knowing that you're here. I'll go to Clare's and we'll talk when we've had time to think about things." He reached into his coat pocket and pulled out the present she'd yet to open. He tossed it onto the coffee table. "Happy Friday, Melanie."

She stared at the present and when she looked up, he was gone.

"Happy birthday," she whispered, her arms wrapped around her body. When she heard the front door close behind her husband, she collapsed on the couch.

CHAPTER 21

Melanie entered the diner and went straight to the coffee machine, quickly pouring herself a cup. She leaned against the counter and sipped gratefully.

"Good morning!" When there was no response, Ida paused in filling the ice bin to stare at her coworker. "Rough night?"

"You could say that." She finished her coffee and quickly poured herself another.

"Isn't that hot?"

"It's hot."

"Don't you usually drown your coffee in sugar?"

Melanie set her coffee down and removed her jacket. "Right now I'm not drinking it for the taste, just the effect."

"What's with the sunglasses?"

"It's a bit bright outside." She removed the shades, squinting at Ida. "Don't you think so?"

"Not any brighter than every day about this time. Seems to me you've got quite a hangover."

Picking up her coffee cup, Melanie drank the hot beverage. Why did Ida always talk so much? She just wanted to be left alone.

"Dare I ask what happened last night?"

"Nothing, Ida. Nothing at all happened, okay?"

Grabbing a coffeepot, she went to check on the only two customers in the restaurant.

She hadn't lied because technically, after Julius left, nothing had happened. Melanie had sat on the couch, debating whether her husband would now file for a divorce or not, finally deciding he would because he'd actually left with a suitcase. So she'd proceeded to drink enough alcohol to make her forget why she'd started drinking in the first place. When she'd awakened on the couch this morning, an empty bottle of Myers Rum on the floor and the shoebox of paper roses spilled across the coffee table, she hadn't remembered anything after Julius leaving, suitcase in hand. She still couldn't believe he'd actually packed a suitcase. Didn't that imply he planned to stay away for quite some time? If there were to be a divorce, she'd have to find a new place to live. There was Rick, of course, but would he even take her back? Was Julius right about Rick wanting her now only because he couldn't have her? Although he obviously thought he could still have her and she hadn't tried to dissuade him of that misconception, had she? And actually there was the possibility that she wouldn't want to go back to him after all. Maybe since her dear mother had turned to God, she could stay with her. She gulped her coffee, burning her throat, just punishment for thinking along those lines. She would not move in with that woman after all the emotional abuse she'd dished out all those years ago. Just because she said she'd changed didn't mean she really had.

Ida placed the coffeepot on the burner. "So did that husband of yours like his birthday present?"

She wondered how Ida would react if she admitted she'd never gotten him anything. She'd probably scold her, accusing Melanie of not caring enough. She remembered the present still on the coffee table where Julius had tossed it. Ida would be right. It was her husband's birthday and yet he'd been the one to give her a present. She hadn't felt right in opening it without him there. Whatever it was, if they were really going to get a divorce, he could return it because she didn't want it. It would always remind her of the night they split up. "He loved it." Melanie closed her eyes, rubbing her temple.

"What did you get him?"

Of course she would want to know that. "I got him a shirt," Melanie lied.

Pedro came out from the kitchen, his coffee cup in hand. "Hola, *mamacita*. Good morning."

She nodded slightly. "If you say so."

Pedro filled his cup and then looked over at Melanie as Ida left them to check on the customers. "Too much partying last night, heh?" he asked, and grinned. "Felipe!" he yelled.

She cringed. "Stop shouting. Please."

Felipe appeared in the kitchen window. "Sí?"

Pedro pointed to Melanie and then said something in Spanish, which made them both laugh.

She turned away from them and leaned against the counter, ignoring their chatter.

Finally, Pedro patted her on the head as he passed her on the way back into the kitchen.

She sighed in relief when the door had swung closed behind him.

"And how was the birthday celebration?" Ida asked, returning. "Must've been pretty wild if you're crawling in here with a granddaddy of all hangovers."

She smiled slightly. "Yeah, it was certainly wild."

"Care to share any of the steamy details?"

"Not this time." She refilled her cup.

"How many cups of that do you think you're going to have to drink today?"

"Ida, did anyone ever tell you that you ask a lot of questions?"

"Probably."

"I'm not surprised." She picked up her jacket. "I'm going to put this away."

"I'll make another pot of coffee."

Melanie ignored her and disappeared into the back of the restaurant, Ida's laughter following her.

Unfortunately for Melanie the diner eventually filled up with the usual breakfast rush, keeping her running all morning when all she wished for was a chance to nurse her headache.

"Door's locked," Ida announced, jingling the store keys.

With a groan, Melanie dropped onto a stool and leaned her forehead against the cool Formica counter. "I am so glad the owners decided to close early today, even if I have no idea why."

"I think it has something to do with inventory, but I could be wrong. Still feeling pretty bad, huh?"

She sat up. "I think all that coffee has made things worse."

"Well, you look like death warmed over, if that makes you feel any better."

"Thanks."

Ida hesitated. "I wouldn't worry, Mel, about the fight you had with Julius. It is sort of the way things work. Couples fight and then they get to make up. And that is by far the best part."

"What makes you think we had a fight?"

"You young ones always think you're experiencing something for the first time ever, that no one else has ever felt what you've felt. I'm not dense, you know."

She was about to deny fighting with Julius, but didn't have the strength. "Thanks."

"Sure."

There was a knock on the glass door. Melanie covered her face with her hands. "We're closed," she muttered. "Go home already."

"Speak of the devil and there he stands," Ida murmured.

Melanie turned to see Julius dressed in his police uniform standing outside.

"Here are the keys. I'm going to start on our side work. Otherwise, we'll be here until Christmas."

She stared at the keys in front of her. She knew she had to open the door, that she couldn't consciously ignore him standing outside, but she wished more than anything that she was someplace else. Slowly, she walked over to the door, fumbling through the various keys until she came to the right one. With a quick glance at Julius's unsmiling face, she opened the door.

"I didn't think you were going to acknowledge me, let alone open up."

"We closed early today for inventory or something. What are you doing here?"

"I saw the sign. I didn't come to eat, Melanie. I came to talk."

"Oh."

"Can I come in?"

She stepped aside and he walked past her. Locking the door, she wondered if she was ready for a confrontation. It certainly hadn't taken him long to think about things.

"Got any coffee left?"

She moved behind the counter to pour him a cup. Setting it in front of him, she hoped he wouldn't notice how awful she looked.

"Is this a bad time?"

She glanced around. "Well, technically no, since we're closed, but I do need to help Ida with our side work."

He smiled slightly, wrapping his hand around the warm mug. "I've been waiting outside for this place to empty out, hoping then we could talk. I forgot all about you having to clean up everything."

"Are you coming from work or going?"

"Coming from."

"If you don't mind waiting a little bit longer . . . ?"

"No, go ahead and get your work done. But can I ask you one thing first?"

Uneasy, she nodded.

"Can I have some cream?"

How polite and formal they were with each other! She quickly retrieved a small dish of creamers for him before escaping to the back of the restaurant and out of his sight, taking a broom with her. She swept the crumbs out from under the booths and wondered what path their conversation would take. Had he decided to file for a divorce? She frowned. At least she could finally stop wondering. And what about Rick? It wasn't fair to Julius for Melanie to be thinking about some other guy. She stopped sweeping and stared in the direction Julius sat waiting. Did she still love Rick? Or had Julius done the impossible? No longer was she certain which man she loved. But maybe it didn't matter now. Maybe Julius had made the decision to end their relationship.

Ida hurried through the swinging door that separated the kitchen from the dining room, vacuum cleaner in tow. "He's waiting for you."

"I know."

"Well, everything's done except the vacuuming. Why don't you get on out of here? I'll be finished with this in no time and would be happy to lock up."

"You've already done more than your fair share. I can't let you allow me to take advantage of you."

"If I'm insisting, then you're not taking advantage of me. So go on."

Melanie hesitated.

"Just go. Go and make up with your husband."

Finally she gave in. "Okay, but just remember you did insist." She disappeared into the kitchen to put the broom away. Ida could definitely be a major pain sometimes, but then she could also be pretty nice. She would have to remember to pick her up a little gift to thank her. Grabbing her jacket, she stopped in the bathroom and checked her appearance. Yeah, she looked as bad as she felt. What would she say to him? She sighed. She had no idea. Turning out the light, she went to meet her husband as Ida turned on the vacuum cleaner.

"I'm ready."

He stood up. "Where would you like to go?"

"I don't really care, Julius."

He nodded, fidgeting with his keys.

The vacuum stopped and Ida appeared. "I almost forgot that I have to let you out. How are you, Julius?"

"All right. And you?"

"Can't complain. Happy belated birthday." She unlocked the door.

"Thanks."

"See you later," Ida said as the couple walked past her and out into the sunshine.

"Bye," they said in unison.

They headed towards Julius's car, careful to keep from brushing up against each other as they maneuvered along the narrow sidewalk.

Melanie was surprised when Julius pulled into the parking lot of the baseball park, the place where he'd first told her he was falling for her. But she didn't comment. After all, where else could they go without people surrounding them?

"Did you want to get out and sit in the bleachers? Or just stay here in the car?"

"Let's just sit here in the car if that's all right with you."

"How's your mother?"

She shrugged. "She's always managed to bounce back from things so I'm sure she's fine."

They lapsed into silence, listening to the wind whip around the car. Finally, Julius cleared his throat.

"I stopped by the house this morning. I forgot my razor."

"Oh." Clare's husband probably had a razor he could've borrowed, but she didn't call him out on his little white lie.

"I saw the empty bottle of rum."

She didn't know what to say.

"You aren't going to start drinking, are you?"

"Like my mother?"

He shook his head. "I didn't say that."

"But you were thinking it."

"I just don't want you to go down that path—"

"Don't overreact, Julius, and blow this all out of proportion. It was a momentary lapse in judgment. So I got drunk. Who cares?"

"I care."

"It's no big deal."

"I also saw the paper roses I made for you. I hadn't realized you'd kept even one of them, let alone all of them."

"Pretty silly of me, huh?"

"About as silly as me making them for you every time I saw you. But I was happy to see that they meant something to you. Because they meant something to me when I gave them to you. My way of being memorable to you."

She pretended to study the scenery, afraid to look at him. It was hard to believe he wanted to be memorable to her. She was no good. Couldn't he see that? And why was he so upset? He was the one who'd left her, suitcase in hand.

He shifted in his seat so that he faced her. "Anyway, I noticed you hadn't opened your present so I brought it with me."

She turned and stared at the present he held out to her. Did she even want to open it when things weren't settled between them? She met his eyes.

"I think that once you open it, you'll understand how much you mean to me, Melanie." He smiled. "And why I couldn't wait for Christmas to give it to you."

She dropped her eyes to study the present again.

"Aren't you going to say anything?"

"Do I have to make my third guess?"

He laughed. "No, I think there's a time limit on guesses and it expired hours ago."

She reached for it, aware that her fingers trembled, and this time he let her take it. She hesitated, nervous about opening it.

"Are you admiring my wrapping? Or just amazed that it's wrapped at all?"

She smiled slightly and slowly tore the paper off. Lifting the lid of the box, she was surprised to see it contained a folded document. This couldn't possibly be divorce papers, she assured herself. He'd had it before all that had happened last night. And he wouldn't be so cruel as to wrap it up and give it to her as a gift. He couldn't. So what could it be? Some sort of love letter?

"You could try to read it without opening it, or you could unfold it and actually read it. But it's your call."

She nodded, unable to even crack a smile at his teasing. After unfolding the paper, she quickly scanned the first page. Turning to stare at him in surprise, she said, "It's the deed to your house!"

"I thought it might help you to feel more secure in our marriage. This way, no matter what, you'll always have a place to call your own." He placed his hand over hers. "But Melanie, I really want our marriage to work out."

"You do?" She couldn't decide if she was happy or not at his news.

"I do. But there are some things we need to clear up."

"Yes." She stared at the paper in her hands. She'd always known he was generous, but this was more than simple generosity. Was he trying to tie her to him? Is that why he'd given her the present before they cleared things up? She put the document back in the box and handed it back to him. "I can't accept this, Julius. I can't allow you to give me your house as a present, and most especially not as a random 'Happy Friday' present."

He ignored the box, shifting so that he again faced forward. Looking out the window, he asked, "Is it because of him?"

She bit her lip. Her husband certainly knew how to get right to the bottom of things. "He's not out of my system yet. It wouldn't be fair to accept your house." She placed the box on the console between them.

Silent, he stared out the window. Finally, he said, his voice thick, "So you're—" He cleared his throat. "So you're going back to him? You're leaving me for a coward that beats you?"

She flinched, but kept her voice steady. "I don't know what I'm doing. I'm confused. What do I feel for you? What do I feel for Rick? I jumped from one situation directly into another without taking time to figure out what I really want. I haven't been fair to you, Julius, I know, but I haven't been fair to myself either."

"What are you saying? That you just need some time to think about our marriage? That you may want a divorce after all? That you may actually go back to that scumbag?"

"I just need some time to think about what I want in my life."

He shook his head. "You know, that sure doesn't make me feel very confident, Melanie. I'm your husband. You're supposed to love me, but instead, you want time to decide if I should even be a part of your life?"

"Don't do this."

"Do what? Challenge your decision? It doesn't just affect you. It's my life, too."

"Don't put me on the defensive. I need some time and you should respect that. Our marriage was rushed. We hardly knew each other. My God, even your mother pointed that out to you."

"Yes, I know all that, but I also know I love you. I don't have to take some time to think about things. So it hurts when my very own wife isn't so sure after all. We're newlyweds!"

She clasped her hands together. "I don't know why you even wanted to marry me in the first place, Julius. I'm damaged! I'm more trouble than I'm worth."

He placed his hand over hers and met her eyes. "Don't ever say that, Melanie. You're definitely worth it to me." He hesitated. "So take some time if that's what you really think is best, but I want you to remain at our house—"

"No—"

"Yes. As long as you are my wife that's where you should be. Stay there and I'll stay at my sister's. It's no big deal; the kids love it. And when you've taken enough time to figure out what you want, what you need, we'll talk."

"Are you sure?"

"Yes. I just want you to be happy, even if that means I can't be with you."

"What about your roses?"

"I can always grow new ones."

"What will you tell your family?"

"What do you want me to tell them?"

"I don't know. I guess the only thing to tell them is the truth. They'll probably hate me, huh?"

"They won't hate you because they know how much I love you. You'll always be welcome in their home, no matter what happens. But for the record, can I just say that I really hope you'll decide you can't live without me?"

She smiled slightly. "Maybe you'll change your mind by tomorrow and hope for the opposite."

"Impossible."

"Can you take me home now? I'm really tired."

"Of course." He started the car.

Melanie stared out the window, wishing things could be different. But this is what she wanted, right? To be alone and think about things without any pressure. *Be careful what you wish for,* she reminded herself. *Too late. You've managed to screw up again.*

CHAPTER 22

Melanie wandered the rooms of Julius's house, restless. Perhaps she should've gone with her husband to Clare's for dinner after all. At least there she'd be too distracted to think about her latest problems. But then she'd brought them on herself so she probably deserved to be alone. After catching herself opening and closing kitchen cabinets for no reason at all, she grabbed her jacket. A walk would help ease her boredom.

She didn't have any destination in mind, but eventually she found herself standing on the sidewalk in front of her mother's house. Should she go in? She turned to leave, but hesitated, glancing back at the house. Something was different, but what? And then she realized the change. The blinds were open, allowing sunlight into the house. Could her mother really have changed after all? Was it possible she'd been wrong?

Tentatively, she walked up the sidewalk to the front porch. With one foot on the steps, she hesitated. What was she afraid of? Stiffening her spine, she climbed the steps and entered the house.

Sunlight streamed into the living room, highlighting the worn furniture and stained carpet. In the corner stood a small artificial Christmas tree, bare of decorations. Christmas carols played softly in the background. A wooden cross hung above the television and a Bible lay on the coffee table.

"She certainly has her props in order," Melanie murmured.

"I thought I heard someone come in, but I expected to see your brother before you."

"Disappointed?"

Annie put the box of decorations she was holding on the floor next to the tree. "I suppose you could say I am disappointed, but only because I know you're happy and he's in jail."

"You are disappointed because I'm happy? Is that what you just said?"

"That's not what I meant. It came out wrong," Annie tried to explain.

"No, you said what you really felt." She crossed her arms. "I've always known he was your favorite. It's good you are finally honest about it."

"It's almost Halloween, Mel. And then it'll be Thanksgiving and, before you know it, Christmas. I'd like to see your brother walk through that door because he's my child and I hate to think of him in jail, let alone spending the holidays there. I do not have a favorite. And I'm really glad that you are happy."

"If you've changed and really become religious, perhaps you should start telling the truth, too."

She stomped her feet. "I'm not ready for this! Not yet!" She closed her eyes and shook her head slightly. "Did you come here to argue?"

Melanie didn't answer. Why had she come here?

She bent down and picked up a tangle of Christmas lights and started to unravel them. "Do you like my tree? I know it's rather early to be putting a tree up since it isn't even Halloween yet, but I needed a dose of holiday cheer and figured this was the best way to get it." She waved towards the small boom box on the stairs. "Listening to Christmas music and decorating the tree . . . well, you probably don't understand. I wish things had been different. I wish you and Benjie could've experienced a real Christmas. Traditional."

"It's a little late for those wishes."

Annie paused, her hands buried in the lights. "I thought so, too. But now you're married to a wonderful man. He'll teach you about the benefits of having traditions . . . and about belonging to a warm, loving family with good Christian values."

"How do you know?"

"I'm not blind. I see things."

"What does that mean?"

"Just that it's obvious. I could see it in the way he touched you when you came to the hospital and in the way he acted towards you at the police station. I know I've been a terrible mother, the worst kind, if you need me to say it, but maybe despite all the terrible things that happened, the way I treated you, I still managed to teach you something because you've ended up with someone like Julius."

"You're going to try to take credit for that?"

Annie frowned. "If you don't intend to forgive me for being such a rotten mother, why are you here?"

She shrugged, plopping down on the couch and picking up the Bible. "Thought you might need someone to run to the liquor store for you now that Benjie's locked up." She idly flipped through the pages.

Annie dropped the lights and turned to face her daughter. "I've stopped drinking, Melanie, and I wish you'd accept that. Why can't you be happy for me?"

She closed the Bible and tossed it back onto the coffee table. "Because I don't believe you. You've always broken your promises and this time will be no different."

"I suppose I have." She stared at her daughter. "Is it too late for us to have a mother-daughter relationship?"

"What exactly is a mother-daughter relationship? Does that mean I tell you your perverted boyfriend has raped me and you push me away and tell me to shut up? Does that also include throwing a flaming roll of toilet paper at me so that my hair will catch on fire and I'll burn to my death? Or perhaps—"

"Enough!" Annie clenched her eyes shut and covered her ears with her hands. "I don't want to relive our past!"

Melanie stood up and strode over to her mother. She pulled her hands away from her ears. "Open your eyes, Mother, and look at me." When her mother had obeyed the demand, she said, "You don't want to relive our past, but I have no choice. The past lives within me and it takes everything I have to keep it buried in my heart. You used to tell me I had a black heart like my father. Well, maybe my heart turned black from the secrets it held. Did you ever think of that?" She released her mother's cold hands and turned away.

"Mellie," her mother whispered, ignoring the tears that dripped along her cheeks. "I'm so sorry. For everything."

She walked out without acknowledging her mother's apology. Pausing on the porch, she fumbled in her purse for a cigarette. Hastily, she lit it and took a long drag. Only after she'd exhaled did she relax slightly.

"Melanie."

She jumped and swung around to see her husband standing on the far corner of the porch. "Julius! What are you doing here?"

"I thought I'd see how your mother was holding up."

She took a drag on her cigarette and then exhaled, her chin raised high. "She's fine. I told you she's never down for long. You shouldn't have come here." How much had he overheard? That was more along the lines of what she wanted to know.

"I didn't think I should interrupt."

So he'd probably heard an earful. She hurried down the steps.

"Melanie!" He raced after her. "Wait a minute."

She stopped at the end of the sidewalk. "I thought you were going to give me some time, some space."

"I am."

"Then what would you call spying on me? That doesn't feel like giving me my space."

"I wasn't spying. I told you I came to check on your mother."

"You don't need to check on her. You have your own mother. Check on her if you need to check on somebody." She took a drag on her cigarette and wondered why he managed to get her so riled up that she began to talk and act like a foolish teenager.

"My mother is fine. Wondering why my wife is never by my side, of course."

"You're not being fair."

"I'm just being honest, Melanie."

"Are you?"

"What is that supposed to mean?"

"Forget it. Tell them I'm working a lot. Or that I'm spending time with my family due to a recent crisis and I'm sorry I haven't spent much time with them."

"Do you think you'll ever forgive your mother for the past?"

"What difference does it make?"

"Did you ever hear the story in the Bible about turning the other cheek?"

"I'm familiar with the phrase."

He put his hands in his pockets. "In order to focus on the future, you've got to let go of the past."

She frowned, rolling her eyes. "Would you speak English, Dr. Freud?"

He stared at her silently until she looked away. "If there is ever to be an 'us,' which I certainly hope there will be, you have to forgive her."

"She has nothing to do with us. Besides, this isn't really any of your business," she said quietly.

"Like it or not, your childhood and how she treated you, good or bad, helped make you who you are today so your relationship does affect us. She does seem sorry for the hurt she has caused you."

"You don't know what you're talking about."

"I have to be a pretty good judge of character in my career so I think I'm right about this. She seems to be truly sorry."

"You think I'm overreacting, don't you? This isn't about my finger getting accidentally pinched in the stroller when I was a child or something equally minor, Julius. This is about . . . it's about . . . "

"Yes?"

"Forget it. It's between my mother and me."

He jingled loose coins in his pocket. "And Benjie."

"Of course."

"Did you ever stop to think that maybe he was just an innocent bystander who got caught in the crossfire?"

"My brother could hardly be considered innocent."

"Perhaps you should talk to him again, but this time about your past. I'm willing to bet his memories are different from yours."

"You'd lose."

He shook his head. "I never bet unless it's a sure thing."

"You've talked to him?"

"No. But I don't need to. Clare and I remember certain events differently. Only after we shared our different perspectives did we come to appreciate each other's point of view."

"Are you still planning on visiting my mother?"

He glanced at the front door. "I was thinking about it."

"What if I asked you not to?"

He studied her. "What are you afraid of?"

"Nothing," she said, raising her chin an inch. "I'm not afraid. I just don't want you to be exposed to her lies."

"Well, then I guess I wouldn't."

"Then I'm asking you to let me handle my mother myself. Don't visit her, Julius."

"I wish you'd let me be your husband, Melanie."

"Go back to Clare's. I'll be in touch." She turned and strode down the street, pulling her jacket tighter around her.

Of all the places in town, she'd never expected to run into her husband at her mother's house. Had he overheard everything? She couldn't be sure. She knew he'd heard their voices raised in argument, but had he been able to understand what they'd said? He hadn't looked at her with pity so she couldn't be certain. Would he now, despite her request, go into her mother's house and ask about the argument between mother and daughter? Or would he, as promised, leave well enough alone and return to the comfort of his own family? And what about her brother? Was Julius right? Had she been too young, too focused on what was happening to her, to see that he wasn't as well off as she'd believed? Could he have been as miserable as she'd been? Was that why he'd turned to drugs? Why he'd stopped laughing and stayed in his room all the time?

"Oh, no," she whispered and started running along Second Street. She ran across the street and around the corner.

At the end of Third Street, she stopped in front of a gas station. Once she'd caught her breath, she dug into her pockets for change. Finding enough, she approached the pay phone. Should she? Taking a deep breath, she dialed. Please, she thought, let him be in and not out on patrol.

"I'd like to speak with Officer Joe Hamilton."

Impatiently, she tapped her foot. "Hurry before I change my mind," she whispered.

"Joe Hamilton here. What can I do for you?"

"Joe? It's me, Melanie. Julius's wife."

"Melanie? Hi. Is everything okay? Julius—"

"Joe, I'm calling about my brother. Is he still . . . there?" She tapped her fingers on the side of the pay phone.

"Oh yeah. He's not going anywhere."

"I want to drop the charges."

"You do?"

"Yeah. Yes," she repeated.

"I don't understand. He robbed your house. We caught him doing it. How can you want to drop the charges?"

"I know. I know what it looked like, but he was right. It was all a big misunderstanding."

He sighed heavily. "Are you sure about this, Melanie? Have you talked it over with Julius?"

She closed her eyes. "I don't need to talk it over. I'm sure. I just—I want to drop the charges."

"We could still prosecute, you know, even without your testimony. He did admit to being there with the intent to rob you."

"Please. Just release him. It was all a terrible misunderstanding."

He hesitated. "Okay."

"Really?"

"Yeah, I mean, you are the alleged victim and if you say it was a misunderstanding, then okay. I'll release him."

She sighed. "Thanks, Joe. Thanks a lot. And tell him, um, no, never mind. I'll talk to you soon." She hung up the phone and wondered if she'd lost her mind. She'd almost asked Joe to tell her brother she was sorry. How had she let Julius convince her that was the right thing to do? Especially without him even having to say the exact words? She turned and began walking aimlessly. Well, at least she'd made the upcoming holiday season happy for three people: her brother, her mother, and her husband. But what about her happiness?

She stopped walking and took in her surroundings. She wasn't too far from Ruben's. Maybe Rick was there. He was just what she needed to take her mind off her problems. Rick wouldn't want to psychoanalyze her; he'd just want to screw her. She could handle that as long as she remembered her New Year's resolution, of course. She smiled without humor and headed for the club.

Mr. Nichols met her at the door. "My dear, where have you been keeping yourself?"

"Here and there."

"You still have interest in working here? I know the contest ended prematurely, but we could work something out."

She stared at him in surprise, having completely forgotten all about the contest she nearly entered because of all that had happened since then.

He smiled, reaching out to touch her arm. "I bet you'd be a natural."

She frowned. Had she been wrong about him, too? What else was she wrong about? "Is Rick here?"

He dropped his hand. "Were you supposed to meet him here tonight?"

"No. I just thought he might be here."

He smiled gently. "Perhaps you should come back another time."

"Mr. Nichols, I really would like to see Rick."

He nodded. "He's here, but he's with someone."

"That's okay." She tried to walk past him, but he grabbed her elbow.

"Melanie, he's here with another woman."

She shrugged, pretending indifference. "We aren't together anymore. He can be here with anyone he chooses."

"I'd heard a rumor of you two splitting up."

"Well, it's not a rumor; it's a fact."

He stared at her and finally nodded, releasing her arm. "You can do better than him anyway."

She smiled weakly and entered the club. Allowing her eyes to adjust to the dimness, she stood just inside and searched the room. It was okay if he was with someone else because she was with Julius, right? So why didn't she feel as indifferent as she'd led Mr. Nichols to believe? She squared her shoulders. So what if he wasn't alone? It wasn't as if they'd planned to get together tonight. And she was confident that he'd see her and dump the chick he was with. After all, he and Melanie had history.

She circulated through the club, smiling at a few of the girls she recognized, but she didn't stop to speak to them. They were working, first of all, but secondly, she couldn't help but be a little suspicious of them. When she wasn't around, were they attempting to seduce Rick? They'd never given her a reason to be suspicious, that is, until Little Miss Candi with an "i" had entered the picture. Now she wasn't sure who she could trust.

There he was. And Mr. Nichols was right. He wasn't alone. She moved over to the bar where she could watch them and ordered a whiskey sour. She sipped her drink and studied the girl he was with. She looked a lot like that stripper Candi with blonde hair almost the same length. But Mr. Nichols wouldn't allow one of his girls to get involved with Rick so she knew she wasn't a stripper. She was certainly voluptuous, though, with cleavage spilling out of the low v-neck sweater she wore. The couple laughed, the girl's hand resting on Rick's arm. Then she stood up, and headed towards the far side of the club where the bathrooms were located.

Melanie snatched up her drink and, after pausing long enough to correct her posture and raise her chin just a notch, she slowly made her way over to Rick's table. "Hey."

Rick turned and, recognizing her, smiled slightly. "Hey, baby. What're you doing here?"

"Thought I'd pop in and have a drink."

"That husband of yours doesn't mind you slumming?"

She shrugged, sipping her drink.

"You are still with him, aren't you?"

"Why?"

"Don't go getting stupid ideas into your head about leaving him and moving back in with me. That ain't gonna happen, Mel. What we got going on the side is fine. Let's leave it like that."

She drained her drink. "So buy me another drink and we can talk about what a good thing we've got going on."

"Ah, no, I can't."

"Well, then let's go back to your place." So much for sticking to her resolution, she thought. Damn her black heart.

"Not tonight. I've already got plans."

"Yeah, I know who've you've got plans with, Rick; I saw her. But surely you can cancel them and spend the night with me."

"I said not tonight, Mel; now go home to your husband."

She frowned. "You've got some nerve."

"Go home, will you? Leave me the hell alone."

The blonde returned from the bathroom to overhear his last remark. "Rick? Is everything okay?"

He swung around. "Oh, Suzanne, yeah. Everything's great."

She placed her purse on the table and turned to look at Melanie.

"Aren't you going to introduce us?" Melanie asked, smiling at the other woman.

He glared at her.

She reached her hand across the table. "Since he seems to have lost his voice, I'll introduce myself. Hello, Suzanne. I'm Melanie."

The woman reached across to shake her hand.

"Rick's wife," Melanie added, her hand tightening on the woman's.

Suzanne snatched her hand back and turned to confront Rick. "Is this true? You're married?"

"Yep. Just look at the lovely wedding ring he gave me." Melanie held her hand out to show her the ring Julius had given her.

Rick jumped up. "I am not married to her. She's insane."

"Insane? I only came down here to find out why you refuse to spend any time with your family. You're insane if you expected me to sit home and pretend I didn't know you were out whoring around."

Suzanne snatched her purse from the table and grabbed her coat. "I think I'd better get out of here."

"Wait, Suzanne. She's lying. She's lying!"

He watched as she hurried through the club and disappeared out of view. Turning to see Melanie smiling, he grabbed her wrist and yanked her closer to him. "Damn you. What the hell did you do that for?"

"Oh, Rick. She was probably a lesbian anyway. Why else would she come to a club full of female strippers?"

"Maybe to pick up one of the horny men watching the strippers?"

"Or maybe under that short, tight skirt, she's really a guy. You didn't follow her to the bathroom, did you? How do you know she doesn't piss standing up? Now do you want to buy me a drink first? Or should we just go on back to the apartment?"

He shoved her away from him and she stumbled, colliding with a man who happened to be walking past. "Leave me alone, Mel." He strode off.

She nodded her thanks to the guy who'd kept her from falling and moved over to the bar, embarrassed and ashamed. What had gotten into her? She ordered two shots of tequila and drank them immediately, wincing at the taste. As she pounded two more shots, she scolded herself silently. She'd just made the biggest fool out of herself. And what about Julius? He didn't deserve to have her treat him this way, using his ring to pretend to be married to someone else. She ordered another two shots and drank them just as quickly. They didn't taste quite as bad this time around. By the fourth round she wasn't wincing at all.

"How about another two shots?" she asked the bartender.

Mr. Nichols appeared at her side. "Melanie, maybe you've had enough tequila for one night."

"Just two more."

"This isn't the way to go."

"It sure feels like it is."

"He doesn't deserve you. You're much better off without him."

"Two more shots. I'll even buy you one."

"Let me call you a cab."

She gazed into his kind eyes and finally nodded. "Okay."

He turned to tell the bartender, but he was already picking up the phone. Mr. Nichols nodded in approval and helped her to her feet.

Once outside, he offered her a cigarette.

Gratefully, she accepted, and after he'd lit it, she leaned against the wall and smoked. "I knew you were a good guy," she said, her voice quiet.

"No," he said. "I'm not."

When the cab arrived, he helped her into the back seat and then handed the driver a fifty-dollar bill. "This should cover the ride, right?"

"Depends on where she's going."

"Within town limits."

"She planning on puking back there?"

"No, no. She's fine."

"Yeah, sure, it'll do then, I guess," the driver answered, pocketing the money.

Mr. Nichols turned back to Melanie, who'd slouched down on the seat and closed her eyes. "You do remember your address, right?"

"Of course," she muttered, opening her eyes and waving him away from the door.

"Good-night, my dear. Sleep well." He closed the door and stepped back onto the curb.

She told the driver her address and they drove off.

CHAPTER 23

"Hey, you alive back there?"

Melanie opened her eyes to see the cab driver staring at her. "Yeah, of course," she mumbled. She struggled to sit up. "How much do I owe you?"

"Already paid for, lady, remember?"

"Right," she said and nodded. Of course she remembered. Did he think she was drunk? Because she wasn't. Sure, she'd had a few drinks, but she absolutely remembered that Mr. Nichols had generously paid for her ride home. She slid across the seat to the door. Gripping the door handle, she opened the door and then glanced up at the house they were parked in front of. "Is this some sort of joke?" she mumbled.

"Come on, lady. I don't have all day."

"This isn't right."

"This is 213 Second Street. Just like you said."

"But this is my mother's house!"

"Listen, I don't care if Uncle Sam lives here, this is where you said and this is where you're getting out."

"No." She closed the door and leaned back on the seat, crossing her arms. "I am not getting out here. Take me to 731 Hickory Lane."

"You got to be kidding me. That's across town."

"So? It'll take like ten minutes. And I believe you got paid plenty of money to take me there."

"You know what? I don't have all night to drive some drunk broad all over town. How do I know you won't change your mind when we get to Hickory Lane?"

"I am not drunk! And I won't change my mind because that is where I live. Now go. Seven-thirty-one Hickory Lane."

He shook his head. "Whatever. You're getting out here. If you don't like it, well, then call yourself another cab because this cab driver is now off duty."

She frowned, finally giving up. "How much more then will it take for you to drop me off at Hickory Lane?"

"Forget it."

She dug into her pocket and pulled out all the money she had on her. "How far will three dollars and twenty-nine cents take me?"

He laughed. "Around the block. Now just go on and get out here, all right?"

"He gave you fifty dollars. I know it doesn't cost that much to get from there to here."

"So call the cops."

"Please?"

"No way."

"How could you just kick someone out of your cab when you know it's not the right address? Don't you have any kind of conscious?"

"You need help with the door?"

"You're a jerk, you know that?" She got out of the cab and slammed the door. He sped off and she gave him the finger.

She could walk home. Certainly she'd walked farther, maybe just not after eight shots of tequila. That had been so stupid of her. She might be more like her mother than she realized—a very depressing thought. She sighed. It could be worse. At least it wasn't too cold and it wasn't raining. She turned towards her mother's house. Was that music? Could her mother be having a party? Had her mother decided to booze it up again? But who would she know to invite over for a party? She smiled to herself. Maybe it was good that she'd given the cab driver this address, as weird as that was. She should definitely investigate.

At the front door, she paused and listened to the voices singing. It sounded like there were quite a few people inside. Over their clapping, she listened to the song. Were they singing some sort of hymn?

She stepped inside without bothering to knock. They wouldn't have heard her anyway. In the corner, two men played guitars while the rest of the group, about ten people or so, were crammed into the living room. Almost everyone's eyes were closed; some people had one hand raised high in the air; others had both hands raised; a few even had wet cheeks from crying; and just about everyone else clapped and rocked slightly from side to side.

"Melanie!" Annie exclaimed in surprise when she finally opened her eyes and saw her daughter standing directly in front of her. "What are you doing here?"

"What in the world is going on?"

Annie blushed slightly, but smiled, drying her wet cheeks with a crumpled tissue. "We're having a prayer meeting."

"So now you pray before you drink? Where's the booze because I've done my praying at the bar."

Her mother paled and took a step closer to her daughter. "Sweetheart, maybe you should go lie down for a little while until your head is clear."

She laughed as the group shifted uncomfortably. "God, why didn't you become an actress? At least then we would've had enough money for both food and your precious liquor growing up."

"Melanie!" Annie grabbed her daughter's arm, her lips pinched and face pale. "Stop it," she hissed.

"Where did you find these people?"

"What is that supposed to mean?"

"I'm just surprised to find the living room full of so many people is all."

Annie glanced around nervously. "These are all people from the church I've joined."

"And why are they here?"

"I don't understand."

"Why. Are. They. Here?" Melanie repeated her words slower and louder.

"I heard you," Annie snapped. She took a deep breath. "I just don't understand what point you're trying to make. I mean, we're all here to pray."

She scowled. "Pray for what?"

A gray-haired woman stepped up, placing her arm around Annie. "We're here to pray for many things. For forgiveness, for understanding, for help—"

"Forgiveness?"

"Sure."

"Is that what you're praying for tonight, Mother? Because I'd like to know what you're wanting forgiveness for. Specifically."

"Oh, you know, things."

"Would anyone care for some coffee or a snack?" the gray-haired woman asked the group.

"No," Melanie said. "Shouldn't you know what kind of woman you're praying with?"

"We all have things in our past we're not proud of, but that is why we pray. We repent our sins—"

"Listen," Melanie said, interrupting the woman. "You don't know what you're talking about, okay? This woman, Annie, my mother, turned her back on her own daughter when I needed her the most. Do you know she used to introduce me as 'the girl'? She never said 'daughter.' She doted on my brother, though. He was her precious son, all blonde and blue-eyed like herself. Did she ever show any pride in anything I did? No. There was never anything of mine hanging on the fridge. She never bragged to her friends about the things I did. I was a child. I didn't deserve to be treated like I was invisible. But she made me think I did. Why? Why did she love my brother and hate me?"

The gray-haired woman stepped forward, arms out, ready to embrace her. "I can feel your pain, Melanie, but God is here for you—"

She took a step back, determined to keep out of the woman's reach. "Oh, shut up. I don't need to listen to any of that crap."

"Maybe this would be the time for that coffee break after all," Annie said.

The crowd murmured in agreement and moved towards the kitchen, allowing mother and daughter some privacy.

"You're drunk, aren't you?"

"Wouldn't you be the expert?"

"I didn't think you had a drinking problem, Melanie."

"Eight shots of tequila went down pretty smooth. Where's the problem?"

"Look at what my prayer group gave me tonight," Annie said, changing the subject. "It's a cover for my Bible. To protect it from dirt and wear and tear."

She stared at the floral, lace-trimmed cover, at her mother's name embroidered in pink on the top. "They don't know you at all, do they? Or is it that they couldn't find any fabric with liquor bottles as the theme?"

Annie's lips tightened and she rubbed her hand along the cloth. "I suppose I deserved that." She put the gift down on the couch behind her. "I was a rotten mother. It wasn't fair to you, but I was. I was jealous of you. I blamed you for all the things that had gone wrong in my life. And I didn't know how to act around you. You were so needy—"

"Needy? I was a child! How can you put the blame on me?"

"Please don't talk like that. And that's not what I'm doing."

"No? I was so needy that you couldn't love me. Isn't that what you're saying?"

"I don't know what I'm saying. Okay? When Benjie was born, your father and I were newly married and we were happy. Things weren't so easy for me when I was pregnant with you two years later. The fairy tale I thought I'd gotten wasn't real and I didn't know how to handle it. If I couldn't help myself, how could I have helped you?"

"You know, you're pretty good at spinning a sob story to get someone to feel sorry for you, but I don't feel sorry for you at all. You've hated me my entire life. Just last month, you were still being mean to me."

"I was still drinking then. I'm sober now."

"That's no excuse!"

Annie shrugged. "I know. But that's all I've got." She took a step closer to her daughter. "I get that you've had a terrible childhood and that it's mostly my fault. It's been tough for you. But you know what? It's time to forgive and move on."

Melanie shook her head. "I'm not surprised that you'd say that. Forgive you? Move on? That would make it easy for you, wouldn't it?"

"I'm learning, Melanie. I'm learning that Jesus forgives and that if He can forgive our sins, shouldn't we forgive each other's sins?"

"Forgive our trespasses?"

Annie looked at her in surprise. "Yes."

"You know what I think? I think it's time to call it quits."

Annie nodded. "Maybe you're right. Tomorrow, after we've had time to think about things, we might be able to clear the air better."

"No, that's not what I mean. I don't want to see you again after tonight and I want you to promise me you won't try to contact me. Ever. And that goes for Julius and his family, too."

"What? No, Melanie. I'm your mother. I can't—"

"When have you done anything for me in my lifetime? Can't you do this one thing for me now?"

"Why do you want to do this now? When I can be a better mother to you because I'm sober?"

"Sometimes change happens too late to be effective, if you've even really changed."

Annie stared at her. "Maybe you're trying to drive me back to drinking. Is that what you're hoping to do?"

"You never know what my black heart is capable of, do you?"

Annie closed her eyes, her fingers moving to caress the gold cross hanging from a chain around her neck.

"Tell me this, Mother. Why didn't you just let me die years ago when I tried to kill myself? Why did you bother to save me? So that you could continue to hate me?"

"No, Melanie. Don't say that." Her lips trembled and she closed her eyes, remembering. "That awful day. I saved you because you were my daughter."

"Your daughter? Oh, I get it. Because people would have talked. There might have been inquiries by social services and then you could've lost Benjie, your precious boy."

"No. No." Her lips quivered. "I know I was a terrible mother to you and I'm sorry. There's no way I can turn back time and change what has happened, as much as I'd now like to. And maybe if you'd chosen to cut your wrists when I was drunk to the point of passing out, I wouldn't have been able to save you. But God was there that day. He was watching over us, only I didn't know it. He was there to help me save your life. He has a plan for your life, Melanie. And for mine."

"I've got to go."

"How else could I have done something so right?"

"You're not trying to convert me to this new cult of yours, are you?"

"It's not a cult. It's Christianity."

"I don't care what you call it. I'm leaving."

"No, wait." She sighed. "Okay, the timing's not the greatest," she said, glancing towards the kitchen, "but I wanted to talk to you about what was said earlier today. Especially since you've decided to forget all about me after tonight."

"What's the point?"

"It's about your father. Can't you stay for a few more minutes? Wouldn't you like to know what happened all those years ago?"

"This should be good."

"I don't really remember what I've told you about him, but today when you brought him up, I realized it was time I told you the truth. Your father left us because I had an affair." She shook her head, her eyes focused on the far wall. "I cheated on him and he walked in and caught me. He left that night."

"You cheated on him with Carl." It wasn't a question; somehow she just knew that Carl had been the cause.

"So if anyone has a black heart, it's me. Carl was his best friend at the time."

Melanie was sorely tempted to slap her, but knew it was a bit melodramatic, a drama more along her mother's line of things. "You changed my entire life because of some tawdry affair. How can you live with yourself?"

Annie sank down on the couch. "I know. I didn't think he'd leave me when he found out about Carl and me. I didn't think he'd leave you and your brother. I thought he'd beg me to stay with him. And then when he left I blamed you because you were daddy's little girl. I think about that now and every night I ask for God's forgiveness."

"*God's* forgiveness?" She shook her head. "Where is he now? Do you know?"

"Who?" she asked, confused. "God?"

"My father. Does he know . . . about Carl? About what he . . . did to me?" It was hard to ask, but she needed to know.

Annie shook her head.

She crossed her arms. "Maybe he would've wanted me to stay with him in New Jersey. Did you ever think of that?" She continued, not letting her mother answer the question. "Instead, you made me move to Florida! Tell me where he is."

Annie clasped her hands together. "He died," she said, her voice wobbly. "There was a car accident. He was driving too fast; the roads were wet. He died that night." She closed her eyes. "Saying it aloud just makes it sound even more unbelievable. Like some dumb B-movie."

"And I suppose you wouldn't be in this dumb B-movie? Maybe as the sad helpless woman who foolishly sacrifices everything including her children for love? Or maybe it was just all about the sex and the alcohol."

"Melanie—"

"All these years you made it sound like he was still alive, but he wasn't."

"It was my fault he died that night. I couldn't admit it, so I didn't."

The front door opened and Benjie walked in. "Wow. I did not expect to see this."

"Benjie!" Annie jumped up and hugged him.

"Ugh," he groaned, pushing her away. "You reek. What kind of old lady perfume are you wearing?"

"Is that how the favorite son greets his adoring mother?" Melanie asked, scowling.

"Never mind what I smell like. You could use a shower, you know. What are you doing out of jail?"

"Cops let me out. Guess they found out the truth after all. Isn't that so, dear sister?"

"I don't know what you're talking about."

"Whatever. Anyway, let's celebrate."

Melanie shook her head. "I'm out of here. This family together-ness is sickening."

"Why don't you stay and pray with us?"

"You've got to be kidding."

"It's just that now that I'm sober I'd like to spend time with my children. I think we should talk about all that has happened. Maybe we can start again and try to be a real family."

"I suppose by real, you mean in an Ozzie and Harriet or *Happy Days* kind of way?"

Annie sighed. "Must you always be so difficult? Can you not attack me at least once?"

"Like the way you didn't always attack me?"

"Melanie—"

"Just forget it." She waved towards the people still hovering in the kitchen, pretending they weren't curious about what was happen-ing in the living room. "Have fun praying or eating live chickens or whatever you're doing." She brushed past her brother and out onto the porch.

Benjie turned on his heel and followed her. "Wait up. Maybe you want to explain what the hell is going on."

"I don't have to explain anything to you."

"No? You're the reason I got arrested."

"Certainly wasn't the first time and probably won't be the last either."

"But we had a deal and I want to know what the hell changed? Why'd you set me up?"

"You don't know?"

"How could I know? I thought we had a deal."

She crossed her arms and shook her head. "Unbelievable."

"What? You could've said no. You didn't have to help me. And if I'd known the kind of help you were offering, I definitely wouldn't have bothered to ask."

"Then why did you?"

"Because I didn't have any other options."

"I don't know about that. There's always male prostitution. I hear that can pull in some bucks." She smiled.

"When did you become such a bitch?"

"I'm a bitch? You deserve worse than being in jail a few nights. A lot worse. I never should've dropped the stupid charges."

"Then why did you?"

"I don't know! But if you want to talk truths, then why don't you tell me why you turned on me years ago when you walked in and saw that bastard raping me?"

"What would you have had me do?"

"Something! But instead you did absolutely nothing. Just ignored me completely. You were my big brother and suddenly I was invisible to you."

"I'm only older by two years! That fat bastard would've killed me if I'd interfered with him porking my sister."

Melanie lunged at him, screaming as her hands flailed wildly.

The door opened and Annie stared at them, her mouth agape. A man from the prayer meeting appeared at her shoulder and then, seeing the siblings fighting, pushed past her and out onto the porch. He grabbed Melanie, struggling to pull her off her brother.

Melanie breathed hard, tears coursing down her cheeks. "I should've left you to rot in jail. My revenge would've been so sweet!"

Benjie touched his face where she'd scratched him. "I guess you could've done worse. You could've tried to poison me like you poisoned him!"

Annie opened the screen door and stepped out onto the porch. "What are you talking about?"

"Little Mellie here set me up. She's just admitted it here in front of us all. Maybe I should sue her."

"I mean about the poison."

"She tried to poison Carl once. Remember that time he passed out in the snow? Back in New Jersey? It wasn't because of too much alcohol, but more than likely because of the combination of alcohol and sleeping pills she'd crushed up and stirred into his soup. Or was it aspirin?"

"Go to hell!" Melanie yelled.

Benjie chuckled. "I think you'll get there first."

Annie slapped her son. "Don't you ever talk like that again."

"Mom!"

Melanie laughed.

The man released her. "I think I'll give you some privacy, Annie. Call me if you need me." He opened the screen door. "Mike, how about we sing that last song again?"

"Thanks, Roger." She turned to her daughter as the screen door closed behind him. "It isn't funny."

"It is to me. You've never raised your hand to him before and the look on his face, well, it was priceless."

"Don't you see that our family is falling apart? I don't know what to do. I can't lose you, either of you. In fact, I will not promise to stay out of your life, Melanie. You can turn your back on me, but I refuse to do that to you. I did that for far too long and now I cannot consciously do that."

She stared at her mother, noting the blonde hair and blue eyes, and remembered how she'd stood in front of the mirror and wished she'd looked like her mother. It had been the only thing she could think of that might win her mother's affection. "Then you'll know how I felt every time I tried to get you to love me and you rebuffed me. Maybe I'll start referring to you as 'that woman who pushed me out of her vagina.'" She hurried down the steps and along the sidewalk. When she reached the street, she hesitated, but stiffened her spine and started the long walk home. She did not look back.

CHAPTER 24

Melanie looked up from the cash register to see Julius entering the diner. She handed the change to the customer. "Thanks. See you soon."

"Hi."

She smiled. "Hi."

"I came in for some lunch. I hope that's okay."

"Of course. Why wouldn't it be?"

"I've been trying to give you plenty of space."

She grabbed a menu. "It's only lunch, Julius." She led him to a booth and he slid in, accepting the menu from her. "Coffee? Or a soda today?"

"How about a Coke?"

She nodded and walked away. Returning with his soda, she asked, "How've you been?"

"Good, thanks. And you?"

"Fine."

"I heard about what you did for your brother. I'm proud of you, Melanie."

"Yeah, well, it is getting close to being the holiday season."

"That's not why you did it."

"It doesn't matter why I did it, Julius, just that I did it."

"No, it does matter because your reasons for doing it came out of

227

love for your brother. You wish you could hate him as much as you say."

She tapped her pen against the pad of paper she held. "Did you come here to analyze me or were you hungry?"

He stared at her. "I'll have the club sandwich on wheat toast and French fries."

She wrote his order down on the pad and walked away.

A few minutes later his order was ready and, although she thought about having Ida take it out, she knew she'd call her a chicken and probably even tell Julius. With a sigh, she grabbed the plate and carried it to his table. Setting it down in front of him, she asked, "Do you need anything else?"

"Yes. What are your plans for Halloween?"

"I don't have any."

"I'd like to take you to dinner."

She hesitated. "I don't know."

He grabbed her hand. "I miss you, Melanie. I'd like to work things out. Maybe this is just what we need in order to get back on track. After all, we've never had a proper date."

"Okay. I'll have dinner with you," she finally agreed, surprising herself. But really what was the harm? After all, they were still married.

He smiled. "Great. I'll pick you up at seven."

She nodded and turned to walk away.

"Melanie?"

She glanced over her shoulder. "Yes?"

"Another Coke before you disappear until I've left?"

"Of course." She smiled happily to herself as she went to get his soda. How had he known that was exactly what she'd planned on doing? It was uncanny and yet nice to have a husband so attuned to her thoughts. She wanted to avoid being asked any serious questions she didn't yet have the answers for and that seemed the only way to do it. Her husband could bring the damnedest things up at the most inopportune times.

She set his soda on the table, along with his check. "How's your sandwich?"

"Delicious." He sat back and smiled at her.

She smiled slightly and walked away.

Later, once he'd finished his lunch and left, she went back to his table. Just like before they were married, he'd left five dollars and a paper rose. And just like before, she picked it up, twirling it between her fingers before finally smelling it. She sat down in the booth and cried, the paper rose clutched tightly in her fist.

On Halloween, Julius arrived at his house precisely at seven and rang the doorbell.

Melanie opened the door, relieved to see it was her husband and not her mother. Annie had left a message on the machine saying she was going to come over and stand on the front steps until Melanie agreed to talk to her. Of course her license had been taken away because of the accident, but she was willing to risk getting arrested if there was any possibility of keeping her daughter in her life.

"Trick or Treat," he said, smiling.

She eyed his suit. "Let me guess. You're an encyclopedia salesman?"

"No!" He straightened his tie. "I'm a handsome, charming date."

"Clever, too."

"Well, yes, I suppose you could add clever to my long list of attributes."

"Modest must be one of the top three on your list."

"Of course."

They stood there awkwardly.

He cleared his throat. "You look amazing."

"Thank you," she said, blushing. She'd picked out the navy wrap dress because of the large hydrangea bloom on the skirt. It wasn't a rose, but she knew he'd appreciate it. She grabbed her purse off the hall table and preceded him outside.

"It's a nice night," he remarked, taking her arm and escorting her along the sidewalk. He watched as a witch, a ghost, a princess, and Superman raced up the sidewalk and rang a neighbor's doorbell. He waved at the mothers waiting at the curb as the children chorused "Trick or Treat" amidst giggles. "So many stars out. And a full moon, too."

He helped her into the car before hurrying around to the driver's side. "Clare sends her love."

"She's very thoughtful."

"I think she's getting a bit tired of having me underfoot."

"Oh, Julius. I'm sorry. I didn't think—"

He reached for her hand. "No, Melanie. We're not going to get into all that tonight, okay?"

Silently, she nodded.

"Good. Now I hope you're hungry."

She smiled. "Starved."

They drove to the restaurant, talking of inconsequential things: Ida, his niece and nephews, the new owner of a small bar called Jack's. By the time they'd arrived and Julius had parked the car, they'd run out of small talk.

Once they were seated, they silently studied the menu. "The linguine with clam sauce is terrific here. My mother usually gets that," he admitted.

"Really? I was thinking of getting the crab cakes. Or perhaps the catch of the day."

"I've had the crab cakes. They were good."

The waiter arrived and Julius ordered a bottle of white wine. "Is that all right with you?"

"Yes, it's perfect," she lied. She would've liked something stronger, something to take the edge off. She'd been relieved when he'd said they wouldn't discuss their problems tonight, but now she was feeling the stress of it. If they were to start fresh, shouldn't they clear the air first? But then again, what would she say? She was no longer even sure what had started this whole thing. It hadn't only been Rick, had it? He'd hardly mentioned her brother so she didn't think that was it.

The waiter returned with the wine and after allowing Julius to taste it, he filled Melanie's glass. Quickly, she drank, finishing her glass by the time he'd filled Julius's.

She licked her lips. "I guess I was thirstier than I realized."

The waiter smiled and refilled her glass.

She itched to drink that glass as well, but could feel her husband's discomfort. She knew he was worried she'd recently turned into an alcoholic like her mother and he didn't even know about the other night when Mr. Nichols had helped her into a cab! He'd probably have immediately enrolled her in a rehab clinic if he knew.

"Melanie? Are you ready to order?"

"What? Oh, yes." She smiled at the waiter and placed her order.

"So do you think you'll make any resolutions for the coming year?" he asked once he'd given his order and the waiter had disappeared. "Or don't you do that sort of thing?"

She thought of the other day when she'd decided she couldn't see Rick again. And then she remembered that she'd easily disregarded her resolution and sought him out at Ruben's. "Not yet. Sometimes I make them. What about you?"

"I'll have one or two this year," he answered.

"You don't want to tell me what they are?"

"Tonight's probably not the best time to mention them."

"Now you have to tell me." She finished her glass of wine and reached for the bottle.

He grabbed the bottle before she could. "Allow me."

She watched as he refilled her glass halfway. That was the problem with drinking wine. Glasses were more often filled halfway than all the way. She wanted a full glass, but refrained from commenting.

"I know I said I wasn't looking to get into things with you tonight, but my first resolution has to do with you and me. Making our marriage work."

She nodded. Maybe she didn't want to hear his resolutions after all. But then again, didn't she want their marriage to work out as well? If she didn't, then what did she want? "That's a good one."

The waiter arrived with their salads and Melanie quickly picked up her fork.

"So then you agree with that? You want to make our marriage work?" he asked, ignoring his salad.

Melanie put her fork down and reached for her wineglass. "Yes, I think so."

He watched as she finished her third glass of wine. "You think so? But you don't know for sure?"

She reached for the bottle of wine and this time her husband didn't offer to pour it for her. She filled her glass almost to the top. "I don't know what you want from me, Julius."

"I want you to love me as much as I love you. I want you to be happy and to want to make me happy. I want you to forget about that ex-boyfriend of yours for good."

She sipped her wine. "Of course I want you to be happy. I wouldn't wish for your unhappiness."

"Well, at least that's something." He scowled.

"What do you mean?"

"Just that I wouldn't want you to ever find a reason to seek revenge against me, Melanie. Like you did your brother."

"Leave him out of this. You don't know anything about my brother so you can't possibly know what you're talking about." She reached for her glass.

"Don't you think you've had enough wine?"

She hesitated, her hand outstretched, and met his eyes. "I know my limit. Thank you for your concern." She picked up her glass and drained it. With a smile, she set the empty glass back on the table.

"Your mother decides to become sober so you take up drinking? Is that it? Have I got things wrong?" He picked up his fork. "Maybe I've misunderstood things. Maybe you'd prefer to emulate your mother."

"What are you getting at now?"

"I'm just thinking out loud. Let's say grace." He bowed his head and closed his eyes, Melanie watching him. "Father, thank you for this wonderful meal we are about to receive and for all that you do for us each and every day. May our words and our hearts honor you tonight as you watch over us. Amen."

They began to eat their salads in silence. Finally, he put his fork down and studied her. "Your mother hasn't been a happy woman for a very long time and maybe you're trying to follow in her footsteps and live your life just as miserably. You've already got the abusive boyfriend; now you're drinking heavily. Pretty soon you might accidentally get pregnant and then that coward you're so fond of may eventually turn to your daughter."

She turned pale. "You were eavesdropping!"

"No, you were yelling. Now what I don't understand is how you managed to do one thing right."

"And what's that?"

"You married me."

"Who said that was right?"

"It's right and you're scared to death that you might actually have to take me into consideration when you're about to do something stupid."

"Something stupid?"

"I know you love me a little bit, but you're afraid to let yourself go and love me with all your heart and soul."

"You are so off the mark." She shook her head, stabbing a crouton. "Stick to being a cop because you'd make a lousy therapist." She took a bite of salad.

"I don't think I'm wrong, Melanie. I might be in love with you, but that doesn't make me blind."

She glared at him and reached for the bottle of wine, but he moved it out of her reach. "I'd like another glass of wine, please."

"You've had enough."

"Fine." She tossed her napkin on the table and stood up. "I'm going home. Happy Halloween, Julius."

"Running away again, Melanie? But whose arms are you going to seek this time?"

She stared at him, her lips pursed, but turned without speaking and walked away. In the waiting area, she stopped by the pay phone, intending to call a cab.

"Who're you calling?"

She turned to see her husband had followed her. "It's none of your business." She picked up the phone.

He took the receiver from her and hung it up. "I'll drive you home."

"No, thank you. I'd prefer to walk if I have to, just as long as I don't have to accept a ride from you."

He stared at her, frustrated. "You really are difficult, you know that?" He produced the valet car keys from his pants pocket. "Here. Take my car. I'll wait for a cab and come by and pick up the car later."

"Gee, do you trust me since I'm an alcoholic now?"

"Take it before I change my mind."

"Fine." She snatched the keys and turned away, expecting him to stop her. But he didn't, and soon she was sliding into the driver's seat and inserting the key into the ignition. She sped out of the parking lot.

She hated him! How could he talk to her like that when he claimed he loved her? He didn't love her; he couldn't. He was scared. He'd probably decided he'd married a lunatic and was afraid he'd never be able to get a divorce. Like she'd want to remain married to him after tonight!

She sped up, not caring that she was breaking the speed limit. How could she have married him? She'd thought he was sweet, but really he was cruel and uncaring. A sob escaped her lips and she clenched her jaw. She was not going to cry over that jerk. He was worse than Rick! She would pack her bags and leave. He could take his stupid house and shove it. But where would she go? She slammed her hand down on the steering wheel. She couldn't go to her mother's, although wouldn't her mother be delighted if she turned up on her doorstep? But she hadn't finished working out in her mind everything that had happened the other night. She couldn't go to Rick's. Julius had hit on a major fear of hers when he'd mentioned how her future daughter could end up being hurt like she'd been hurt, which was why she'd insisted on getting birth control years ago. Not that there was much chance of starting a family with Rick. He'd made his intentions with her abundantly clear the other night. A hotel? But she couldn't afford to stay longer than a couple days. She angrily brushed away the few tears that slipped past her eyelashes. Damn him! Ida. She'd ask Ida if she could crash at her place for a while.

But the thing was she knew she would miss him. He'd burrowed his way into her job at the diner, into her life, into her heart. He'd done what she'd thought was impossible: He'd gotten her to believe she might have something to offer someone after all.

She turned the corner, tires squealing, and saw Julius's house ahead. Out of the corner of her eye, she caught a flash of light before a cat ran out in front of her. Slamming on the brakes, she closed her eyes, her knuckles white on the steering wheel.

At the telltale thump, she cried out and, as the car came to a halt with a jerk in the middle of the street, she tumbled from the car.

She knelt on the pavement next to the gray cat, uncaring that she might ruin her new dress. She reached out and with trembling fingers, touched the soft fur wet with blood. "Oh, God, no," she whispered. As she stared at her wet fingers, she was instantly catapulted back into time. Suddenly she was twelve years old and once again, she hadn't been able to save her Yoda. She pulled the dead cat into her arms, rocking it back and forth. She didn't care if the neighbors were looking out of their windows at her. She only cared about this cat. She stroked the cat's head and whispered to it, the words similar to the words she'd whispered to her own cat years ago as he lay dead in her arms, a bullet through his body from her mother's boyfriend's gun.

Headlights highlighted Julius's car as a vehicle turned the corner, but Melanie didn't notice. She didn't hear the door slam shut after the cab had pulled over or rapid footsteps as the passenger raced over to her.

"Melanie?" Annie bent over her daughter.

There was no response other than slim fingers slowly petting bloody fur.

"Melanie!" she said again, but sharper this time.

Her daughter looked up. "He's dead."

Annie knelt next to her daughter, her fabric-covered Bible forgotten as it fell from her arms, and stroked her hair. "I know, honey. I'm sorry. I should've been home. I should've tried to save Yoda. To save you."

"I've lost him," she whispered.

A police car rounded the corner and stopped in the middle of the street. Julius jumped out of the passenger side and hurried over to where the women knelt. Joe stepped out of the car, but didn't venture closer.

"What happened? Melanie, are you hurt?"

"She's going to be okay. She hit a cat."

He stared at them openmouthed. "What?"

Annie continued to stroke her daughter's hair. "She never told you about Yoda, did she?"

"Yoda? The *Star Wars* character?"

With a glance at her daughter, she shook her head. "Yoda was her cat. When she was about twelve, my boyfriend Carl shot Yoda in front of Melanie." She sighed. "He could be very cruel," she added, her voice dropping slightly. She met his eyes. "I thought she'd gotten over it, but she hasn't. Or maybe she had until tonight."

He moved closer and touched his wife gently on the shoulder.

She glanced up at him, her eyes full of unshed tears. "Julius . . ." She didn't know what to say, how to tell him she was sorry for Rick, her brother, everything.

He knelt next to her. "It's okay, sweetheart. I love you."

"You do? Still?"

"Oh, yes. There's nothing you could do that would make me not love you."

"But—"

"No. You captured my heart a while back. We'll work through this together."

Leaning into him, she nodded slowly and glanced at the cat in her lap. The last time she'd allowed herself to love, she'd loved her cat. And then when she'd failed to save him, she'd vowed never to love anyone that deeply again. Maybe it was time to try.

Turning to her mother, she didn't know what to say. It would be hard to forget everything that had happened between them in the past, but it would be nice to have a mother. Someone she could talk to, someone who would worry about her and be proud of her, someone who would fill the spot in her life like Gretchen filled in Julius's life. She spotted her mother's Bible, the lace now tinted red with blood. Maybe she *had* changed. "Your Bible cover . . . the blood . . . it's ruined!"

Annie shrugged. "It wasn't really me anyway. Too frilly. Besides, it's the inside that counts."

Maybe she could forgive her family, and then eventually the good memories would erase the bad ones. Melanie squeezed her hand and was rewarded with her mother's smile.

Acknowledgments

You know when the long shot at an awards ceremony wins the statue and then in the excitement of the moment forgets to thank some of the people essential to their success? That's about how writing this acknowledgments page feels to me.

I started this novel years ago, and then I finished it and put it in a drawer and moved on to other projects, got married, moved a bunch of times, had a few kids, lived life like we all do. And every so often I'd pull it out, think about it, talk about it, share it, and then put it back in the drawer. And because of that I know I'm going to forget to thank someone, someone who was instrumental in helping me get *Trespassers* into your hands all these years later. If you are reading this book and wondering why I neglected to thank you, it is because my memory fails at some of the most inopportune times. That being said, here are a few people I mustn't forget:

God. I thank God for all the blessings in my life, and I pray that this book speaks to at least one person.

My parents. You have supported me and encouraged me and believed in me and I couldn't have accomplished anything without your support and love.

This Administration. El Hefe. The Love of My Life. The Father of My Children. Otherwise known as my husband, Greg. You are the gold in our Golden Couple and I thank God for you every day.

My children. I am blessed to have three beautiful, rambunctious, sweet boys and my life would be incomplete without you in it. If I never publish another book, I hope that by publishing this one, you'll be encouraged to always follow your dreams.

My friends. You know who you are. And especially to my local Birmingham friends: Krystal Gibbs, Carmen Harrelson, Mary Kennedy, Julie Patterson Davis, and Beth Pulles. Thank you for your encouragement on those (too many) days when I doubt myself. And thank you to Cheryl Handley Tolbert, Dan Lai, Marty Metzl, and Sarah Urbancic for reading drafts of this novel.

My teachers. I've had some really great teachers in my life, from high school all the way through graduate school, who've encouraged me and guided me and critiqued my writing: Randy Albers, Andy Allegretti, Matthew Bogdan, Madonna Johnson, Tom Nawrocki, Ann Smith, and especially S. L. Stebel, whose guidance and encouragement were invaluable as I wrote this book.

Cait Levin and Brooke Warner at She Writes Press. Thank you for your encouragement, support, and hand-holding as I navigated the publishing world. Without you this book would still be a stack of papers in a desk drawer. And thanks to Katie Caruana for her terrific editing and to Sheila Cowley for my beautiful book cover.

My readers. Thank you for taking a chance on me and on this book. I hope you liked it and I look forward to sharing my next novel with you.

Questions for Discussion

In order to provide reading groups with the most informed and thought-provoking questions possible, it is necessary to reveal important aspects of the plot of this novel.

If you have not finished reading *Trespassers*, we respectfully suggest that you may want to wait before reviewing the following discussion questions.

Julius eats at the diner on a regular basis as a way to see Melanie. What do you think attracted him to her? Do you think Julius likes his job? Or do you think a part of him wishes he'd stuck to his former occupation as a landscape architect?

Melanie thinks that Mr. Nichols, the strip club owner, is a good guy. Do you find that believable? What kind of insight does that give you into Melanie's character? Later, when he tells her he's not a good guy, does his honesty say more about Mr. Nichols's character or Melanie's?

Melanie has some confusion about good versus bad; she believes that her mother and brother are good, that Mr. Nichols is good, that even Rick is good. Julius is a Christian, and he does not instantly label Melanie's mother as a bad person, but rather sees her as a person who made bad choices. However, he is quick to judge Rick as a bad person. Do you think that by teaching tolerance instead of truth, today's society makes the lines between good and bad more blurred for everyone?

When Melanie goes with Julius to the baseball field on her birthday, she thinks of him as being more real. What do you think she means by that? Why?

Melanie wonders whether, if her upbringing had been in a "white bread" household, she would have fallen for someone like Julius or would still have fallen for the "bad boy." What do you think she means by "white bread household"? Do you think some people are just drawn to "bad boys," no matter what their upbringing?

Does Rick's reaction to the roses and the information that Melanie received a marriage proposal surprise you? Do you think he really does love Melanie? What kind of childhood do you imagine Rick had, based on what you know about his character and his chosen career?

When Melanie runs into Gretchen at the mall, Gretchen offers her Julius's deceased father's wedding ring. Do you think Gretchen is happy about the upcoming wedding? Do you approve of how Gretchen talked to Melanie, or do you think she should've been more straightforward with her thoughts?

Julius invites Annie and Benjie to their wedding without talking to Melanie first. Are you surprised by his initiative? Does that tell you anything about his character? What do you think would've happened if they'd seen the invitation? Would they have gone to the wedding? Would they have been disruptive, as Melanie feared?

On Melanie's wedding day, Gretchen tells Melanie about Julius's sister who died when he was little. Do you think that was appropriate? Do you think, based on her conversation with Melanie, she will be a good mother-in-law or not? Why do you think mothers-in-law are often portrayed negatively?

Melanie decides pretty quickly her marriage will be passionless. Do you think she's being too hard on Julius? Do you think the lack of passion she initially feels has more to do with her experience with abusive men and less to do with reality? Do you think Melanie is capable of sharing a healthy relationship with anyone?

Melanie comes up with a plan and convinces her brother he will benefit from it financially, but really it will land him in jail. Do you think her plan is a good one? Do you sympathize with Melanie or with her brother at this point?

Melanie makes a lot of bad decisions in this novel. Which decision surprised you the most?

Julius refers to himself as cowardly because he won't ask Melanie if she's cheating on him with Rick. Do you see Julius as a coward? Or is he brave for wanting to work on his marriage, despite his suspicions of her infidelity?

Melanie and Annie have a pretty honest conversation about the past, and Annie asks if they can ever have a mother-daughter relationship. Discuss the differences between mother-daughter and father-daughter relationships. Do you think Melanie should forgive her mother?

Julius tells Melanie she must forgive her mother in order for them to be together. Do you think he's being fair? Do you think he's right?

How have Melanie, Julius, and Annie changed by the end of *Trespassers*? What do you think will happen next in their relationships with each other?

About the Author

© Cooper Martin

A ndrea Miles earned her Masters of Professional Writing from the University of Southern California. Originally from Pocomoke, Maryland, she currently lives in Birmingham, Alabama with her husband and three children. *Trespassers* is her first novel. To learn more, visit her at www.andreamiles.com.

SELECTED TITLES FROM SHE WRITES PRESS

She Writes Press is an independent publishing company founded to serve women writers everywhere.
Visit us at www.shewritespress.com.

The Belief in Angels by J. Dylan Yates
$16.95, 978-1-938314-64-3
From the Majdonek death camp to a volatile hippie household on the East Coast, this narrative of tragedy, survival, and hope spans more than fifty years, from the 1920s to the 1970s.

Fire & Water by Betsy Graziani Fasbinder
$16.95, 978-1-938314-14-8
Kate Murphy has always played by the rules—but when she meets charismatic artist Jake Bloom, she's forced to navigate the treacherous territory of passionate love, friendship, and family devotion.

A Cup of Redemption by Carole Bumpus
$16.95, 978-1-938314-90-2
Three women, each with their own secrets and shames, seek to make peace with their pasts and carve out new identities for themselves.

What is Found, What is Lost by Anne Leigh Parrish
$16.95, 978-1-938314-95-7
After her husband passes away, a series of family crises forces Freddie, a woman raised on religion, to confront long-held questions about her faith.

Clear Lake by Nan Fink Gefen
$16.95, 978-1-938314-40-7
When psychotherapist Rebecca Lev's father dies under suspicious circumstances, she becomes obsessed with discovering what happened to him.

Say It Out Loud: Revealing and Healing the Scars of Sexual Abuse by Roberta Dolan. $16.95, 978-1-938314-99-5.
An in-depth guide to healing the wounds caused by sexual abuse, written by a survivor who's lived the process firsthand.